Forbidden Love
Bad Boys

Issue one

Featuring

Brenna Lyons

CJ England

Terri Pray

Under the Moon

Forbidden Love
Issue One: Bad Boys

Copyright 2006 Under the Moon

Editor in Chief: Terri Pray
Cover: Carrie Hall
Authors: Brenna Lyons, CJ England, Terri Pray, Ally Blue
Astrid Cooper, Phylis Sullivan, Rian Monaire
Interior Artists: Veronica Jones, Diana Stien, Carrie Hall, Richard
Savage, Thom Scott, *Avatar Art's* Mates Laurentiu
Editors: Morrigana Townsend, Stephanie Althof
Layout: Samuel Pray

ISBN 1-934153-55-9

Table of Contents

Forbidden Love
and
Under the Moon

are proud to announce the addition of Claudia Christian to their lineup of fine authors and artists. The cult-classic Babylon 5 regular (Commander Susan Ivanova) is not only an accomplished actress, both on the large and small screens; she's also an established writer, musician, singer and director, and she'll be stretching her wings at Under The Moon.

Claudia's initial debut with UTM will come in the form of her long-awaited CD, Once Upon A Time. The CD will be carried in the UTM catalog and bundled with some of the magazines.

But, Claudia's involvement won't stop there. Fans will then be able to sample some new dark erotic romance work from her in issue #2 of Forbidden Love Magazine: Wicked Women. Claudia's story, Revenge Is A Bitch To Swallow, will be one of the two cover stories for that issue!

Check out the Web Store
http://www.genreconnections.com/shop

Forbidden Love
Issue 2: Wicked Women
Coming in February

Debuting Claudia Christian's, of Babylon 5 fame, entry into the realm of women's fiction and from the wicked minds of Brenna Lyons, C.J England, Terri Pray, Sapphire Phelon, Under the Moon is proud to present tales of Wicked Women.

From Pirates to Shape Shifters, these are women who will do whatever it takes to get the job done. They will use their bodies, their minds, their wits in order to win, regardless of the cost. Are you ready to face these dangerously wicked women?

Recommended for mature readers only.

Check out the Web Store
http://www.genreconnections.com/shop

Playing Games

PLAYING GAMES
By Brenna Lyons

Dedicated to...

Fran and Bob, who played matchmaker to get me into the family. I know you watch from behind the veil.

Chapter I:
The Game Begins

May 1, 1987

Denise Roberts shook her head at the report again, dropping it on the passenger seat of her car. It didn't make sense, and reading it a hundred times or a thousand times didn't help that situation.

The victims were primarily female, young and attractive. Only one of the ten was male, and only two were over the age of twenty-five. They had all been found at the doors of one of the four local hospitals, hypo-anemic and confused, unable to recall what had happened to them. They were in good health except for their condition when they were found, not using drugs or drinking on the night of the attacks. It was rare to find a mark on them save the one that baffled all the experts.

It was a single puncture over a major artery, too large to be even the largest medical-grade needle for drawing blood...by far. She could pick up the file and find the precise grade she was looking for, but until something led her to a suspect or crime scene, what was the point of that?

"It's not like I'd recognize a single gauge of needle, even if I did know which one I was looking for," she sighed. This was decidedly not her usual beat.

Moreover, the marks left were healed sites that the victims and their families all attested had not been there hours earlier. The wound had somehow been used to draw off blood, but how was the mystery Denise was ordered to discover.

How was the blood drawn off without leaving an open puncture anywhere on the body? The experts had been over every victim with a fine-toothed comb. There were no scabs, no evidence of a deliberate blood draw.

What caused the discoloration reminiscent of a childhood scar, the pale or silvery oval, smaller than a fingertip, that refused to fade over time?

What caused the memory lapse?

That bothered Denise most. No drugs were found in the blood they took, urine, saliva, or even in the spinal fluid. There were no signs of head injury, indicating that they had been rendered unconscious, and it was simply unbelievable that they would all choose to lie.

While Denise found it intriguing, the street cops were frustrated over the lack of evidence, the media was scared shitless and the forensics specialists were ready to rip out someone's throat themselves. There had been ten victims in less than five months and not a shred of evidence to link them to an assailant or to each other. There was never evidence on the victim, and since they were all taken from popular sites, there was no hope of finding evidence at that end, by the time the victim could state a location or the guys on the street found the victim's car.

Denise was their last line of defense.

She sighed and clicked off the overhead light in her car, cursing herself as a fool again. Denise had been on this case for two months and had made no more headway than anyone else. It was embarrassing, an insult to her professional track record.

What Denise did was hard to describe. Even her boss didn't care how she did it. She just found her way to results that no one else seemed able to. If they were desperate enough to assign her for no better reason than that, they were more desperate than she had seen them in years.

So, what am I doing? Skulking around the alleyways where these people last recall being. Why? What am I going to find that no one else has and that I haven't up until now?

What do I hope to accomplish by coming here at night?

Denise shifted nervously. She needed to catch a sicko who drained blood from unsuspecting victims, before someone else got hurt, but this was crazy.

If Adam knew she was doing this, her boss would handcuff her to her desk. As it was, Adam was nervous that Denise had been requested for this assignment. He'd called her into his office more than once to lecture her on all the rules she already knew, his green eyes showing moments of deep emotion while he spoke. Her night excursions without an escort would drive him batty. Worse, Adam would have her banned from the case for her blatant disregard of protocol.

The alley was between a restaurant and a dance club. It led from the main street to the parking lot where she'd left her car. The last victim had disappeared from this alley more than two weeks earlier, and another would go soon. There was never more than three weeks between attacks.

Denise turned on her flashlight and panned it over the ground and walls. There were no doors that opened onto the alley or hiding places large enough for an adult to use. The fire escapes and dumpsters were at the back of the buildings, nowhere near the mouth of the alley. Both ends were well lit and the alley not poorly lit either. There was no conceivable way to sneak up on a person. The victim hadn't been with anyone else when she entered the alley. So, how--

"Lose something?" a deep voice inquired, a rich voice with a faint accent.

Denise turned with a yelp, losing her balance and landing on her ass with a grunt. She swung her flashlight up at the man standing over her.

He blinked stunning sky-blue eyes in the glare of her light then shaded them with one large hand. His hair was a mass of bright blond curls spilling over his forehead almost into those beautiful eyes. "Are you all right?" he asked.

She felt her cheeks heat. Denise pushed to her feet awkwardly. "How did you do that?"

He furrowed his brow. "Do?"

"How did you sneak up on me?" she demanded. "Where did you come from?"

He rolled his eyes. "I didn't sneak up on you. I walked, and I came from the street."

Denise ground her teeth in frustration. He did sneak up on her, and she had to know how. Denise didn't get lost in her own mind. She was always aware of her surroundings.

He smiled. "Are you sure you're all right?" He reached a hand out as if to check the temperature at the back of her neck.

"Polero," a new voice barked. "Face me."

Denise swung toward the new arrival, taking in the tall, dark man dressed all in black. He pulled a wicked-looking dagger more than a foot long from a sheath at his waist; the metal was dark, some alloy that didn't reflect the light as a steel blade would, making it seem to appear from and disappear into the shadows. When she could see it clearly, she wondered at the design; it was like nothing she'd seen before: flat on one edge, slightly curved on the other. The thing had to be heavy, and yet he was hefting it as if he held a butter knife. *Of course, he is six feet five, at least.* She back-pedaled, expecting to hit the wall of the blond's chest.

She didn't. Denise glanced over her shoulder and felt her breathing hitch. He was gone, disappeared without a sound, though he had to have traveled more than fifteen yards to leave the alley. Denise turned back to question tall, dark and dangerous, but he had disappeared as well--silently. She ran a shaking hand over her forehead. "People do not just disappear," she assured herself. Denise turned her light to the ground, scowling that the blonde had been on the

cobblestones. She spun back to the other
man's position, sighing in relief at the boot prints in the dirt break. "Okay. They do exist," she decided.

The blonde would be long gone. He'd been on the street side of the alley and could have turned any direction at the other end. The dark man was on the parking lot side. Unless he could run the hundred in ten flat while hauling that hardware, she'd see him.

Denise vaulted toward the lot, stilling and turning back at a sound behind her. Dust danced in the beam of her flashlight. Her hand shook. Denise sank to her knees and touched the cool soil where the footprints had been.

* * * * *

Polero smiled, watching the policewoman examining the alley feverishly. She was special in many ways: intuitive, determined, and intelligent. Her confusion and denial of the truth was the best part of the game so far.

When Jörg had ordered him to play this game with the Lord Jäger and his brothers, Polero hadn't been pleased. After the disaster of trying to take Lord Jäger's daughter and his near miss with Stephen's young bride, Polero didn't want to be within two states of those Warriors, but Jörg was his master, and Jörg's word was law.

Sometimes, Polero cursed his moments of weakness: the moment when he entered Jörg's service and the moment he accepted this damned half-life to escape death at the hands of Jörg's enemies. Polero hadn't realized how the loss of kind emotions would eat at him, as the centuries fell away.

He smiled at the policewoman again. Denise. There were only two things that made Polero feel truly alive now, and pretty Denise could provide him with both. And, she would provide...willingly.

Polero dematerialized and drifted toward her. Denise wanted answers. Her thirst for that knowledge would be her undoing. In nearly three centuries walking the Earth, Polero hadn't found a woman who wasn't consumed by curiosity.

He took shape behind her, watching her sift the dirt through her fingers, listening to her internal list of possible explanations, none of them remotely close to the truth.

"I take it he didn't harm you," he noted quietly.

Denise jumped to her feet, laying a slap across his cheek, her heart pounding and her mind a riot of thoughts tumbling over each other. She blushed in the sudden realization that she had lost her

11

composure. It wasn't something she was accustomed to doing.

"Y--You," she stammered. "Who t--the hell are you?"

Polero smiled. Being able to tell her was half the fun of this game. "Antoñio Pablo Polero, at your service." He executed a formal bow for show.

She took a step back, her eyes widening in surprise. Denise motioned toward the parking lot. "And Conan?" she asked lightly.

Ah yes. Stephen of Jäger. "An adversary."

Denise raised an eyebrow, regaining a bit of her composure. "You must be good at dodging."

"I have means of protecting myself."

"Where did you disappear to?" she demanded.

"I was leading him away from you. I knew he'd rather hurt me than you."

She didn't miss a beat. "Why would he want to hurt you?"

"Because I am a threat to his safety, and you are not."

Denise laughed harshly.

Polero started speaking before she could. "Don't laugh, Officer Roberts. The police cannot touch him. It isn't safe for you here. You should leave...before he comes back."

She paled.

He nodded. "Yes. I know exactly who you are, Denise." Polero turned toward the street, counting the seconds it took her to recover enough to try and stop him. She moved on five, surging toward his back, her quick steps eating up the distance between them.

"You're withholding information in a police investigation, Mr. Polero," she growled. "You're not leaving here until you give me those answers. Or would you rather leave in cuffs?"

Polero stopped and shot her a look of amazement. Denise was a formidable woman. And a surprising one; even he hadn't expected her to consider arresting him without some sort of aid in the task.

He crossed his arms over his chest. "Your superiors won't believe what I have to say," he warned her.

"What I've seen so far defies logic. How much worse can it get?"

"Don't ask what you don't want to know."

Denise strode to him. "I do want to know. That's why I'm here."

Polero shivered. Stephen is back. The youngest of the Jäger brothers had always left a slight tremor in his wake when ghosting that his brothers weren't sloppy enough to leave. That tremor had saved Polero's life more than once.

Forbidden Love: Bad Boys

He launched toward her, covering Denise's mouth before she could scream. He ghosted them both. "Shhh," he soothed her. Polero scooped his crucifix from beneath his t-shirt and held it between them, as if it had meaning.

She stilled, looking at the couple walking through the alley in confusion. Denise furrowed her brow, her mind desperately trying to analyze why they weren't reacting to her obvious distress.

He nuzzled against her ear, closing his eyes to the sweet smell of her fear. "Shhh," he reminded her, taking his hand away slowly. "He's back."

Denise's eyes darted back and forth, searching for some sign of Stephen. "I don't see him," she whispered.

"You will not, unless he wishes to be seen."

As Polero expected, Stephen heard at least part of their exchange, but still he didn't allow himself to be seen.

Stephen's challenge came from nothingness. "I know it's you Polero, you baby-stealing monster. Using the woman as a shield won't last long. Either you'll move or reveal yourself. I have all night."

Denise's eyes widened, and her fear intensified, but with it came her innate curiosity.

Polero pressed a kiss to her ear, speaking in a voice too low for Stephen to hear. "I will lead him away again, but you must promise to leave immediately."

She nodded slowly.

"If you wish to know the truth, meet me at the attack site preceding this one three nights from now."

She nodded again, her heart pounding in excitement.

He kissed her ear again, smiling at how easily she was falling into his trap. Polero pushed away from her and released his ghosting, relinquishing the game...for the moment. "Come for me, cursed one," he spat, as he turned and ran.

It was a chance. The Cursed Warrior could choose to stay behind, to educate the woman in what Polero was, but the odds were against it. Most Warriors would choose to leave an uninjured victim that had not been used for feeding behind for the possibility of making a kill.

Polero laughed aloud, laying on speed as he left Denise's line of sight. Stephen was close behind, as Polero knew he would be. Any Warrior would follow. To revenge themselves for the loss of the Lord Jäger's wife and child, any Warrior of Jäger would pursue Polero to both their deaths.

May 4, 1987

Polero materialized behind Denise, running his fingertips down her arm slowly. Denise turned to him, her hand fisted on the grip of her handgun. She met his eyes, relaxing with a sigh.

"Mr. Polero," she greeted him stiffly.

He chuckled. "Antoñio will be fine," he assured her. "Shall we go, Denise?"

She backed off a step, her eyes narrowing. "Go? Where are we going?"

Why didn't I tell Adam and get backup?

Because, he would have had a cow about the first night out, let alone this one!

Well, what would he say to you going somewhere with-

"You want to know the truth?" he interrupted her internal argument, dizzy in the strength of her mind. It had been a long time since he'd encountered a human whose thoughts were projected so clearly. She would be all the more enjoyable because of it, though there was the risk that she would be able to fight his control, in the end. He bit back a smile at that; what challenge could be found in a game with no risk involved?

"Of course." Adam is going to kill me.

"Then come with me."

She hesitated. "Tell me why that man called you a baby stealer first."

Polero affected a sigh. "It's not what it sounds like."

"You took his child," she accused.

"No. His master took my brother's wife. He nearly killed Jörg to take her. I was trying to take Anna-- I was trying to take her and her child back."

He paused for effect--and to push back the true anguish of his failure. Anguish wasn't a kind emotion; as such, he was more than capable of feeling it. Anguish and regret...would that men never knew them. No, there were too many beasts like that already, insane men who were without kind emotions in their human lives, so they didn't possess them as beasts.

He continued. "She's dead, and her daughter will never know her. I failed utterly."

"How utterly?" she asked suspiciously.

"There's a reason they want my brother and I dead. If I ever get

the chance again...”

She shuddered.

“Do you want to know the truth?” he asked.

Denise nodded. She didn’t pull away when he wrapped an arm around her hip and led her along the nearly-deserted streets. This was the most amusement Polero had gotten from the game thus far, giving Denise just enough of the truth and avoiding just enough lies to make it more interesting.

He’d chosen this site for a reason. One of his holes was close to this alley. Polero had surrounded himself with books and icons over the centuries, copying or stealing texts to keep a stable library, even on those rare occasions when Warriors discovered one of his holes. Tonight, Polero would sacrifice one to his pleasures.

She entered his hole, an apartment over an abandoned clothing store, willingly and looked around at some of his treasures. He’d collected both Christian and Warrior icons: artful recreations of the crucifix, religious robes, a few amulets stolen from dead Warriors, and even a sacred weapon. He’d copied religious texts from both religions, some calligraphed meticulously and some rewritten to suit his own needs.

Denise ran her fingers over a twentieth century Roman Catholic collar. “You mugged a priest?” she joked.

Polero chuckled, dragging off his sweatshirt in favor of the muscle shirt beneath. “I was a priest,” he answered honestly. Not in this time, but I was once of the order.

She turned to him in surprise, running her eyes from his jean-clad legs to the ladder of muscles up his abdomen to the tattoo of the cross on the front of his right shoulder. “You?”

He nodded. “Surprised?”

“To say the least,” she admitted. “What happened? You were a priest.”

Polero shrugged. “The organized religions aren’t into the hunting of evil, as they once were.”

“Evil?” she asked dubiously.

He strode toward her, pressing lightly to her body as he reached for one of the volumes on the shelves at her back. Polero kept his eyes locked on hers as he brought the book down for her.

Denise gasped as he hardened, gazing down between their bodies.

Polero backed away, biting back a smile at her interest. “Natural reaction to a beautiful woman,” he confided, opening the book and feigning interest.

Denise blushed. "But, you're a priest," she protested weakly.

"No, I was a priest. That was a long time ago, and even priests react to a beautiful woman."

Polero had certainly reacted to Yzabeau. Whether it was Jörg's possession of her or something nameless about her, Polero could never say. Regana's souls had always captured men, Warriors, and beasts alike.

"Beautiful?" she scoffed.

He moved his eyes over the bun of auburn hair and dark eyes to the ample breasts, half-disguised beneath her jacket, to the outline of her mound through her jeans. "Yes," he answered bluntly.

She blushed deeper and cleared her throat. "Answers," she reminded him.

Nevertheless, she was pleased that he thought her beautiful, and she wished another man thought so--

Adam.

The man must be a fool.

Polero looked back to the book. "Of course."

Denise was the type of woman Polero enjoyed. It wasn't so unusual that she didn't find herself attractive, though. Americans of the present day leaned toward willowy females, not a woman with lush curves and breasts a man could become lost in.

He sat on the couch, in the circle of light cast from the lamp he'd left burning, and waved for her to join him. She sat on the opposite end, and Polero scowled at her.

"You speak Latin?" he asked bluntly.

She shook her head, easing next to his body.

Denise took the book from his hands, gasping at the illumination on the first page. Polero swallowed a laugh. He'd chosen this volume purposefully. Long ago, Polero had designed this seduction piece for nights like this. When he surrendered this hole to the Warriors, it would be the one treasure he carried away with him.

Her breathing was ragged as she surveyed the illumination of two beasts sharing a woman while they fed from her, the victim's face a study in exquisite pleasure.

Polero remembered the night in question well. Every illumination in the book was a recreation of some sensual pleasure in the years since he'd abandoned the church to follow the more powerful gods of the beasts. Having the trappings of his former life around him served only two purposes. It was once a comfort, and it put humans at ease to associate him with the position he once believed in.

"They're..." Denise's eyes went wide in understanding. He's cracked. "But that's not--"

"Real? I assure you, the beasts are very real. What you see there is a new beast awakening after his change."

"A what?"

"A turned. A beast made by one of the elders, a master. Some of the elders would just fuck the new recruit while he fed, but that is not as striking a picture as them sharing the turned's first victim." And, Jörg is not like other elders.

Polero hardened further at the memory of taking Jörg's blood, Polero's beast demanding other pleasures.

Jörg ordered him to close his feeding site, looking to Polero's engorged member in something resembling pity then ordering him not to make a move. It was maddening, feeling the burn to climax and not having the leave of his master to seek it. For a long moment, Polero believed it was some sort of punishment Jörg was handing down, though he couldn't think clearly enough to reason why Jörg would want to punish him that night.

Polero watched as Jörg drew the woman between them, the elder's hands teasing the woman sexually as he began to take her blood. She cried out in ecstasy as Jörg pushed his cock into the depths of her ass.

Polero's fangs itched to taste the blood he smelled. He stroked his cock, needing to taste other depths. Perhaps Jörg would give the woman to Polero when he tired of her, but the waiting would drive him mad, seeing and smelling their blood and sex.

Jörg closed his feeding site and met Polero's eyes. "Join me," he invited. "Feed your beast, but feed it slowly. Feed it gently."

From that day to this, Polero had never felt anything as sublime as sharing that woman with Jörg: kissing her as they thrust inside her, sharing her blood, taking her body in every conceivable combination that night. He and Jörg had shared women on many occasions, but there was something unforgettable in that first time, a dark rush of power, the fellowship of blood...before it became jaded and forgotten as every other kind emotion had been.

Polero forced his mind back to the subject at hand.

Denise flipped the page, swallowing hard at the illumination of him taking a woman over a ship's railing.

Ah, yes. The captain's mistress had been luscious and willing.

The captain had been a bought human. He'd had her himself after Polero was done with her, though for her comfort, she had no memory of anyone but her lover.

Polero forced his fangs back, as Denise's body prepared for him. Given enough time with her, he could fully sate every one of the fantasies her fertile mind was concocting at the book's suggestion. But, they wouldn't have that much time together.

She turned another page.

The minister's daughter he'd deflowered, his tongue taunting her spasming body as he drank from her engorged tissues.

She bit her lower lip, moving her thighs against each other restlessly. Denise turned another page, her breath hitching at the next scene.

Oh, yes. She likes that. Polero smiled, morphing his member larger as he had that night.

She'd been a streetwalker he'd picked up for his amusement. Polero had enjoyed watching her mouth spread wide around his increased size.

"No one is that big," Denise whispered.

Polero chuckled. "Really?" he drawled.

Denise glanced at his face then panned her eyes down to his lap. She darkened and looked at the book again, running a hand through her hair nervously. He was a priest? What a waste!

"These beasts," she choked out. "Vampires-- Tell me about them. What does all of this say? Besides their love for screwing anything that moves, of course."

She was sweating, shaking. Her body needed completion almost as much as his own did, but she directed him back to the subject at hand. Self-preservation. She's afraid to take what she wants.

He reached across her body, pointing to the text. Denise's eyes strayed to the inked drawing often. Polero snuggled closer to her as he eased his fingertip across the page.

"It talks about the limitations of the beasts, the ways to kill them."

"How?" she asked urgently.

"There are icons."

"Crosses? Holy water?"

Polero laughed harshly. "No. I believed the old stories, too. Nothing so mundane works against them. I learned that the hard way."

Denise searched her eyes over him frantically, locking on the marks Jörg had left on him when Polero entered into service with him. She touched the marks, rising to her knees. Her breath was hot on his skin. "Do you remember this?"

"Yes." Jörg wanted him to remember every searing second of that feeding without the pleasure he typically gave his bought humans. It was a punishment, a warning of what cruelty he was capable of if Polero ever crossed him again.

"Why did they leave your memory? That is how they're taking away memories. Right?" She touched the marks gently, as if he would break.

"Yes. The beasts reorder or blank memories to hide their existence." He cupped her hip. "I imagine the one who did this was playing with me. I was a priest, after all."

"You tried to use the usual means to stop a vampire?"

"He walked into my church, killed a bishop, and nearly killed me. Nothing worked against him. It was years later when I found these texts, when I learned that my fellow clerics knew much more than they let on." Ah, Jonrie. Working for the enemy all that time.

"You confronted them?"

Polero rubbed her lower back. "Yes. It's amazing the things the church doesn't admit to."

"So, you set out to do this on your own?" she asked in awe.

"Armed with some texts I'd liberated from the church and a few loyal men with the same beliefs."

"Your brother?" Denise asked, sitting down and meeting his gaze.

"Yes. Jörg and I have always been in this together." Polero smiled sadly at that. *Little comfort that is. I cannot even find comfort in our connection. I cannot find comfort in anything but what Denise can offer.*

"Why?" she mused, her mind abruptly elsewhere, on a track and moving so fast, Polero had trouble following her.

"Why what?" He ran his hands further up her back, easing the tension in her muscles.

Denise sighed.

So typical. My past always makes them feel so safe.

"Why is the vampire doing this? I mean, he has to eat, but it's more than that. He wants these victims found. What is his reason?"

"It's a game," he confided.

"A game? What kind of game?"

"Look at it from the culprit's mindset. This brings attention the pursuer does not want or need." *At a time when he needs the distraction* least. "It flaunts the ability of anyone to stop him. It sends pursuers scrambling to end it."

She nodded. "He's amusing himself."

Not yet. "They live to appease their hungers and still their longings. They want endlessly."

"Blood," she mused.

Polero picked up the book from where she dropped it between them and flipped another page, turning it for her to see. "And other pleasures."

Denise looked at the book for a long moment, barely breathing in her excitement. She blushed deeply.

"What is it?" he asked, though Polero knew well enough that she wanted him desperately. She'd resigned herself to the fact that she could never tell her co-workers about all of this. What Denise learned now was for her own avid thirst for knowledge.

"W-who wrote and illustrated this book?" she stammered.

"Priests," he offered in half-truth. "Working from the actual accounts of copulation of beasts with human women."

"They're drawn-- They all seem to be enjoying themselves."

"That surprises you?" he asked.

"Yes," she practically shouted. "They... And they drink blood, and...and--"

He smiled at her unsettled mind. "Ah. I see. The beasts feed off of emotion almost as much as they feed off of blood. They don't feel kind emotions of their own."

"They want to make the woman happy to experience the rush of her emotions?"

"Absolutely."

And much more.

"*The beast demands satisfaction sexually while it feeds, satisfaction for the beast. Any powerful emotions mollify the beast. A woman's terror in rape is enough. The stillness-- The peace in feeling her pleasure is for the tattered remains of the man, not for the beast. One who forgets the pleasure and peace to be had for the man should be exterminated.*" Jörg had taught Polero that on the night he turned.

Denise fingered the illumination, staring at it again. "There was no sign of sexual assault," she noted.

Polero grimaced. "You're not listening. It wouldn't be an assault."

"You're saying the women willingly screwed a beast?"

"If you want a man badly enough, don't you?" he prodded.

She darkened further and cleared her throat. "How would he convince them so quickly?"

He smiled. "A being that reads minds? He knows exactly how to touch her, exactly what to say to her."

"It can't be that easy."

Polero rolled his eyes at that. It wasn't the easiest thing Jörg had ever charged him with doing. "He picks his victims carefully."

He dragged a finger up her arm. Yes, Polero had chosen Denise very carefully.

"And the man?" she asked slowly.

"He's not into men. That was a simple feeding."

"Why vary the typical plan?"

He scowled. "Irritation. Pure and simple. Days without finding a suitable woman. The beast got hungry."

She nodded and leaned back, flipping through the book. Polero counted the pages, mentally picturing each illumination as she went, gauging its effect on her. Gods, but her scent was driving him mad.

"What is it like?" she asked suddenly.

"Like?"

Polero traced the outer seam of her jeans from knee to hip. Though she pretended not to notice, he knew she was aware of every touch, reveling in it, wanting it.

"Tracking them. Dodging them."

"Lonely." Loneliness wasn't a kind emotion. Loneliness was something Polero felt every day of his life.

Denise turned the page again, and Polero bit back a chuckle. The illumination was so close to their current situation that Polero knew she would be affected. Her perusal of the book was giving him a very clear picture of what would excite her.

"You don't interact with other people much," she guessed. "Not even your brother."

"He's mourning," Polero excused Jörg immediately.

Until he claimed his mate, Jörg would always mourn them. *No. He mourns the lost souls even as he revels in the one he holds. There is no peace for Jörg.*

"You've never married?"

"No. I have never been blessed with something so precious," he decided bitterly. From priest to bought human to damned beast, there was never an appropriate time to marry.

Her hand touched his thigh and lingered, brushing over the

muscles, taut in his restraint. She started to pull back, but Polero covered her hand with his. Denise met his gaze and moved her hand beneath the cover of his, toward his inner thigh and up to his crotch. He matched her movements, encouraging her.

She wanted to seduce him. Denise wanted to be bold. That was the fun of this game. He'd known when he'd chosen her that Denise would pursue given the chance to do so.

He tensed as her hand covered his aching length. She stilled, uncertain.

"Don't stop," he gasped. Polero tipped his hips beneath her.

Denise traced the bulge breathlessly. "So big," she whispered.

Taste it, he begged silently, restraining the mad urge to coerce her. *Nothing the Warriors can see until it's too late*, he reminded himself.

Polero moved his free hand to the space between her slightly-parted legs, skating his fingertips over her damp jeans, over the heat he'd created in her. His hunger spiked at that, at her excitement and the blood rushing in her veins.

"The hungers of the beast are formidable. He who cannot order his beast doesn't deserve to live another day."

Denise pushed up on her knees and brought her lips to his, tentatively, questioning Polero silently. He captured her mouth, stroking her more purposefully, letting her feel his hunger.

She did feel it. Warriors believed there were few human sensitives, but Polero secretly believed that every woman was one, to some extent. They all felt the darkness of the beast. Some were drawn to it. Some were repelled by it. Those who were drawn to it required no coercion to make them hunger to taste the darkness. Denise hungered for it, and the hunger made women behave in unbelievable ways. Denise pulled up at his shirt, and Polero released her long enough to allow her to pull it off.

Strictly speaking, clothing wasn't a necessity for Polero. He could project the illusion of clothing right down to the feel of the fabric against his own skin and the skin of anyone who touched him. He certainly didn't need them to shield his body from the elements. Even in a solid form, the elements didn't touch him, and dematerialized, he was impervious even to attack.

But, Polero preferred clothing. He was one of the highest level turned there was. Elders and others like himself were capable of dematerializing solid, inanimate objects worn on their bodies. The illusion of clothing was one of the few powers he possessed that Polero seldom used. He preferred the reality of true clothing, and he preferred feeling women remove them.

She kissed him, sinking into his hunger, matching his rising lust. Denise unbuttoned his jeans with a single pull. Polero groaned at the sensation. He loved the feel of the new jeans: acid-washed, relaxed fit, soft and form fitting. Nothing, not even leather or silk, felt as good against his body.

Denise's mouth closed around the head of his aching cock. *Almost nothing feels better than jeans, but a woman's body tops the list.* She strained to take him in, and Polero wished he'd made himself smaller just to feel Denise take all of him. He smiled. She would take all of him very soon.

Polero dragged her shirt up her body and unhooked her bra, playing at the tips of her breasts. "I will be returning this favor," he promised her.

She met his eyes, peeling her jacket, shirt and bra off as she drove him on, inviting Polero blatantly to use her body. He smiled, the predator raising its head and taking in her scent.

Polero wanted Denise more than he'd wanted a woman in years. She was a classic beauty. Her hips were made to carry sons that some lucky human man would give her. Her breasts were lush and full, capped with rose-colored nipples.

Only one thing was wrong. He reached out and pulled the clips from the bun, letting the heavy waves of auburn hair cascade over her shoulders.

"Now," he ordered. "I have to taste you."

Denise stood before him, unbuttoning her jeans and easing them down those wonderful hips. Polero took over as her curls appeared, sweeping her down onto the couch and stripping off her remaining clothing and shoes. Her gun thumped to the rug, forgotten by its owner.

He buried his tongue in the well of her honey, drawing her essence out and tasting her. Far from assuaging his hunger, it fueled him. Her musk and her cries made him ache for more.

The minister's daughter danced in his mind much as she had danced naked for Polero, begging him to possess her again. He could take Denise's blood now, drawing it from her as she shattered, her blood and climax mixing in his mouth, but the Warriors would be on him before he could find further pleasure with her. Polero rose up over her, determined to feel his cock buried deep inside her.

Denise's eyes opened wide as the engorged head parted her. "No," she gasped.

He ground his teeth, tapping down his frustration. If she told him to stop now, he'd use coercion. He'd feed. Polero would taste her climax any way he had to. "Yes," he countered urgently.

Denise's hand circled him. "Let me get on top." She didn't plead for what she wanted. She ordered what she needed from him.

Polero smiled, visions of Denise stolen from her mind making him pulse in anticipation. He eased off of her and sat on the couch by her feet, stroking his length in invitation. "Yes," he growled his agreement.

She sat beside him, dropping to encase him in her mouth one last time and releasing him before Polero could protest. Denise placed a hand on his shoulder and swung her leg over him.

He guided his cock, still wet and tingling from her mouth, between the slick outer lips of her sex. Denise lowered herself, sheathing his increased size, inch by torturous inch.

"Yes," he hissed. "Take me. Take all of me." His hands tightened on her hips as Denise settled in his lap, taking him to the root.

She started moving over him, taking what she needed from him, her body and mind a riot. Polero teased at her breasts, guiding her over his length faster, pounding hard into her.

Denise was close, ready to plunge over the edge. It was time. Polero nuzzled her throat, allowing his fangs to extend as she threw her head back.

"Why?" she whispered.

"Why what?"

"Why one puncture? Why not two?"

He kissed at the artery, feeling the pulse of blood to her brain speed. "He's a turned. Long before his master turned him, they went head to head, and one of his eyeteeth was broken in the exchange. It extends, but it isn't sharp enough or long enough to pierce flesh."

Denise sighed as she wrapped her fingers in the waves of his hair. "How do you know?"

"I was there."

Polero sank his single good fang into her, shuddering as the pain drove her over. Denise screamed in ecstasy, her muddled mind trying to piece together what he was doing to her. Her hands fisted in his hair, and her body clenched rhythmically on his length.

He suckled at her, drinking deeply of both her blood and emotions, wrapping her at last in the pleasure he could give her while he fed. He was a master at this, at gauging how much pain a woman would bear in orgasm before he had to trick her mind into finding his feeding a joy.

Polero pulled back as he climaxed, filling Denise with his sterile fluids, the peace he came to associate with sex, blood, and death washing over him. His beast was sated, though the smell of her blood rushing over her chest called to him, and Polero resumed his feeding. The spilled slick teased at their bodies, as he took her in slow, sensuous strokes.

He spoke to her through their newly-forged link, needing to explain to her as he'd never explained to the others.

"Soon. I will clean you and dress you. I will leave you where you will get immediate medical care. I wish I could leave you this memory, but I cannot."

Denise moaned her protest, wanting to hold to this moment as they all did...until they weren't in the arms of the beast and wrapped in the alluring cloak of darkness. Few women pursued the game that far.

"You have earned a page in my book, Denise. You will forget this night, but I never will."

The game was all that was left to tickle his morbid sense of humor after all the centuries of living with his beast. Polero began his reordering of her memory with a heavy heart. Of all the women over the years, few made the game as amusing as Denise had.

* * * * *

Denise groaned, clenching her eyes shut against the harsh light without opening them to it, shading her eyes with one hand and reaching for the light switch next to her bed with the other. The switch wasn't there. The wall was tile instead of wallpaper.

She opened her eyes a slit and furrowed her brow at the sight of the IV stand over her. The scent of antiseptic was heavy in the air. It was a hospital, but what the hell was she doing here? Denise fought for a clear memory, but her head ached with the effort--almost as much as her body ached.

"Finally," a voice growled at her.

Denise turned to it tenderly. "Adam?"

He nodded grimly. Her boss looked sleep-deprived. Dark circles shadowed his beautiful green eyes, and it looked like he hadn't had a shave recently.

"What the hell did you think you were doing?" he continued.

She closed her eyes, trying desperately to remember what she did to end up here. Denise wasn't a street cop. There was no reason that she should have been shot or beaten, though beaten didn't sound far from the truth by the feel of it.

"You didn't think to ask for backup? You didn't call me?"

"Backup?" she repeated.

"Backup. Something you were ordered to take along if you were going to do something this monumentally-- You met a possible suspect alone," he hinted in irritation.

"What suspect? I would never--"

He held up her pocket brain, his eyes flashing in fury.

A pulse of sexual excitement coursed over her nerves. Denise pushed it away, disconcerted. "And?" she asked weakly.

"You tell me. It's your handwriting, and we retrieved it from your car."

"Adam, all I know is that my head hurts, my stomach is upset, every muscle and joint in my body aches, and you're yelling at me."

And all I can picture is you alone with me somewhere private. What the hell is wrong with me? She'd always fantasized about Adam, but it had never taken over her mind like this. Maybe her walls were down.

"You don't remember arranging to meet a Mr. Antoñio Pablo Polero?" he demanded, flipping the notebook open to a page three or four in.

"Who the hell is--"

"Six feet, two-ten, blond, curly, halfway down his neck, light blue eyes, slight accent, maybe Spanish...*with* a question mark," he snapped, his body trembling.

"Sounds cute," she quipped. "Sort of like you, except for the accent and your pretty green eyes. Where can I find this Adonis?"

Adam raised an eyebrow in surprise.

Denise ran a shaking hand over her forehead, swallowing down a wave of nausea. *Why did I say that? I am never going to live this one down.*

Adam shook his head, suddenly uncertain. "Denise... What day is it?"

She glanced at the sunlight streaming around the window blinds. "Daylight," she noted. "Saturday."

He paled. "What's the last thing you remember?"

Denise grimaced at the spike of pain thinking about it caused. "Punching out," she groaned. "I think. No. I had soft tacos for dinner," she continued hopefully. "Taco Bell... The one by--" She grimaced, the headache raging abruptly out of control.

"By? By where?"

"I don't know. I..." The pain spiked again. *Don't want to know.* She panted, waiting out the agony, praying it was over.

"Friday?" he asked urgently.

"Of course, Friday," she snapped. "Adam, what the hell is wrong with you?"

He sank into a chair next to the bed and extended his hand toward her, touching her cheek with a pained look. Adam turned his arm to offer his watch for her inspection. Denise looked at him in confusion.

"Read it," he ordered quietly.

She squinted at the digital numbers. "Eleven-twenty," she noted. "I don't--"

"The date."

"The-- Have you lost your mind? I told you the date."

"The date," he insisted.

Denise shook her head, biting back a sick swirl. She locked her eyes on the watch again, her heart stuttering. "The fifth? Adam, please tell me your watch is fast," she managed weakly. "Otherwise, I've been unconscious a long damn time."

"You've been unconscious for thirteen hours, but you've lost four days."

"Then I did even worse than the civilians," she complained bitterly. *Oh, I will never live this down.*

"Not entirely."

"What do you mean?"

Adam took her hand, squeezing it and offering her a rakish smile. "You came back with two descriptions and a name for the clear description. At least we have somewhere to start. That's more than anyone else has given us."

Denise nodded. "If it does us any good."

He stroked her knuckles, an almost unconscious move. "What do you mean?"

"Just a feeling that someone is playing games with us."

His smile disappeared. "What makes you say that?"

"I have no idea." She blushed. "I just...know it."

Adam nodded grimly. "That was why you were requested. Wasn't it?"

"Yes," she admitted. "Yes, it was."

Chapter 2:
Blackout

Denise straightened her spine, forcing her breathing to remain slow and steady as the room fell silent around her. She wouldn't accept their pity. She'd meet their eyes steadily when they wanted the simplicity of looking away from her.

"You don't have to do this," Adam whispered. "You don't have to see this."

"I do. I have to know." Ten days earlier, her life had come to a screeching turn, one that she could neither remember nor explain. If the answers were here, she wouldn't leave until she had them.

"It's only been four days since you were released from the hospital. You can see the videos later and--"

"I'm fine...a little weak but strong enough for this."

He nodded and handed her a pair of latex gloves. Denise pulled them on and ambled along the shelves, touching antique books and religious icons, trying to fathom the mind that would surround itself with these things, a mind she supposedly touched in those four lost days.

"Some of these things are priceless," Det. Ross said, examining what appeared to be a jewel-encrusted, golden Celtic cross in awe.

She fingered an etched disc hung on a frayed loop of silk string. It was a strange design, not unlike and old bit of heraldry, crossed swords with a howling wolf head above. She brushed her fingertips over the faded word beneath. "KlingeStütze," she read.

"Sword bearer," Sgt. Peters stated without looking up from the book in his hand.

She turned to him. "What did you say?"

Peters darkened and didn't quite meet her eyes. "That's what it means. I had someone check. I mean... It's one of those things that's not like the others, so-- It will take us months or even years to translate all of this. We're dealing with at least ten languages here, some of them dead languages."

"Oh. I'll keep that in mind. What language is this?" She pointed to the disc.

"German."

"Thanks."

He nodded and turned back to the shelf, studying a green stole embroidered with black a little too intently.

Denise moved on, acting unaffected when she wanted to scream. When she'd woken in the hospital, she'd been afraid she'd never live down the laughter of the other officers. She'd been wrong, and the truth was worse.

The guys weren't laughing. They were terrified. Whoever their maniacs were, they weren't afraid to take down a cop.

Still, Denise had done the impossible, which only seemed to heighten their unease. She may have been found, blood weak and near death at the ER doors of Central, but she'd come away with descriptions on two suspects and a name for one scribbled in her pocket brain, though admittedly she had no memory of either of them. The information had netted them nothing so far, but it was more than any of the other victims had come away with.

Officially, Denise was still on medical leave. Unofficially... *Adam would have to handcuff me to the bed to keep me away.* That was an image she didn't need. She pushed it away and resumed her personal tirade. *Memories or no, I have to see this.*

She scrunched her nose at the rancid smell emanating from the far reaches of the room beyond the rows of shelves. That was what brought them here, the smell that convinced the building's owner to call the police in to investigate the supposedly-abandoned site. It hadn't taken her brothers in blue long to identify the blood as hers, and Denise had insisted on visiting the scene with Adam.

There's no time like the present. She turned and strode toward the back of the room.

Without missing a beat, Peters and Ross blocked her path. Abrams joined them, shaking his pale face.

"You don't want to do this," Abrams assured her.

"Don't, Roberts," Ross agreed. "It's not pretty."

She managed a cold smile. "I didn't expect it to be. Let me past."

Adam stepped to her shoulder. "It's okay. I'll go with her."

Denise ground her teeth at that, swallowing her protest that she didn't need a babysitter. Adam had agreed to let her come here only because of her badgering. He could ban her from the scene just as easily.

The officers parted, resuming their disconcerting avoidance that simply.

She looked at the opening, her heart pounding and her mouth dry. Her feet felt nailed to the floor, and she was acutely aware of the empty space where her gun would have lain had she not been on leave.

"You don't have to do this," Adam breathed at her shoulder.

He was right. Denise planted her feet, stifling the mad urge to turn and run the other direction. She didn't *want* to do this. "I have to," she whispered, her voice wooden.

Ross winced.

Denise didn't give herself time to reconsider. If she did that, she'd manage to talk herself out of this, and she would never forgive herself--or win back the respect of these men. She strode past her coworkers, her head held high.

The space behind the shelves was set up as a living room. She panned her eyes over the touchier floor lamp, a stack of books at its base, freezing at the sight of the sofa, blood soaked heavily into the green cushions, dime to half-dollar-sized droplets dotting the floor and a bloody handprint on the back cushions of the couch. Bile rose in her throat, and she swallowed it down painfully.

She didn't question that the print was her own, but that raised more questions than it answered. There hadn't been a drop on her when she was found. Of course, she could only assume the clothing she'd been found in was what she wore out to meet Polero, since she had no memory of dressing and no witnesses to what she'd been wearing that day.

Adam's hand closed on her shoulder, and his breath was rough.

"He bled me," she choked out. She'd known that, of course, but there seemed to be more blood spilled on the sofa than she'd expected to see. *Blood weak... How much blood did I lose?*

As if he read her mind, Adam answered her. "It's not as much as it looks like...not even as much as you lost, according to Wilks from forensics. It's not precise yet, of course, but they're fairly sure of that."

Her mind fought the idea that finding the site was a good thing. They'd never had a site to dig into before. Surely, something would come of this.

Denise pressed a hand to her forehead, noting the sweat coating her body numbly. The air suddenly seemed thick and hard to draw into her lungs.

She stared at the sofa, arousal beating at her nerves, her nipples coming to uncomfortable points against her bra. Heat radiated from the wound on her throat outward, akin to the feeling of hot breath swirling against her neck. She braced herself, dizzy in the unexpected response.

Her mind rebelled. A maniac had bled her here and dumped her at the hospital in what she knew was some sadistic game. What was there to be aroused about?

Forbidden Love: Bad Boys

Her body ignored her mind's protestations, a disconcerting heat pooling at the apex of her thighs.

"Denise?"

Adam's voice wrapped around her, stoking the embers of excitement into a roaring conflagration. Phantom hands skated over her body, and she swallowed a groan of pleasure.

A flash of a memory crackled in her mind, a book in her hands though she couldn't read the page, the lamp burning brightly in the dark room. There was someone beside her.

Not here. There!

Denise shook off Adam's hand and vaulted toward the sofa. The smell assaulted her, and she pushed it away, standing with her calves pressed against the unstained portion, unwilling to sit there even to acclimate herself. "I sat here," she whispered.

She vaguely noticed that the other officers had put down the objects they held and congregated at the mouth of the isle between the first two shelves, waiting to see what would happen next.

"He..."

She turned her head, barely breathing. At first, there was nothing, just the room in its state of disrepair.

"Denise," Adam rasped.

Denise... The ghostly voice whispered in her mind, rich in a thick accent and--excitement?

The face floated before her, insubstantial as smoke. The entire room changed, growing darker, the far corners lost to shadows, the single beacon of light at her side...and him.

"Antoñio."

She met his eyes, light blue eyes the color of a summer sky, eyes that pleaded for something--or did they demand it? It was hard to reconcile that point.

His blond hair was wind-ruffled, and he was smiling. The tattoo of an ornate Maltese cross peeked from behind a black muscle shirt. Muscles, he had in abundance: washboard abs, strong arms and thighs that strained the seams on his faded jeans.

Everything about him was sinfully decadent. He was eye candy, but something about him screamed that one taste of him would be addictive and dangerous.

He laughed, and her eyes locked on the one imperfection. His left eye tooth had been broken at some point in the past.

Pain sliced through her mind, and Denise clasped her hands to her temples, whimpering, her balance deserting her.

"Denise!" Adam caught her, swearing profusely and supporting her against his chest. "I shouldn't have let you come."

"No," she pleaded, stumbling along as he turned her toward the shelves. "Paper. I need paper."

"Denise--"

"Now, Adam. While I still remember--" A new spike of pain assaulted her, and her knees buckled.

Adam lowered her to the floor with her back to one of the shelves. "We have to get you some help and--"

She grabbed the pocket brain from his jacket pocket then fished for the pen stuffed deeper in. Denise wrote everything she could remember about the man's physical appearance. *Antoñio...* Her hands shook wildly, and more than once, she had to stop because the pain made thinking impossible.

At last, she handed the notebook to Adam, her breathing labored. She met his green eyes, abruptly drained.

Adam took the notes from her hand, staring at them in disbelief. "Abrams," he managed. "Get this information added to the file." He met her gaze as the other three officers poured over the new description. "Can you work with an artist tomorrow?"

Denise rubbed her aching forehead, nodding. "I think...I can," she gasped.

"Good. Then let's get you home."

* * * * *

Home. Denise looked at Adam out of the corner of her eye, watching guiltily as he washed their dinner dishes. Since she'd been released from the hospital, her home had been his, and he rarely let her lift a finger.

The first night, he'd claimed concern for her medical condition. After that, he'd argued that her attacker or attackers might come back for her while she was so weak, knowing she might remember more than she already had.

Adam wrapped his hand around the back of her neck as if checking for a fever. "Your headache gone?" he asked.
She nodded, her eyes straying to his bare chest.

"I still think we should have someone check you over."

"No. I'll be fine," she lied. In truth, every time she focused on the black hole that encompassed four days of her life, it felt as if her head would split in two. Dealing with the artist was likely to make her puke.

32

Worse, nothing more had come of her attempts to remember the lost time.

"What is it?" he asked.

Denise shook her head hopelessly, stepping toward him and letting him pull her to his chest. She closed her eyes, greedily breathing in his scent. These moments were the calm in the howling hurricane of her life.

Adam massaged her neck, his breath stirring her hair. "What did he do?" he murmured. "Why does it hurt you to--"

"No," she pleaded, tipping her head back. "Please, don't talk about it any more today."

For one agonizing minute, they stared at each other. Then his mouth closed over hers. Denise closed her eyes, giving herself up to the cascade of feeling that submarined her every time Adam touched her, nearly every time he looked at her.

It was like no first kiss she'd ever experienced. There was no hesitation, no exploration. It was purely carnal, dark and rich as Godiva chocolate, and all-consuming.

Adam pulled back, his breathing coming in sharp gasps. "Oh, God. What are we doing?"

"Do it again." She wrapped her hands around his neck and guided his mouth back down to hers.

The second kiss was no less involved. He pulled her against his body, nestling her to the rigid proof that he wanted her, despite his protestations.

Denise sighed into his mouth. She could have taken the time to argue with him that it wasn't what he thought. He wasn't taking advantage of her in a heightened state of emotion. She'd wanted him for at least the last year they'd worked together, moreso since she'd awoken in the hospital with Adam hovering over her. She didn't waste her breath explaining it when he wasn't actively refusing.

He pulled back again, every muscle in his body rigid. She opened her eyes, staring into the intense green of his. It couldn't stop here. Denise couldn't let it.

She started unbuttoning her shirt, and his eyes followed, his tongue darting out to wet his lips.

"This is going to complicate things at work," he grumbled, not taking his eyes off of her bra.

Denise shucked the shirt off of her shoulders. "Do you really care?"

Adam shook his head slowly, trailing his hands up her spine and unhooking her bra.

She peeled it away, feeling a wanton thrill at standing topless with him in her kitchen. "Adam?" she purred, her voice strange in her own ears.

He held her lightly to his body so that the tips of her breasts brushed his chest, still staring between them. "Yes?"

"I think we should go to bed."

"Definitely." But, he made no move to accomplish it. Adam pulled her closer to him, rolling his hips against her as if in amazement. "Now," he breathed. "Right now."

He turned Denise and crowded against her back all the way to her bedroom. His hands cupped her breasts, pinching and kneading the ample globes lightly until she ached for more. "Take off your jeans."

His voice was a growl that made her shiver in need. Denise spread her feet slightly, pressing back into his hips and forward into his hands as she opened the jeans and peeled them down onto her thighs. She paused, unable to go further while he held her this way.

She gasped as he slid his hands down the soft expanse of her stomach. One pushed her jeans further while the other skated down between her thighs, teasing at her seam then dipping inside. Denise murmured protests as his fingers retreated.

Adam circled her, scanning her body slowly. "Take them off," he ordered again.

Denise considered her move for only a second, pushing away the nagging voice asking when she'd become so sexually bold. True, it wasn't at all like her. She'd always found her slightly-plump form an embarrassment, but Adam's blatant perusal made her feel sexy.

Adam was more than she'd ever hoped for in a man. He was worth seducing, if needs be, and she didn't believe in seducing men as a rule.

Moreover, Denise wanted him at the edges of control. Out of control. She wanted him to shed the careful patience he showed in the precinct house and show her the man beneath.

She released the knot of hair at the back of her head, letting the auburn tresses tumble down. Denise arched her back, pushing her breasts up and forward, her hair fanning over the back of her buttocks and thighs. At Adam's groan, she turned her back to him, folding herself and pushing the material to her ankles, exposing herself to him.

"Oh, yeah." The unmistakable sound of a zipper spurred her on.

Denise pulled one foot free of the denim and spread her legs further, kicking it free of her other foot. She placed her hands flat on the floor and cast a sly smile at Adam from between her legs. She'd always been flexible, and it was time she used it to her advantage.

His jaw was taut and his eyes slightly manic. One hand circled his length while the other rolled a condom down. His jeans lay crumpled at his feet.

Then he moved, stepping to her, grasping her hips in his hands, and thrusting inside her with a primal growl. Denise cried out, scrambling for balance and sighing in relief that his grip held her upright.

Adam slid his hands down, gripping her inner thighs and lifting slightly. He turned toward the bed, holding her off the floor, impaled on him. "Kneel," he gasped, though she didn't doubt that he gasped in pleasure and not in the exertion of lifting her.

He leaned forward, and she folded her legs onto the edge of the mattress, laying her cheek on her folded arms and opening herself to his resumed thrusts.

"Oh, yeah," he repeated, a sound of complete satisfaction.

Denise panted back her release, memorizing the sensations of every slide he made within her. Adam was fierce, driven; and she could almost taste his lust.

Disturbing images flirted at her consciousness and were shoved away. She didn't want to remember anything now. Adam was what she wanted...and she'd have him again. She'd taste him and seduce him into her body again.

She pushed back onto Adam, determined to force him over just so she could tease him up again. He growled a series of curses, his hands tightening on her hips and his length pistoning in and out of her.

Waves of delight lapped like an incoming warm tide up her body, taking more of her with each thrust. Denise screamed at the sensation of those waves crashing into foam and disbursing along her nerves.

Adam forced himself deep and flattened her beneath him across the mattress. His heat teased her through the latex, and he buried his face in her shoulder.

He laid a kiss on the join of her neck and shoulder. "He'll never touch you again," he vowed.

And, the memory exploded in her mind, nearly blinding her in its intensity.

The room she'd been attacked in loomed around her, dark and forbidding, as she'd seen it that afternoon. Antoñio was under her on the sofa...naked. She was riding him, enjoying the exquisite pleasure and pain of her orgasm.

Denise squeezed her lids shut at the spike of pain behind her eyes, her climax quickening, squirming against Adam.

Some corner of her mind argued it. Not that it was true! Somehow... For some mad reason, she'd obviously screwed Antoñio Polero--and screwed her life completely in the bargain. But, taking pleasure in it while she was having sex with Adam was too much.

He nuzzled her jaw aside, oblivious to her inner struggle. His next kiss was placed over the faint scar on her throat. "Never," he breathed.

Antoñio pulled back, his eye teeth lengthened into fangs, one flattened where the tooth was broken. Blood stained them, running in thick rivulets down his chin and splashing onto his chest as he exploded into her. The copper smell assaulted her, and she looked down at herself in a detached sort of understanding, at the blood pulsating down her body from her punctured jugular, pooling at their joined bodies and spilling over onto the green fabric beneath them. He pulled her toward him, the blood between them sensitizing her to every touch of his body. His mouth returned to her throat.

Adam groaned against her throat, still aroused. She jerked her neck away from his mouth with a sob of pain and disgust mixed.

He left her body abruptly, turning Denise into his arms, touching her face, his eyes wide and frantic. "What? What did I--"

"Vampire," she whispered, her stomach rebelling at the image in her mind as much as in the sick headache remembering gave her.

"What?" he demanded.

She felt her pale cheeks darken slightly. If she told him the truth, he'd send her to the psych ward; he'd think she had cracked. She'd never have a chance with him. But, how else could she explain it?

"His delusion," she forced out. "He's playing vampire. That's why there's less blood at the scene than I... He doesn't carry it away, Adam! He dr... Oh, God!"

Denise clamped a hand to her mouth and staggered to her feet, bolting to the bathroom. Adam was at her back with a cool cloth in hand in the blink of an eye, smoothing her hair and whispering his assurances that she would be all right. When she'd emptied her stomach, he helped her clean up and guided her back to the bed. She snuggled into his chest, reveling in the warmth and comfort he offered.

"How did he draw the blood?" he asked, correctly assuming she had the answer to that now.

"I...don't know." How could she ever explain it? That rubber room beckoned if she ever tried.

"How could he stomach it? It should make him as sick as--"

She groaned at the renewed mental image of his blood-soaked face, compounded by the sick pain in her head and the one in her stomach as her nipples tightened.

"Forget I asked that."

"Thanks. I don't really know. Practice, I guess."

Adam paled. "Not an image I needed."

"Me either." She closed her eyes, exhaustion dragging her down.

He stroked his hands over her back, cradling her to his chest gently. "Denise?"

"Mmm hmm," she yawned.

"What did he do to...subdue you? Do you remember that?"

"No," she lied. "I have no idea." That was one thing she would never share with Adam. She couldn't. "I hope I never do."

About the Author

With a BS in accounting and computer programming, backgrounds in everything from teaching to tracking fraud suspects, it is a strange irony that Brenna Lyons will become best known for her first love, writing. Brenna is an award-winning bestseller in e-published and independent science fantasy, straight genre through dark erotic romance, journalism and poetry.

She became the youngest Taproot winner of her time at age eleven and earned an externship in poetry at the University of Pittsburgh at age 15. In her first three years published in novels, Brenna has finaled for five EPPIES, three PEARLS, two CAPAS, a DREAM REALM and a lucky thirteen P&Es.

A former Navy wife, Brenna now lives in MA with her husband, three children and a zoo of pets. She's the current president of EPIC and belongs to WRW, EWAG, ERWA and Broad Universe. She can be reached via her site at

http://www.brennalyons.com.

An Unholy Embrace

An Unholy Embrace
by CJ England

To my family, who supports me without
question,
And
A special thank you to my Editor, Terri Pray,
Who recognized in me the ability to 'think
outside the box'
And appreciates it!
Thylyrn Os Paes...Follow Your Dreams

Chapter One

She heard the sounds of running footsteps behind her. Pursuing her as relentlessly as the smell of her own fear.

They were going to catch her. She couldn't run from them forever. Somehow, she'd always managed to evade them in the past. Through fate or cunning, she didn't know. Her heart fluttered and her mouth went dry at the idea that this time... her luck had run out.

She darted through the twisted trees of the forest, tripping over exposed roots and brush. Branches clawed her bloodied face and pulled at her dress with bony fingers. The sharp crack of a foot stepping on a fallen limb behind her spurred her faster. They were so close.

Sobs of frustration and fear clogged her throat and tears blurred her eyes. She tried to take in a deep breath, but she choked instead. Burning pain spread through her lungs at her labored breathing. There was no one to help her; no one who would come to her rescue. Her heart broke with the certainty of that. She had no one who cared enough. In fact ... if she disappeared, no one would even miss her.

Hope was something that belonged to those who had love in their lives. It was for those who knew the joy of waking up with the certainty that they were valued. She

however, knew exactly what her worth was and why she was being chased through this desolate wood. She was good for only one thing in the minds of her pursuers.

"Teran!" an angry voice shouted. "You can't run forever! Make us angry and we'll only hurt you more."

She bit her lip in fear. They'd hurt her as he promised and enjoy doing it. She dodged a large boulder and ran down a deer path deeper into the woods.

"The bitch has gone into the forest," another man shouted. "Get her! I want to hear her scream when I fuck her!"

Teran blinked back more tears. She raced up the path, but her legs were quivering with fatigue. She was slowing down and it wouldn't be long before the men caught up with her. She risked a look over her shoulder and her heart nearly stopped when she saw a man's form leave the shadow of the trees. His lust filled gaze captured hers for a moment and she faltered.

"I've got her!"

She twisted back around and dodged into the trees, hoping that they would hide her from the man behind her. It was pitch black, but she blundered forward knowing it was the only chance she had.

When she came up hard against a solid form, her heart fell to her shoes. Arms came up to surround her and she screamed.

She was caught.

With her last ounce of strength she struggled. She kicked and bit the man and she heard him hiss in anger. Her head lifted quickly and their eyes met.

Every bit of moisture in her mouth evaporated. The man's eyes gleamed red and watched her with an animal like intensity. They were both frozen for a long moment.

Suddenly, he smiled, revealing sharpened fangs.

It was all too much. Teran screamed again and fainted.

* * * * *

He had lived in the forest a long time. Longer than many of the trees that surrounded him. Longer than the mortals that called it their own. He used them as he needed. They were his food, his sustenance. Now, one had literally fallen into his arms.

Sebastian gazed down at the unconscious woman. He'd thought at first she was a child, but she was just small boned and very thin. Yet, he could feel her womanly curves as he held her close against him. Her clothing was threadbare and patched, but clean, with the faint scent of flowers.

He brushed the long black hair from her oval face, frowning at the marks he saw there. They did not belong on such beauty as this. Her skin was like fine porcelain with high cheekbones and a full pouting mouth. Her long black lashes fanned down over eyes he'd seen were a dark blue.

He saw the hot blood racing through her veins. His body tightened and his mouth watered. He wanted to bury his teeth into her neck and taste her living energy. Passion grabbed him in a burning fist. He wanted to bury his cock into her heat and let himself go like he hadn't in decades.

His thoughts were pulled back by the sound of men crashing through the trees all around him. His eyes narrowed. The men were chasing this woman. Why?

He tucked the small human under his arm and moved so he was nothing more than a shadow in the darkness. One of the men blundered past him and with the speed of a striking rattlesnake; Sebastian reached out and knocked the man to his knees. Moving faster than the mortal

41

could see, the vampire knelt and gripped the man's head with his large hand, using his enthralling powers to keep him still.

He snarled as the reasons for the chase were made plain. These men were rapists, intent on ravaging the beauty he held in his arms. He looked down at her bloody face and his anger flared. He would not allow this.

He bent and put his mouth close to the enthralled man's ear. "Not this time," he whispered. "She has escaped you." Making a fist, Sebastian clubbed the would-be rapist, sending him sprawling to the dirt.
Then lifting the woman into his arms, he melted away into the shadows.

* * * * *

Teran's eyelids fluttered. She felt like she was slowly pushing up, up, up, through a thick mist. She smelled the scent of burning wood and something very soft was stroking across her cheeks. Her eyes flickered again and this time she made out the form of a man sitting beside her. It was he, who was caressing her so carefully, so gently.

"Can you hear me?" His voice was deep and rough. It stroked over her nerve endings like a soft kiss.

"Who are you? Where am I?" she croaked and then blushed at the raspy sound of her voice.

"My name is Sebastian and you are in my house. I... came upon you in the woods."

Teran's eyes cleared. "You rescued me."

His lips twitched. "I spirited you away."

She shuddered, remembering the lechery in her pursuer's eyes. "I'm Teran. I owe you my thanks."

"Should you not fear me as well?"

Teran studied the man who sat beside her. Tall, dark and definitely handsome, he had a brooding quality about him that gave her pause. His face was long and thin with sculpted cheekbones. His sensuous lips were framed by a mustache and small goatee. He had shoulder length dark hair and deep piercing brown eyes that seemed to gaze into her very soul.

Wide shoulders and muscular arms were easily seen under his tight fitting, black silk shirt. His dark slacks covered hard thighs. Teran blushed when she saw that the bulge between his legs was as big as the rest of him. Heat curled tightly in her belly.

She raised her eyes to his, struck by a longing to be closer to this man. She shook her head dazedly. She'd never felt quite this way before, but he was right. She was alone in his home and she didn't know him.

42

Forbidden Love: Bad Boys

She shouldn't trust him. She should run from him the same way she ran from those other men. Still... there was something about him.

Something in his eyes that made her feel... safe. Safer that she'd felt in a long, long time.

Chapter Two

"I'm not afraid of you."

Sebastian stared at the lovely woman in astonishment. She wasn't afraid of him? Impossible! Even those who were unaware of what he was instinctively feared him.

Standing, he made his way over to the fire and stared into the flickering flames. "You would do well to be cautious, little one. Such trust can be used against you."

Swinging her legs to the floor, Teran sat up and closed her eyes tightly as she waited for the room to stop spinning. She laughed bitterly. "I don't trust anyone. I've learned not to."

Sebastian narrowed his eyes at her tone. "Why were those men chasing you?"

She sighed, pushing back her tangled hair. "It's a long story."

He sat down in a large stuffed arm chair. "I have no place to go. Tell me."

Teran chewed her lip. She hated to talk about it... she never talked about it, but he had saved her. Maybe he did have a right to know. She sighed again. "My mother grew up very poor. She helped out her family by taking in laundry. Apparently, one day she was offered money to do something more than wash shirts." She looked away from Sebastian's intent gaze.

"She prostituted herself?"

She flushed. Even after all these years the fact that her mother was a whore, shamed her. "She made more money on her back than she ever did at a wash tub. She became a rich man's mistress. He kept her well until she became pregnant. She didn't tell him, but when she got too big to hide it; he tossed her out into the street. It was too late for an abortion so she had to have the child."

"And that child was you." Sebastian's voice was harsh.

Teran flinched. "Yes."

"And does she still sell her body?"

Her lips trembled. "Yes." She lifted pained blue eyes to him. "And they think that now that I am old enough... I should be willing to do the same."

Fiery outrage coursed through his body at the thought of this delicate woman whoring herself. Then he cursed inwardly. It shouldn't matter to him what she did. He calmed himself with an effort. "But you do not."

She shook her head vigorously and then grimaced as if the movement hurt her head. "No... never!"

Sebastian took a deep breath in relief, then swore again when he realized that it did matter... too much. "And your father?"

Teran shrugged. "I've never spoken to him. He doesn't claim me." She looked into the fire. "I've always lived with my mother."

"How did you come to be in the forest last night?"

"I'd delivered some shirts to one of our clients. Afterwards, I took a short cut through the woods. My mistake. That's when those men saw me." She shuddered. "They thought I was like my mother. They wouldn't take no for an answer. So I ran. I escaped into the forest and they almost caught me until..."

She frowned, suddenly recalling how she'd run from one man right into another. One who had looked so... strange. Now she remembered his face. Her eyes flew to Sebastian's as she gasped out loud. "It was you."

He inclined his head.

"But... your eyes... your... teeth..."

The dark man sitting before her smiled, revealing a set of sharp fangs. His eyes took on an unholy glow. "Is this what you saw?" he asked silkily.

Teran's mouth dropped open in shock. She'd seen pictures of his kind in the church archives. He was one of the undead. The priest would call him a monster. Her heart beat a little faster in nervous excitement. Shouldn't she be afraid? He was a killer, wasn't he?

Then she remembered the tender way he had cleaned the blood from her face. How he had saved her from the men, protecting her. No... even knowing what he was, she still felt safe with him.

Sebastian was surprised at her reaction. She knew the truth, he could hear the blood in her veins rushing faster at the revelation, but he still didn't sense any fear from her. Surprise, yes. Wariness... there was that as well, but it was because he was a male. He didn't understand it.

"Are you not afraid? I am a vampire, Teran. I use your kind for nourishment."

Curiosity filled her eyes as she gazed up at him. "Is that why you were in the forest?"

"Yes."

"Do you live here? Do you really drink blood? How old are you? Can you die?" The questions tumbled out of her.

He shook his head, nonplused. He was supposed to frighten her, not make her curious. Didn't she understand what he was?

"Can I see your teeth again?"

Sebastian narrowed his eyes. His emotions threatened to rage out of control. This was why he didn't have contact with humans. He hated to be on display. As his irritation grew, so did his lust. She was so close to him, he could smell her own special sweet scent. He wanted to grab her and drive deep in her body with both teeth and cock. The thought made his mouth water again.

"No," he snapped.

Teran looked hurt. "You don't have to get all mad about it."

He shot to his feet, looming over her. "I am not angry. I am hungry. You prevented me from feeding last night."

A tingling feeling of arousal went through her. She stared up at the handsome vampire. Her heart pounded and it made her limbs weak. A thought leaped unbidden to her mind. What would it be like... to be fed off of? Would it hurt? Would else might he do to her? She trembled. She was already attracted to him. Something she had never felt before.

His eyes were glowing even redder now. He stared at her with the same animal intensity he had in the forest, but still she wasn't afraid. She was drawn to him in such a powerful way. Did she want him to use her for nourishment? Was it more than just curiosity that made her want to get closer to him? She bit her lip in sudden indecision.

She would be putting her life in someone else's hands. Something she never did. But, she argued with herself. He needs you. And he did help you. Before she even consciously knew she was making the choice, she reached her hand out to him.

"Do... do you want to... feed from... me?"

Sebastian stilled. He searched her face for fear or disgust, but instead he found... acceptance. Who was this woman? He shook his head, getting more confused by the
minute. She was reacting differently than any human he'd ever met. He had to remember what she was. She was human, so she was food. No matter what how she made him feel, she could never be anything more.

"I will feed from you," he rasped as he took her outstretched hand and pulled her against him. He ignored how perfect it felt to hold her. "I will take your blood to give myself strength. He ran his hand up her smooth throat, pushing back the tangled hair. "You will allow this."

Teran trembled. She felt his mind reach out to hers and was suddenly afraid. She wanted to do this, but on her own terms. She

Forbidden Love: Bad Boys

didn't fear much, but like earlier, the fear of being out of control of her own destiny terrified her. She didn't want to be turned into a mindless automaton. She jerked away from his grasp.

He growled and his eyes lit with red fire. "You cannot escape me."

Taking a deep breath, knowing that she was making a choice, Teran shook her head decisively. "I don't want to."

Chapter Three

The vampire stopped, confused by her words. "What?"

She swallowed as the enormity of what she was doing struck her. She lifted her chin and met the flaring red of Sebastian's eyes. "I won't run from you. You saved me from

certain rape in the forest. I owe you. If you need to eat, then go ahead. All I ask is that you leave my mind alone. Don't steal away my will."

Sebastian stared at her. She'd surprised him again. She was offering herself to him? His body twisted in sudden arousal. She was strong, brave and beautiful and he wanted every part of her. He stepped closer and ran a long finger down to the pulse he could see throbbing in her neck.

"It will hurt if I do not enthrall you."

Her breathing quickened at his touch. "I'd rather have the pain. It tells me that I'm still alive."

He frowned at the bleakness of that statement. It gave him a glimpse into what her life must truly be like. Unthinkingly, he smoothed her wild hair, pulling her closer. He had the sudden urge to protect her forever. Then he laughed inwardly. Why was he even thinking such a thing? She was his for the day. He would slake his hunger for her blood and her body, and then let her go.

She didn't want him to enthrall her? So be it. He would seduce her in other ways. His eyes darkened to a deep blood red.

"I will not kill you, little one." He ran his hands down her back to her shapely rear. "I have reasons to keep you alive." Bending, he caressed her neck with his lips.

Teran gasped as desire swept through her. This was something she hadn't experienced before. Because of her mother, she'd kept all the boys in town at a distance. Now... this man... this vampire, stirred her like no other. He bit down, gently and she moaned. Oh, God... it felt so good.

As if he heard her thoughts, he gathered her closer to him. He licked down her neck and then up to the shell of her ear. She instinctively cocked her head to give him better access. He growled, deep in his throat. Instead of scaring her, it aroused her more. She wrapped her arms around Sebastian's strong body and snuggled closer to him.

He caught his breath and his mouth trailed over her cheek. "Teran..." he muttered softly. "Allow me to kiss you."

Forbidden Love: Bad Boys

Without hesitation, she raised her mouth to his. He took it like he was starved for her. His mouth slanted over hers, his tongue sweeping across her tender lips. When she gasped at the feeling, he plunged inside, touching and tasting every part of her until she trembled against him. Need crowded out every other thought.

Sebastian drowned in the scent, the taste and the feel of her. His body shook as he ravaged her mouth, needing her like he'd never needed another woman. He knew in that instant that he wouldn't let her go. Whatever he had to do... she would stay here with him, both as food and as lover. He would have it no other way. Suddenly ravenous for her, he lifted his head and looked deep into her dark blue eyes.

"Are you sure, Teran?" he questioned roughly. "I can make it so much better if I take away the pain."

She shook her head. "No... promise me that you won't enthrall me. I want to come to you on my own."

His body tightened in a glorious rush. He ached with unspent need. "Then I will do as you ask."

"Promise me. If you break your word, I'll leave."

His gaze was fixed on the pulse beating at the base of her neck. "I promise."

She closed her eyes and offered her slim throat to him. His hands shook; the need to feed was so strong. He licked her, her taste already making his mouth water. Unable to wait a moment longer, he bared his fangs and buried them into the vein in her neck.

Teran cried out. The pain was worse than she had imagined. She struggled instinctively, but Sebastian's arms tightened around her. Since she wouldn't allow him to blunt the pain, he fed from her as gently as possible. After a few moments, she stilled as the pain dulled.

She sighed. Even with the hurt, she felt so safe, so wanted in his arms. A part of her wished she could stay in his embrace forever. She moved and he growled at her. Ignoring him, she stroked up and down his muscular back, wishing that she could touch his bare skin. Her face heated. He made her act like a wanton. Would he think she was like her mother?

He pulled her closer and she felt the hard line of his erection against her. She gasped and lust unfurled within her. Her heart beat even faster. Oh God... he wanted her too.

Sebastian couldn't think, couldn't concentrate on anything but the flavor of Teran's blood as it flowed unceasingly into his mouth. The taste was different than any that he had savored before. He sucked it down like a thirsty man would drink down his last glass of water.

Understanding filled him. He had found her... the one who could sustain him throughout eternity. Her body quivered in his arms, her hands molding themselves over him and desire roared through him. He would take all that she was. She would belong to him.

Suddenly, she went limp and Sebastian jerked his head up. Her face was frighteningly white. He cursed himself. He'd been so distracted by the longing he felt, he had taken too much from her. She had fallen unconscious.

Lifting her in his arms, he carried her up the stairs and into his bedroom. He pulled back the covers and laid her down on the white sheets. Her dark hair spread over his
pillow and Sebastian swore at himself again for loosing control. Instead of being able to bury himself inside her to slake his need, he would have to wait. She would sleep for some time as her body replenished the blood he had taken.

Carefully he undressed her, his cock thickening, when he saw that her nipples were pinched with arousal. Curious, he ran a finger through the thatch of dark hair between her legs. One touch made him groan and he struggled for control. She was drenched in dew. He lifted his fingers to his mouth, reveling in her taste. He smiled. She was sweet all over.

Quickly, he pulled his own clothes off and slid in beside her, pulling her back into his arms. When she awoke, not another moment would go by before he laid final claim to the body.

* * * * *

Teran yawned and snuggled back down in her bed. There must be an extra cover on her because for the first time in her life, she was delightfully warm. She didn't want to get up yet. All she had waiting for her were chores and responsibilities. If she could snatch a couple more minutes of comfort and sleep, she would do it.

Oh, the warmth was heavenly. She cuddled closer to the source of the heat. She buried her face into her pillow and promptly sneezed when she inhaled a mouthful of
tickling hair. Her pillow chuckled and moved. Teran came abruptly awake.

Sebastian leaned over her, his head propped up on one hand. His long hair was messy and his eyes were sleepy as if she had awakened him. She stared at his naked chest. Had he been the pillow she sneezed on? She lifted her head and met his eyes. He smiled slowly at her and her

50

entire body began to shake. She wasn't even properly awake yet and she wanted him. She trembled at the force of the attraction between them.

Without looking away from her, he bent and touched her lips with his own. Once, twice, a third time, before a deep masculine groan rumbled out of his throat and he pulled her against him. His mouth wasn't hesitant any more, but possessive, as if he was declaring it was his right to touch her.

He kissed her deeply, his tongue touching all the places that had made her shake the night before. She leaned into the kiss, needing it... needing him.

She gasped as he rolled her over on her back and came down on top of her. She stiffened when she realized that they were both naked. Skin against skin, she felt him hard against her. He soothed her with his mouth and she relaxed, knowing that this was what she wanted. She wanted him to make love to her.

His lips trailed across her cheeks, her eyes and then back to her mouth. She sought his touch as a flower seeks the sun.

"Sebastian..." she whispered.

"I am here, little one. Soon I will be deep inside you."

She shivered at his words. He'd taken her blood. Now he would take her body. "I've never felt... I..."

He stopped her with a deep kiss. "I will have you." His hands moved over her and her heart beat faster. How could he know how just to touch her? She moaned and arched into him, giving herself completely.

Chapter Four

Sebastian gritted his teeth, fighting for control. He wanted her desperately, but he wouldn't rape her like those animals in the woods would have. She'd offered herself to him, blood and body. He would not betray her by hurting her. He would make her forget any others she had been with before. He bent and kissed her again, groaning at the way she responded. He would seduce her so completely, she would never leave him.

Carefully, he traced his fingers down over her mouth, down her lovely throat to her peaked breasts. They were no more than a handful, but the silken feel of her sent waves of need spreading through him. He touched her, softly and then with more strength as her desire for him rose. Her moan set fire to his senses.

As his hand teased her nipples, his mouth caressed her throat. He kissed his way down to the wound he had made the night before. He licked it and his groin tightened when she cried out in pleasure at the sensitivity of the injury. Sebastian fought the urge to bury his teeth in her. It was too soon to take her blood again. He kissed his way back up to her mouth. His tongue plunged in and out, mimicking what he would do with his body.

Soon she was writhing beneath him. Her breasts were swollen, her nipples pointed and dark with passion. Her lips begged him to take her deeper. He nipped at her ear.

"Do you want more, Teran?"

Teran stared up at him. His eyes glowed with a dark red heat that made her shiver. The feel of his hand on her drove her mad with need. She reached up and pulled his head down to her breast.

"Please, Sebastian," she choked out. She didn't know how to ask for anything more.

To her relief, she felt his mouth touch her. The swirl of his tongue around her nipple made her come up off the bed in pleasure. Surely, a woman could die from this feeling. He continued with caressing her, treating both of her breasts to the same wonderful sensations. His hand trailed down her body and began to rub gently at her mound. When she instinctively spread her legs for him, he groaned again.

Suddenly his movements took on a new purpose. No longer were they gentle and slow, but hard and arousing. His mouth sucked at her nipples and she cried out from the pure pleasure of it. His hand also became more insistent as his fingers parted the soft hair and searched for the source of her desire. When he found it, he took her clit between two strong fingers, rubbing gently.

Heat pooled in her belly and she moaned uncontrollably. Her legs trembled and when Sebastian inserted a finger into her hot wet channel, she bucked against him. He held her down effortlessly and continued to pleasure her. Pinpricks of heat started in her toes and worked their way up her legs. Heat coursed through her breasts. She whimpered.

"Let go for me, little one. Just let go." His voice was a soft murmur in her ear. Teran writhed under him, her breaths coming in short pants as the feelings in her body boiled inside of her.

She screamed as her world imploded. Pleasure such as she had never felt before shot through her. Diamond shaped colors danced behind her eyelids. She sobbed out his name, but he never stopped touching her until she had climbed the peak a second time and leaped again into the inferno of desire.

Sebastian shook like a man with palsy as he stared down at Teran sprawled beneath him. He'd never wanted a woman more than he wanted her, right now, at this moment. His cock throbbed so hard it was painful. He wanted to tease her more. To let her touch and taste him in return, but there was no way his heated body could handle that. Maybe later… when he had slaked his lust.

Roughly, he kneed her legs apart and settled between them. The feel of her heated flesh against the head of his cock almost made him come right then and there. He gritted his teeth and eased inside her slick channel.

She moaned and wriggled and he froze. She was so hot, so wet and tight. Her little moans aroused him so much he was afraid he'd disgrace himself right then and there. He took several deep breaths before he felt he was in control once more. He slowly pushed inside her.

Sweat beaded on his forehead. She felt like a fist around him, she held him so tightly. He pressed further inside and stopped dead when he came against the thin
membrane that proclaimed her innocence.

Knowing he was the first shattered Sebastian's control. Without thinking, he sent his enthralling powers over her, wanting to protect her from the pain of the rending of her virginity. Unable to wait any longer, he thrust through the thin tissue, burying himself deep inside her.

Teran gasped when his full weight settled on her. She could feel him throbbing deep within her. There had been no pain, only a fullness that as he began to move, gave her unbelievable pleasure. Instinctively, she wrapped her legs around his waist, wanting to be as close to him as possible. He shuddered and thrust against her, pulling almost all the way out, before driving himself deep in her again.

The pleasure she had felt before quickened again. She moaned and buried her mouth into Sebastian's chest. Her lips found one of his nipples and she laved it, knowing by his instant reaction that he was as sensitive as she.

He groaned out her name and plunged hard against her. A spear of pleasure shot through her but she barely registered it before he began moving again. All she could do was follow as he led her in a sensual dance. He throbbed within her and his movements became even more forceful. Suddenly, he roared out her name and buried himself deep inside her. His climax triggered her own as she soared off the peak one more time.

It was a long time later when he lifted his head, his body replete for the moment. He gazed down at the woman beneath him and smiled at the dreamy look on her face. They had given each other much pleasure and it would not be the last time. She fit him perfectly. She now belonged to him.

He bent and licked at her throat, feeling her pulse quicken at his touch. The knowledge that he excited her sent all the blood rushing back to his groin. He watched her eyes widen when she felt him swell within her.

"Oh..." she stuttered, her face turning rosy.

He grinned. "You inspire me, little one."

Teran smiled shyly. "It was wonderful. I didn't know it could be like that between a man and a woman."

He bent and kissed her. "You are mine. Our bodies belong together. It is for that reason our mating felt so perfect." He moved deliberately and saw her eyes darken. "And I find I am pleased that you were a virgin. That I was the first."

"It didn't even hurt," she marveled, tracing her fingers across his wide chest. "I thought it would be painful."

Sebastian nipped at her chin. "I chose not to allow you to feel the pain. I wanted you to remember your first time with joy."

Teran stilled and her eyes met his. "I... I don't understand."

He smiled again, his look dark and possessive. "I used my powers so you would not be hurt. I numbed the pain in your mind."

She just stared at him. Then her eyes filled with tears and she pushed at his chest. "Get off of me."

He frowned, but allowed her to push him off so he lay next to her instead. He frowned when he saw her leap from the bed. "What is wrong with you?"

"With me?" she repeated incredulously. "You're the one who broke his word. You promised not to enthrall me!"

Chapter 5

Sebastian stared at her in surprise. She was angry because he'd numbed her pain? Ridiculous! Then he remembered the promise he had given her that he would leave her mind alone. Guilt curled in his stomach. He frowned as she gathered up her clothing. "What are you doing?"

She glared at him. "I'm leaving."

A cold rage filled him. Leave? She could not leave him. "You are not going anywhere."

Teran pulled on her dress. "Yes I am," she said fiercely. "You broke your promise. I can't trust you."

Swiftly, he came to his feet and stalked over to her. "Trust is not necessary. You belong to me now."

She shook her head. "I belong to myself. I told you if you lied to me I would leave. So I'm going!"

Sebastian snarled at her. He was furious that she would even think of leaving him. "I was trying to protect you, foolish girl! I did not want you to feel pain when I took you."

"It was my choice. And you took that choice from me. How can I trust you after that?"

He grabbed her shoulders. "As I said before, trust is unnecessary. You will stay with me. I will feed from you as I need to and we can pleasure each other. I know you enjoy how I make you feel."

Teran blushed and her eyes filled with tears. "I... I thought I could love you, but I could never love a man I can't trust."

Her words shot through him like an icy dagger. Love? He'd never thought of love. It was for mortals, not for one such as him. Preposterous! What vampire would even consider such a thing? He glared down at her, noting her stiff body and trembling lips. He would put an end to such thoughts once and for all.

Quicker than she could even see, he swept the dress from her body. At her startled squawk, he lifted her and tossed her back onto his bed. She bounced once and then was up and running for the door, but he caught her easily. She fought him, kicking and hitting at him as she had done in the forest.

"Let me go!"

He ignored her, tumbling her back into the sheets and coming down hard on top of her. She squirmed beneath him, firing his lust even more.

"Be still!" he roared. "I do not wish to hurt you."

Teran glared up at him, her breasts heaving in agitation. "I don't want to stay here. Let me go!"

"You have no choice, little one. You are mine."

"I gave myself freely, but I won't any more. You will have to rape me. Is that what you want?"

A dark pain shot through him. "It will not be rape," he murmured as he touched his mouth to her throat. "I can make you want me."

"You are no better than the men in the woods," she spat at him. "You're giving me no choice. I hate you."

He bared his fangs at her in his anger, feeling something tighten around his heart at her words. "You would compare me to those dogs that chased you?"

"How are you any different? You take what I don't want to give, just as they wanted to!"

Furious with her, he kneed her legs apart and thrust hard inside her, ignoring her gasp of surprise. "They would not give you pleasure, Teran. They would take you like the animals they are and leave you lying in the dirt, bleeding from their possession. I... I will give you more pleasure than you can comprehend."

Tears spilled from her eyes. Her body warmed at his touch and she fought the need to pull him against her. It wasn't fair that he could do this to her. Angry with herself as much as with him, she blinked and tilted her chin.

"I will never give in to you," she stated stubbornly. "You will have to force me every time."

Sebastian growled with frustration. Couldn't she see he meant her no harm? He had wanted to protect her, not hurt her. But the obstinate woman couldn't see past his broken promise and it infuriated him.

"So be it," he gritted out. "I will take you as I choose. I will use you for my own pleasure, but you will find your own as well. I will not have to ravish you."

Teran shook her head sadly. "Then you rape my mind as well as my body. You force me to feel things I don't want to feel."

"Enough!" he growled. He was done trying to talk to her. He took her mouth, wanting to drive himself deep inside her. He would show her so much pleasure that she would beg to stay with him.

*****

He didn't leave her side, all the following days and nights. They slept and when he was done sleeping, he would slip inside of her and pleasure her awake. By the time Teran woke up enough to realize what was happening, her body had taken over. Afterwards, she would lie in his arms, silver tears trailing silently down her cheeks.

Several times while she was sleeping, he disappeared bringing back with him something for her to eat. Her heart warmed at his thoughtfulness, but it couldn't forget that she was a prisoner.

Twice he'd taken her to shower with him and he taught her the ways of loving under the spray. There too, she fought until her body betrayed her. She hated herself for giving in. Each time they were done, she swore that it would be the last. To protect herself, she refused to respond to anything he said or did. It was only when he made her body sing, that she came to him freely.

Sebastian hated the fact that she'd withdrawn from him. He was furious that the only way he could get her to respond to him was to force her flesh to react. His body took what it needed, but their first time together had been so wondrous, it had fed his soul as well. Seeing her weep after each mating infuriated him.

He'd been sure that after a few times together, she would see the light and forgive him for enthralling her. But instead she became more and more withdrawn. She wouldn't speak to him and she wept after each joining.

He made sure that each time she was satisfied, yet she continued her angry silence. He refused to apologize for taking her pain away the first time. She would have to come to terms with the fact that he'd done what was necessary. He would brook no interference from an angry woman.

Sebastian put off feeding, knowing she would hate him even more, but as the days passed, he knew he would have to have nourishment. He thought of going out and finding another human but the idea of partaking of any blood other than hers turned his stomach. He wanted Teran only. That knowledge surprised him. Never before had a lover enthralled him, but she did. Her body, her blood, even her uncertain temper. She had become necessary to him.

How necessary, was brought forth when he awoke from his slumbers late one afternoon with the sudden, absolute knowledge that her blood was the only kind that would sustain him. He was starving. He had to feed.

Knowing how she would react, he started out by bringing her pleasure. As usual, she fought him, but it wasn't long before her need for him took over. He kissed her, murmuring softly in her ear as his hands stroked her sensitive flesh. Every moan, every gasp was a triumph for him.

Teran writhed beneath him, lost to everything but how he made her feel. She pulled him to her and cried out as he suddenly plunged inside her. He began to move in her, slow steady thrusts that made her skin tingle and her insides heat. She didn't even flinch when he swept the hair from her neck and trailed his tongue over the healing wound.

"I will not enthrall you," he whispered to her. "I will keep the promise I gave to you."

Teran moaned. His cock inside her was stroking every nerve ending. It was hard listening to anything else. He moved quicker, one hand trailing down between their bodies. He found the swollen jewel of her desire and squeezed it gently. Teran's eyes flew open as sensation rocked her body. She stared at him for a long moment as he rubbed her clit. Then, in the next heartbeat he thrust deep within her, at the same time plucking at her again. She screamed and bucked against him, mindless with pleasure.

Sebastian kept up the pace of his thrusts, but hunger of another type overwhelmed him. As she screamed her release, he bit down into the vein that held her life's blood. The taste of her fueled his climax and he shuddered as he exploded inside her.

Chapter 6

Teran screamed again, this time in pain. She fought him, but she wasn't strong enough. He held her easily. She could do nothing but lie in his arms and weep as he took the needed food.

This time, Sebastian stopped before he took too much from her. He wanted to show her that he could be trusted. He licked at the wound, cleaning it and then kissed her throat. But when he tried to kiss her lips, she pulled away. His eyes narrowed angrily.

"Still, you turn from me?" he demanded. "I am sorry for the pain, but if you would allow me to enthrall you--"

"I don't want you to touch me!" she cried, pulling away from him. She curled up in a small ball. "I just want you to leave me alone!"

Sebastian growled and rolled off the bed. His heart ached. He had fed fully and wanted nothing more than to mate with his lover again, but her words wounded him.

Suddenly he'd had enough. "Then I will... for now. I will leave you to yourself while I shower." He walked around to her side of the bed and tipped up her chin so she would have to look at him. "Then little one... I will have you again." He bared his fangs at her in a cold furious smile and turning on his heel, left the room.

Teran shuddered and wrapped her arms around herself. She was loosing herself to him, she could feel it. His touch, his scent, everything about him still pulled at her. If only she could trust him, things could be different, but he'd shown his true colors. He was a man... no a vampire with no feelings.

She heard the shower running. Suddenly, she realized that for the first time, he'd left her alone. Did he think her so beaten that she wouldn't escape? She leapt from the bed and raced to the window. Throwing back the heavy curtains, she blinked as the harsh sunlight filled the room. Her heart pounded. It was late, but the night was still a little ways off. If she could just get outside, she would be free.

Vampires couldn't walk in the daylight.

Grabbing up her dress, she quickly pulled it on and grabbed up her shoes. She would need nothing else. She ran out of the bedroom, but her heart stopped when she couldn't hear the water any more. She didn't have much time. Swiftly, she turned and ran down the stairs and through the comfortable sitting room where they had shared their first kiss.

Forbidden Love: Bad Boys

"Teran?"

She looked back over her shoulder, her eyes wide with fear. He was still upstairs, but he was looking for her. She ran to the front door. Her hands, made clumsy by lack of blood and fear, fumbled with the locks.

"TERAN!!!"

She gave a sob. She was discovered. She got the first lock open and started on the next. She heard the pounding of his feet on the stairs behind her. The second lock opened and with a frightened cry, she pulled open the door.

"NO!"

A hand crashed down on her shoulder, but with a strength borne of desperation, she jerked away and fled outside. Sunlight bathed her face. She ran far away from the house and then turned.

Sebastian stood on the porch, gloriously naked; his long wet hair sending trails of water streaking down his body. For the first time she really saw him... saw how beautiful he was. He looked like a master's painting of a fallen angel. His body was lean and hard, with corded muscles that flexed as his hands curled into fists. His shaft, still semi-hard, made her eyes widen in wonder.

His chest heaved as he glared down at her. His eyes were the color of angry rubies. Holding her eyes, he stepped off of the porch... and into the sunlight.

Teran held her breath. Were the old stories more lies then? Her eyes filled with tears. Was she still his prisoner?

Several steps into the clearing, he stopped and flinched. His eyes still glowed angrily, but now they were filled with pain as well. She cried out when she saw that his flesh was beginning to smolder and peel. Her heart almost stopped beating.

"Oh God, Sebastian... go back... you're burning up!" She wept then, knowing in that instant she loved him as much as she hated him.

He took another step toward her, and then another, but finally the agony was too great. With a shout of rage, he turned and ran back to the shelter of the shaded porch.

Teran collapsed where she stood, still weeping in reaction. She buried her face in her hands. He was safe. Oh God... he was safe and he couldn't leave the house. That meant... she was free!

"Teran..." his voice entreated. "Do not do this. Come back to me."

She lifted her wet face and stared at him. In his eyes she saw a desperation that she didn't understand. Was she more than just food?

Did he want more than her body? Could he actually need her? Could he learn to love her?

Then he held out his hand. "Come to me, Teran."

Her brain suddenly struggled to think. When she felt the pull of his voice, she shook her head groggily. She was so tired. Maybe she should just go in and lay down. He wouldn't hurt—

Her heart crashed to her feet. It was him. After everything she'd said, he was still trying to steal her mind.
"Stay out of my head!" she screamed at him.

Sebastian dropped his hand, knowing that she was too far away for him to enthrall properly. The only reason she felt anything was because of the intimacies they had shared. He clenched his fists, furious at her and at himself. "I will come after you," he growled. "You will not escape me."

Teran stared at him. "Let me go," she whispered. "Don't you understand? It will never be right again."

Despair washed through him. Would she always fight him? He'd been so sure that he could use her need for him against her. Didn't she know that what they shared was special? The pain that he saw on her face almost destroyed him. Even if he stole her away from the village, would she ever be truly his? His chest hurt, as he wondered how he could bring her back to him. He wouldn't let her go... he couldn't. He watched in silence as she put her shoes on and then stood.

She hesitated for a long moment, as if she wanted to say something. She searched his eyes. Then she sighed and brushed away her tears. "Goodbye, Sebastian."

He watched as she walked out of the clearing and into the forest. How long he stood there, he didn't know, but dusk was licking at the porch steps when he finally sank to his knees. His voice was a cry in the night.

"TERAN!!!"

Chapter Seven
(one month later)

He was driven from his house by hunger. Ever since she had left him, he'd been existing on the blood of animals, but tonight was All Hallows Eve. The one day a vampire had to take human blood or die.

He slipped through the forest like a shadowy, dark wraith. His soul... alive for such a short time was cold and dead again. Nothing mattered to him now. Sebastian had learned too late that Teran was the only one who could sustain him. The perfection of their mating was because they were soulmates, destined for each other. He had destroyed it by abusing her trust.

He'd gone after her as he said he would. As soon as night came, he'd followed her trail to a small shack on the edge of town. He'd waited in the shadows of a nearby oak until he'd seen her walking back from town. When she was close enough for him to touch, he'd stepped out into the moonlight.

She'd frozen like a rabbit when confronted by a predator. They'd stared at each other for what seemed to be an eternity, before he reached out and gently touched her cheek. She trembled, just as she did before coming apart in his arms during a climax. He wanted her so badly that he had moved to lift her into his arms. It was then that he saw the tear.

It hovered on an eyelash, turning it into a watery piece of art. Then, even though she was held motionless by his gaze, it fell, landing on her face to slide in a silvery trail down her soft cheek.

It told him a story. It said that even if he took her back to his home, he would never truly have her. Her body might be his, but that wasn't enough. Now he wanted more. He knew he couldn't steal her away. He, one of the strongest vampires of his time had been defeated by a woman's tears.

So he'd left her, turning on his heel and melting back into the shadows from whence he came.

That had been a full moon cycle ago. He glanced up. The moon was at its fullest, just in time for All Hallows Eve. He wondered if he would have to actually go into town to take his prey, or if he would be lucky and some human might stray across his path. What would he do if he came across her... Teran? Would he be damned by taking what was rightfully his? Or damned by walking away from her? His heart twisted in a pain he had felt all too often in the last month.

His head shot up and his heart stopped when he heard the scream. Every instinct in his body shrieked to life. Without thinking he turned and ran towards it. It was her.

Teran was in trouble.

With supernatural speed he raced through the trees. He heard her scream again, but this time it was cut off in mid cry. His gut clenched. For the first time in centuries, he sent a prayer up to heaven. Let him be in time.

He burst into a clearing and snarled at the sight that met his eyes. Teran… his Teran was tied to a tree. Four men surrounded her, one with his pants around his ankles. As Sebastian started toward them, one of the men slapped Teran across the face and laughed.

Fury swept through him. It would be the last time the mortal drew a breath.

Teran cringed away from Silas. He'd already had his hands on her and when she had screamed, he'd back-handed her and then gagged her with her own blouse. Now she was trussed up and helpless and very soon each of these men would rape her. She gave a muffled sob, knowing no one would save her this time.

Her frightened mind flashed to Sebastian. He alone had wanted to protect her. He'd made mistakes, but she'd been a fool to leave him. Even if he didn't love her, he wanted her. It had been her stupid pride that had kept them apart. Now it was too late. She wouldn't survive what they had planned for her.

She looked away when Silas dropped his pants, but when he tried to rip her panties off, she kicked him right in the groin. There was no time to celebrate, because he slapped her so hard, everything went black for a moment. She felt his hand at her crotch and she tried to scream again. It was then that all hell broke loose.

It was Sebastian!

Silas was lifted from her and tossed like a rag doll across the glade. The other men screamed and tried to run, but she watched in a kind of horrified glee as Sebastian picked up one of them and literally ripped his head off. He gave a roar of rage and threw the bloody head into the trees. The mangled body fell at her feet.

The second man was slammed to the ground. Sebastian straddled him and with one slash of his hand, ripped his heart out. But he didn't stop there. His anger was so great that he ripped the man's body apart as easily as a child might pull the legs off a fly.

When he was finished, he searched for the last man, but he was gone. One look at Sebastian and he'd taken to his heels. The vampire bared his teeth and glanced around. Spying the hapless Silas, who was crawling away on his hands and knees, his eyes glowed.

He was on him before the rapist could take his next breath. Sebastian lifted the man and slammed him against a tree. He took him by the throat and squeezed.

Silas clawed at his hands, his eyes bulging in his face but Sebastian ignored him. He leaned in and licked the side of the man's throat. The sweet-sour smell of urine filled his nostrils as the man's bladder let go. He gave the man a shake that rattled his teeth.

"You dare to touch what is mine. For that you will die, human."

Silas's mouth gaped as he tried to draw in a breath. He read his death in the vampire's eyes. He struggled again, but to no avail. Sebastian bared his fangs and ripped the man's throat out.

He let the body fall to the ground, spitting out the taste of the man's blood. He wiped his arm across his mouth, already tracking the man who'd run, in his mind. If he hurried, he could still catch the bastard.

A small noise made him pause. Suddenly, he stiffened remembering the bound woman behind him. He whipped around and met Teran's wide frightened eyes. The fleeing man disappeared from his thoughts.

Sebastian's heart sank. She had seen him kill. Not just kill, but utterly destroy. Now she knew of the beast that lived in him. His shoulders slumped. No matter that he'd done it for her, now that she'd seen his true nature, he would have no chance of winning her back.

He walked to her, kicking the one body out of the way. Her flinch made him grit his teeth, but he stepped in front of her and removed the gag.

"Are you alright?" he asked hoarsely.

She nodded as he untied her hands from above her head. Then he froze in shock when she wrapped her arms around him and buried her face in his chest. She burst into tears and his arms came up to cradle her gently.

"Shhh, little one. It is over. You are safe now."

Chapter Eight

For the first time in a month Teran felt whole again. Being in his arms was all she dreamed of at night. She replayed the times they had been together, over and over again. It was all she had in her lonely bed at night. She had left a part of herself behind when she'd left him. She'd learned very quickly that she wasn't whole without him. As his hands moved over her gently, soothingly, she couldn't believe she'd run from him in the first place.

She rubbed her face against his strong chest, uncaring of the blood that covered him. All she knew was that she was home. Finally home.

Sebastian's throat tightened as he held her close to him. He wasn't sure exactly what was happening, but he'd missed her so much. Having her in his arms again made his whole body throb in need. But he wouldn't touch her. Not in that way. She'd made her choice and he would have to honor it. Even if living without her was killing him... literally. He would make sure that she was safe, no matter what happened to him.

When she raised her face to his, he drew in his breath at the expression on it. He'd never thought to have a woman look at him in such a way. Wonderingly, he touched her cheek, his chest tightening with hope.

"Teran?"

She smiled and her tears overflowed again. "I love you, Sebastian."

His own eyes burned as he crushed her against him. He wanted to shout his joy to the moon. "But... you ran from me. And now you see that I... I am an animal."

She shook her head as she met his eyes. "You were wrong to have numbed my mind, but you only did it to protect me. I shouldn't have been so angry. And what you did here?" She shook her head. "Again, you were protecting me. How can I fault you for that?"

Sebastian couldn't believe what he was hearing. He cradled her face in his hands. "I am what I am, Teran. A vampire. I can never change that. This..." he gestured around him, "is just one of the things I am capable of. You take a risk being with me."

She grabbed his wrists. "I see that you can kill. But I also know what else you are capable of. You saved me... twice." She lifted her hand and traced her fingers over his sensuous mouth. "You are gentle and caring and strong... passionate and loving. The only risk I can see is living my life without you. I've done that for the last month and I can't take any more. I would have come back to you, I swear it. I was dying inside, Sebastian. Please don't send me away now."

He shook his head slowly, still not able to believe what she was saying. "How can I send away the one thing that makes me want to continue my existence? You were not the only one who was slowly dying, Teran. My arms have never felt so empty. I have not tasted human blood since you left me. I would have no other, but you."

Teran's eyes widened in surprise. "You haven't fed?"

"Not on humans. You are the only one who can satisfy me."

Her eyes glistened with tears. "You could have died."

He touched her face gently. "Without you... death was preferable."

She buried her head back in his chest. They'd come so close to loosing each other. She thanked God that she'd been sent out on a wild goose chase. She didn't know she had spoken aloud, until she felt Sebastian stiffen.

"Wild goose chase?"

"My mother." Her voice was bitter. "She wants me in the family business. When I told her to forget it, she set me up. Sent me on an errand. But instead of shirts, I found those men waiting for me."

Sebastian growled deep in his throat as anger welled up in him. Vampires were thought of as monsters. But a human's talent for cruelty surpassed anything that his kind would ever do. "Your mother did this foul thing?"

She nodded. "I have no one else, Sebastian. No one... but you. Please let me stay with you. I love you."

His eyes darkened and he pulled her against him, plundering her mouth with his own. They both groaned at the taste. It had been so long since they had touched each other.

When he raised his head, his look was totally male and possessive. "You are mine."

Teran smiled shakily. "Then take me home, Sebastian. Take me home."

*****

Teran stepped out of the shower, straight into Sebastian's arms. Without speaking a word, he lifted her and strode straight to the bed. His body was hard with urgency when he came down on top of her. She felt the throbbing of his cock against her thigh, signaling his readiness to mate. More than anything she wanted to feel him deep inside her... but...

67

there was something she needed to do first.

She pushed against his broad chest. "Wait!"

He froze, staring down at her. Anger and need warred in his face. "You would not deny me now!"

"No, Sebastian. Oh no, no." She kissed him. "I'll never deny you again."

"Then why do you stop me? We do not have much time." He trailed his hand down to the curls at the apex of her thighs. "Soon they will come for me."

She clutched at his shoulders, distracted by his touch. "What are you talking about?"

"One of the scum that attacked you got away." His eyes darkened with regret. Even now he wished he'd gone after him. "He will tell the townspeople what I did. They will seek to destroy me. I cannot stay here any longer."

Teran's heart pounded in sudden fear. "You don't mean to leave me behind?"

His eyes gazed sadly into hers. "When you came to me, you dreamed of being safe in this place. I cannot give that to you now."

She narrowed her eyes at his words. "My dream is to be safe in your arms, not in this house. I love you. As long as we are together, I will be safe." She swallowed, not knowing how he would take what she next had to say.

"I want you to turn me, Sebastian. Make me like you are."

Sebastian stared at her, torn between surprise and joy. Part of him had longed for her to say those words, so he could keep her and spend eternity with her, but she didn't know what she was asking. What she would be giving up. Gently he gathered her to him, searching for words.

"What you ask of me, I want more than anything." He bent and kissed her, his need to do so overwhelming him. "But becoming a vampire will not be easy for you."

"I don't care," she said stubbornly. "I want to be with you forever."

He nipped the pouting lower lip. Then his eyes turned serious. "If I turn you, Teran, you will belong to me forever. As your sire I will always hold sway over you. As a fledgling, I could take away your ability to choose, make you do what ever I desired. Do you understand what I am saying? It is only as you mature in your abilities that you would be able to stop me." He squeezed her tightly. "Think carefully before you say yes to this. It was only upon the death of my sire, one hundred years ago that I was truly free."

He would have total control over her. Her right to choose was again in danger. She had run from him once because of this. She stared into the dark eyes that were banked with red fire. She hadn't trusted him before and because of it, they had both nearly died. They needed each other.

Oh, she knew that there would be times where he would expect her to obey him without question. And there would be times they fought about it. But this time, he was giving her a choice. And that choice had been made the second she walked back into his arms.

She reached up and cupped his cheek. "I trust you, Sebastian. You would never knowingly hurt me."

His arms tightened. "Are you certain? Once I start, I will not stop." His eyes searched hers.

"Please, Sebastian." She wriggled under him, feeling his body harden even more. "I want you. I love you. Make me yours."

He'd given her every chance to say no. She freely made her choice, even if it meant giving him access to her mind. Joy filled him and desire flared anew. "Then you will have your wish, little one. I will make you immortal."

She bit her lip, suddenly afraid. "Will it hurt?"

He shook his head and smiled. "No... just trust me, remember?"

Teran took a deep breath. "I do... because I love you."

Sebastian growled low in his throat. His eyes brightened with red fire. Her words, the feel of her body beneath his, the smell of her blood, made him shake with lust and hunger. He crushed her mouth beneath his and with one strong thrust, joined their bodies together.

She cried out in surprise and pleasure. It had been so long and he filled her so completely. When he started to move within her, she forgot everything but the sensations that he wrought inside her. His kisses ravaged her mouth as his hands moved swiftly over her soft aroused flesh. She touched him in return, tracing her way down his sides and then back up to his masculine nipples. He shuddered beneath her hands and Teran knew her first taste of feminine power.

The need built quickly. Soon all the nerves in her body were screaming for release. He pulled almost all the way out of her and then slammed hard back into her. She sobbed out his name, crying for him to take her over the edge.

He pulled out again, this time tilting her head to the side before he drove himself deep in her clinging heat. He ground his hips against her and her orgasm hit her so hard she screamed. As her body convulsed, he bit down into her throat, his hunger for her taking over him. As he fed, he numbed her mind so she would feel no pain.

He continued to drive in and out of her. It only took a few more thrusts before he too, climaxed. Even as he shuddered against her, he continued to drain her life blood. He felt the magic of the change sweep over him. It filled his lonely, hungry soul.

When he judged he had all but drained her, he stopped feeding. Looking down at her, his stomach clenched at her waxy face and blue lips. Quickly, he bit into his own wrist and then placed the bleeding arm against her mouth.

"Feed, little one. It is your turn to take my blood."

It took a few moments, so long that Sebastian was afraid he'd left it too long, but suddenly Teran's mouth clamped down on him. He grimaced in pain as she fed, sucking down the blood that would make the change complete.

Suddenly noise and sound filled Sebastian's head. He stared down at her in astonishment. They were connected! He could hear her thoughts, read her mind. He sensed her groggy excitement and sleepy joy at what was happening to them. Felt her surprise at the knowledge that he could feel all she was feeling. She tried to speak through the mind link, but she was too weak from lack of blood. He instinctively soothed her... smoothing her hair and kissing her sweat dampened forehead.

He held her as she fed, until she went limp in exhaustion. He licked the blood from her lips and then pulled her back into his arms. He lay back in the bed, cradling his precious burden carefully. She would sleep now. When she awoke, the change would be complete. And she would be his... forever.

Epilogue

They stood on the roof of the house watching the flickering flames of torches draw nearer. As Sebastian had thought, the townspeople were out in force to destroy the monster.

"Do you regret?" His voice was whisper soft.

She faced him and smiled, her new fangs shining white in the moonlight. "How could I regret loving you? You have given me new life."

Sebastian turned and cradled her face in his hands. His throat tightened at the adoration he saw in her eyes. How could he have lived without her? He bent and gently kissed her. "And you have given me something I never thought I would ever have. I have lived over four hundred years and never knew what it was to love a woman. But now... now I do. I love you, Teran."

Her own throat clogged. Tears filled her eyes. "You do?"

"I do. From the moment I saw you, though at the time I did not understand what I was feeling. I saw you and my world stood still. I had never felt that way before. I knew then that you were mine."

She buried her face against him. "I am yours. For all eternity."

"You will never escape me, little one. Not again."

Teran laughed up at him. "Try and get rid of me."

His eyes gleamed with love and humor. "I think I will pleasure you instead. I still have much to teach you."

Her eyes glowed in answer. "And I promise to be a very good student." She kissed him lingeringly. "We can begin our studies as soon as we are safely away from this place. But how do we leave without alerting them to our presence?"

Sebastian cast a brief glance at the gathering crowd and then grinned. "Do not worry. Let me give you your first lesson. Are you ready?"

When she nodded, he lifted his arm, wrapping her in his long black cape. "Come then, my little love. Let us find a new haven to call home."

"Wither thou goest, so do I," Teran murmured. "But I have already found my home... and it is you."

His eyes flared, but he made no sound. He pulled her tight against him and drew on his powers.

The air shimmered. Where they once stood, two owls now perched. The darker one nuzzled the smaller bird with his beak. She answered with a soft loving hoot. In unspoken agreement, the two predators launched themselves from the roof. They circled once, over the house that had sheltered him for over four centuries. Then, they soared into the sky and disappeared into the forest and into their future.

About the Author

CJ England credits her passion for writing to her second grade sweetheart, Steven, a blond haired cutie with dimples, who dumped her for a girl who could swing on the monkey bars. She wrote her first story about love and loss after that tragic episode.

Always feeling a little different from everyone else, CJ was never content to spend too much time doing the same thing, so she enjoys her writing for the simple reason that in a book, she can do anything she wants to do, and never gets bored.

In her life she has modeled, competed in rodeo as a barrel racer and trick rider, taught preschool, performed as an actress and singer, birthed and raised three children (Jessaca, Jeramiah and Jasiah), served cocktails at Disneyworld, specialized in production work, and got carried away by Spiderman when she worked with him at Universal Studios.

She calls herself a gypsy, due to her curiosity and "itchy feet". She has spent time in fourteen countries, and has visited forty two states in our own.

Married to her own personal hottie, Jonathon, who is her inspiration, lover and bestest friend, they plan to travel the world together, writing about all the places they visit.

CJ says her goal is that her books will spark the imaginations of her readers. That each time they read them, they feel like they are meeting friends. And that somewhere, in their hearts and souls, they too will begin to believe that anything can happen... if you follow your dreams.

For more information on CJ and her new releases, visit her web site at
http://www.cjengland.com
CJ England and husband, Jonathon

Forbidden Love Issue 2 Wicked Women: Debuting Claudia Christian's, of Babylon 5 fame, entry into the realm of women's fiction and from the wicked minds of Brenna Lyons, C.J England, Terri Pray, Sapphire Phelon, Under the Moon is proud to present tales of Wicked Women.

From Pirates to Shape Shifters, these are women who will do whatever it takes to get the job done. They will use their bodies, their minds, their wits in order to win, regardless of the cost. Are you ready to face these dangerously wicked women? **Recommended for mature readers only.**

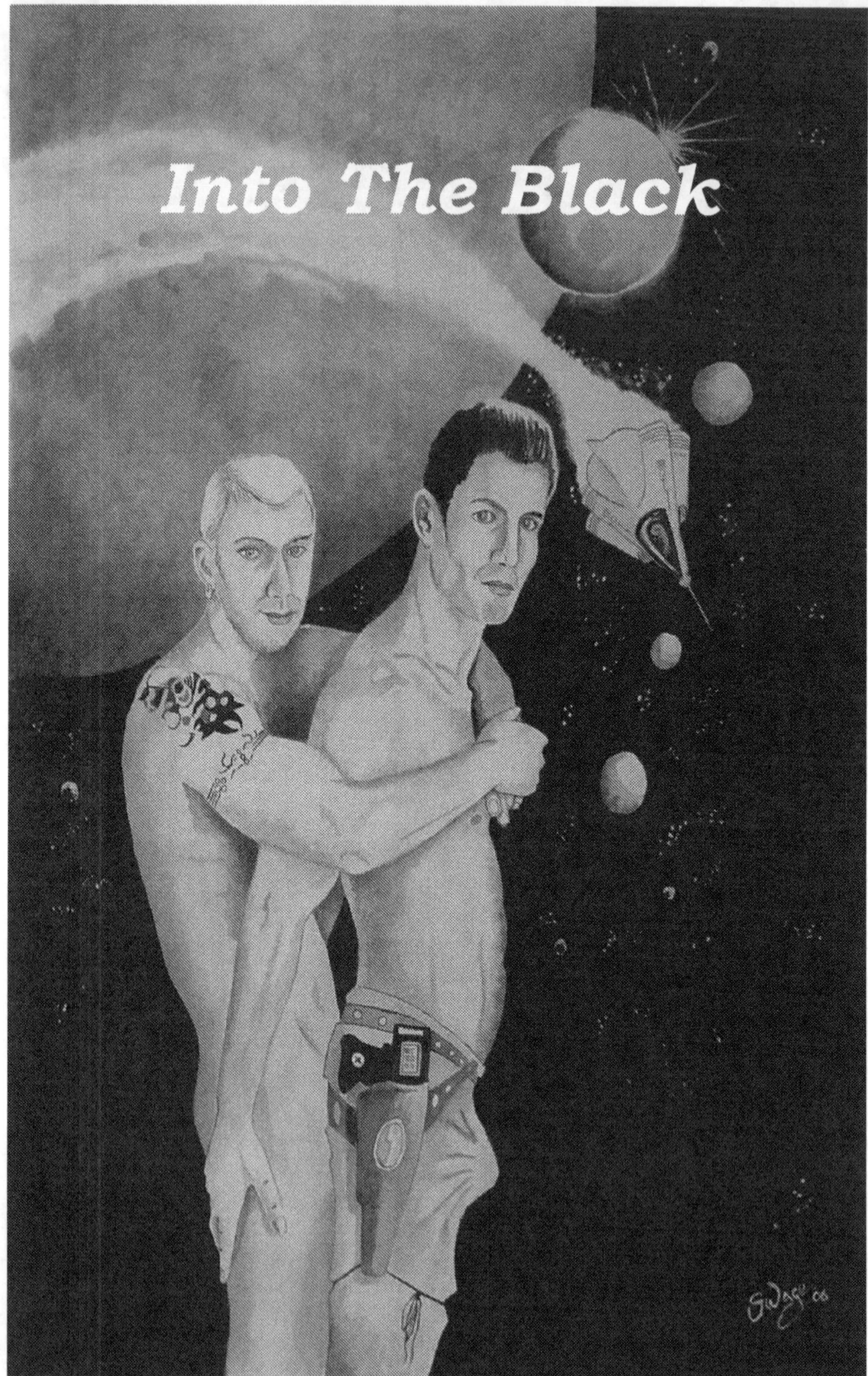

Into The Black

Into The Black
by Ally Blue

Dedication:

"To Firefly, for being the best space Western
ever and giving me the vision."

From space, the stars of the Milky Way resembled a swirl of diamond dust, shining hard and bright out of the endless Black. On Earth, their light would be dimmed or hidden altogether by the soupy, toxic atmosphere. At least that's what Colt had heard from the old-timers who claimed to have been there before it became uninhabitable. He, himself had never seen the stars from any vantage point other than here on the upper level of Hell's End, the last space station before the void.

"Daydreaming again?"

Colt turned toward the voice with a smile. "Hi, Taz. Just looking at the stars."

"You're always looking at the stars." Taz sauntered over from the lift, a rare genuine smile curving his rosebud mouth and putting dimples in his round cheeks. "I doubt the view's changed that much since yesterday."

"It changes." Colt swung his arm toward the far side of the huge transparent dome, where Pluto loomed gray and menacing against the abyss. "There's a new crater today."

"Well, there's a shock," Taz said dryily. "An asteroid hitting Pluto, imagine that. Call the newsfeed, we've got a hell of a story here."

Colt laughed. "Were you coming to look at the stars too?"

Taz's smile vanished, his clear blue eyes hardening into chips of ice. "I came to find you. Boss has a job for us."

"Both of us?"

"Yeah."

Colt felt himself tense. If Etienne L'arisian wanted them both, it wasn't going to be pretty. It usually meant he'd have to use his size and intimidating looks to threaten someone, distracting them while Taz did the real job.

Taz's cherubic face and slight build caused most people to underestimate or even ignore him, and he used it ruthlessly. He'd flash that deceptively sweet smile, huge blue eyes wide and vacant, and get himself instantly labeled as harmless. He'd blend into the background, striking when his prey's attention was firmly fixed on Colt and his perceived menace.

The quarry never knew who'd robbed them blind when their back was turned, or slit their throat. Taz made sure of that. He also made sure that Colt never had to get blood on his hands. But Colt still didn't like these jobs. It hurt him when Taz had to kill, even though his partner did it without emotion or regret.

"What do we have to do?" Colt asked, trying not to look as miserable as he felt.

"One of the dealers on the lower levels screwed the boss's mistress out of several grams of Rapture. She paid for one hundred,hundred; the dealer only gave her ninety. Boss wants us to convince him to give us the other ten."

"And if he doesn't?" Colt already knew the answer. Rapture was horribly addictive and expensive, but nevertheless wildly popular on the space stations orbiting the Outer Planets, where the air reeked of tight-packed humanity and despair and everyone wanted an escape, however temporary. Cheating anyone, never mind the mistress of the head of the L'arisian family, out of what they'd bought was an almost guaranteed death sentence.

Taz smiled again. This time, it was the smile that everyone who knew him had learned to fear. "If he doesn't? We off him."

Colt turned away, his stomach churning. He'd belonged to the L'arisian family for ten years, ever since his parents had sold him at age eleven to buy their own lives, and the lives of their first two children. In all that time, he'd killed only once, in self-defense. It had left an indelible scar on his soul.

"Hey." Taz's arms came around him from behind. He felt the press of Taz's cheek between his shoulder blades. "I'll do it, if it comes to that. You know I won't make you."

"I know." Colt laid his big hands over his partner's small ones. "It's just, I don't like for you to have to kill people either. It's not right."

Taz was silent for a moment. Colt felt the rise and fall of his chest as he breathed. "It's not a question of right or wrong. We do what the boss says, or we die. Better some fucking Rapture dealer than us, yeah?"

Colt didn't answer. Nothing he could say would make Taz regret what he had to do to survive, just as nothing Taz could say would ever make Colt believe it wasn't wrong.

Taz let go of Colt long enough to turn him around, then stood on tiptoe, arms raised. Colt bent and swept Taz into his arms, lifting the smaller man right off his feet. Taz tilted his head up, lips parting. Colt took the kiss Taz offered, accepting his silent comfort as the gift it was.

In all the years they'd known each other, in all the time since Taz had first come to Colt's bed, Taz had never said 'I love you'. But Colt knew it was true nonetheless.

"Let's get this done," Taz whispered against Colt's mouth. "Then we'll go home and fuck. You can do me tonight, okay?"

A lump rose in Colt's throat. He could count on one hand the times that Taz had let him top in the three years they'd been lovers. Taz liked being in control in bed as much as he did in every other area of life. Colt didn't mind. He loved the feel of Taz's cock in him, loved being able to give himself completely to Taz.

However, the nights when Taz opened his pale, slender thighs for Colt, allowing him to take something no one else had ever taken and lived to tell about... Those nights were rare and precious. Not because Colt loved topping so much, because he really didn't. Those nights were special because when he moved inside Taz, his lover's cold eyes would thaw, the walls he'd built to keep the world at bay would crumble, and Colt could look right down inside to the person he'd fallen in love with all those years ago. The man who'd taken a terrified young boy under his wing, protected him and taught him how to survive in a world that had no place for mercy or tenderness or love.

Colt kept those memories close to his heart, hoarding them as greedily as the dragons he'd read about as a boy, before he was sold.

"Thank you, Taz.," Colt said softly, letting everything he felt for Taz shine in his eyes. "I l—"

"We gotta go," Taz interrupted. He pushed on Colt's shoulders. "Put me down."

* * * * *

They rode the lift in silence. It took several minutes to travel from the Star Dome where Colt spent so much of his free time to the bottom of the huge space station. When the lift doors opened on the noise and stench of the first level, Taz took Colt firmly by the arm and led him through the crowd.

"The dealer we're looking for is called Shilo," Taz said as they made their way through the shoulder-to-shoulder press of hookers, dealers, and Rapture junkies. "Boss said we'd find him in the Inferno."

Colt gulped. He'd never been to the Inferno, and didn't want to go now. "Monk says the Sorensens run the Inferno. He says they kill L'arisian's people on sight."

"Monk's a fucking idiot." Taz smiled benignly at a grizzled old woman who was giving him a narrow stare. She turned away, muttering. "Yeah, the Sorensens run it. They run the whole level. But they don't kill L'arisians on sight. Boss would have Lorena Sorensen's ass for breakfast. She may be crazy, but she's not stupid. She wouldn't risk pissing off the L'arisians."

"Why'd the boss let his girl buy from the Sorensens?" Colt

78

wondered. "He had to know they'd fuck her over." It was a question that niggled at Colt's mind.

Taz's expression turned thoughtful. "I don't know. Maybe he didn't know she came down here to buy. Maybe she got the whip for it." Colt winced in sympathy.

"So what's the plan?" he asked, slowing down as they approached the section of the station that housed the Inferno.

"I'll go in first. You wait two minutes, then follow me. When I find Shilo, I'll stand next to him and twirl my hair, like this." Taz demonstrated, winding a shoulder-length golden curl around his index finger. "You come up and explain to him what he did wrong. If he gives you the ten grams, fine. You'll take it and leave, and I'll follow you out two minutes later. We'll meet by the lift."

"What if he refuses?" Colt asked, trying to keep his voice steady. "How do we get him alone so you can... you know."

"If he refuses, punch him in the face and tell him he has twenty-four hours. Make it look good. Make it look like you mean it."

Colt frowned, relieved but puzzled. "I thought you said—"

"Shh!" Taz hissed. He tugged Colt's arm until he leaned down. "Yeah, I will."

"How?"

Taz's mouth curved into a sly, secretive smile. He reached into the front pocket of his vest and pulled out a tiny syringe. A plastic cap covered the short, thin needle.

"It's a poison boss's doctor developed," Taz said, his eyes gleaming as he put the syringe back in his pocket. "I swiped it from the doc's stash before I came to find you. I used it last month on that pimp that sent the boss's son a girl with the rot, you remember that one?"

"Yeah," Colt said, nodding. "But the newsfeed said he died of a brain hemorrhage."

Taz's smile widened. "He did. That's what the poison does. It takes five minutes to work, and it causes bleeding in the brain. We'll be gone when Shilo keels over and dies. We won't be in any danger."

Colt didn't answer. They'd reached the other side of the station, where the Inferno huddled like a malignancy against the thick metal wall, squat and black with fading red flames painted on the door. Taz's hand crept into his, lacing their fingers together.

"I won't let anything happen to you," Taz promised. "Trust me."

"I trust you." Colt gave Taz's hand a squeeze, then reluctantly let go. "Be careful."

"Always." Taz stared at him, eyes hard and cold. "Two minutes, Colt. Put your badass face on."

Taz turned and walked across the teeming street to the Inferno. Colt watched him disappear through the doorway. He tried to suppress the familiar surge of anxiety. Taz could look after himself, better than anyone else Colt had ever known, but Colt never got used to watching him walk alone into deadly danger.

Two minutes crawled by. When it was time to go in, Colt drew a deep breath, plastered on his most threatening expression and headed for the Inferno.

The second he opened the door, Colt knew something was wrong. Not one person in the crowded bar looked his way, but he felt eyes watching him nonetheless, sidelong glances from under lowered lashes or hats pulled low. The men and women packed into the place looked almost posed. Everything seemed too still, too...

"Fake," he whispered to himself. "Shit."

Colt sauntered toward the bar, glowering at everyone he passed. He spotted Taz perched on a barstool. Taz's eyes cut briefly toward the door. Colt followed his gaze, making it look like he was simply perusing the room. Two tall, muscular women leaned against either side of the door. Both had the Sorensen brand, an elaborate 'S', burned into their upper arms.

Colt met Taz's gaze, a question in his eyes. Taz shook his head almost imperceptibly, and Colt's guts clenched.

Shilo wasn't here.

Colt leaned against the bar, heart thumping. Helpless anger at the betrayal coursed through him, nearly drowning out the fear knotting his guts and making his mouth dry as dust. He shot a wide-eyed glance at Taz, silently willing him to take charge of the situation.

As if hearing Colt's thoughts, Taz slipped off his barstool and sidled up to him. "There's a back door behind the bar," he murmured. "When I say 'go,' throw me over the bar. I'll take out the bartender. You cover my back. Ready?"

Colt glanced around the room. Sorensen's two women were easing toward them through the crowd. He mentally gauged how long they had, then turned back to his lover. Taz had dropped the sweet-and-innocent act altogether. His blue eyes blazed with a dangerous fury. It scared Colt to see that, because it meant that there was no longer any point in pretending. They were down to survival: live or die, us or them.

Taz always said that made things simpler. Colt recognized the truth of that, but he much preferred duplicity and complex machinations to the possibility of watching Taz die.

"Yeah," Colt answered. He ignored the metallic taste of fear on his tongue, channeling the rush of adrenaline into increased perception and quick reflexes. "I'm ready."

Taz's eyes locked with Colt's for one searing second, then focused on the bartender, who was eyeing them with deep suspicion. "Go."

Without hesitation, Colt picked Taz up around the waist and tossed him across the bar. He had a split second to watch Taz twist in mid-air and kick the bartender in the face before the Sorensen women leapt on him. He didn't waste time fighting them. He threw them off, planted his hands on the bar behind him, and kicked, catching each woman in the gut with a large, heavy boot. It sent them both staggering back, buying him the time to leap over the bar and slip out the back door behind Taz.

Outside, Colt slammed the door shut and ran after Taz, who was already scampering along the narrow alley between the buildings and the wall. "They'll be after us any minute," Colt said as he caught up. "Those two womean were coming over the bar right behind me."

"I know a place," Taz answered, shooting a glance at Colt over his shoulder. "They won't find us."

They ran in silence. Taz took them on a winding course through the bewildering streets of the first level. Colt was soon hopelessly lost. He jogged along at Taz's side, trying not to think of how utterly fucked they both were.

* * * * *

They ran for almost two hours, near as Colt could figure, occasionally climbing one of the enclosed ladders to a higher level. Colt kept looking around and behind them, expecting at any moment to be nabbed by a group of Sorensen's people, but he never saw anyone following them. By the time Taz led him out of the shadows to a decrepit old building on level ten, Colt had begun to relax just a little.

"What's this place?" Colt asked as Taz picked the lock with his knife and pulled him inside.

"Old apartment building," Taz said, shutting the door behind him. "It's condemned. I hid here once. The Ortegas fucking own this level. Sorensen's people don't come here."

"Oh. Okay." Colt turned in a slow circle, taking in the stained and crumbling walls, the floor thick with dust, and suddenly it all hit him like a sledgehammer. He sat down abruptly on the floor beside the gray metal

81

staircase, shaking all over. "Taz, what're we gonna do? What the fuck are we gonna do?"

Taz laid a hand on Colt's head, absently stroking his hair without looking at him. "We'll be fine."

"How the fuck you figure, huh?" Colt demanded, frustrated and a little angry. "We got the Sorensens after us. Our own fucking boss sent us in there, knowing they were gonna try and kill us. We got no place to go, Taz! We're fucking dead!"

Taz's eyes went wide with surprise, then all the heat bled out of them, leaving them cold and empty. Colt felt a thrill of fear. He'd seen that look leveled at many men and women in the last ten years, but he'd never been on the receiving end before, and it was terrifying.

He held that blank gaze as steadily as he could. Either Taz would kill him, or he wouldn't. He'd much rather die quick and easy by Taz's hand than spend weeks in agony in Lorena Sorensen's legendary torture chambers. He was surprised and very much relieved when Taz's lips curled into a rueful smile.

"Yeah, it seems that way, doesn't it?" Taz shocked Colt to the core by sinking to the floor and crawling into his lap. "I'm not giving up, though. I'm gonna find a way out of this mess."

Colt raised a tentative hand to stroke Taz's back. Taz sighed and leaned his head on Colt's shoulder. Colt took it as an invitation. He wrapped both arms around Taz and held him close, cheek pressed to his hair.

"We could go into the Black," Colt said softly, voicing the wish he'd harbored ever since he'd been brought to Hell's End. "Steal a ship, go, and explore the galaxy. Just you and me."

Taz laughed without humor. "Can you pilot a ship?"

"I can pilot a shuttle. Done it for the boss once or twice."

"The shuttles won't go any further than Pluto and maybe a couple of the deep space stations between here and Neptune. We'd need one of the interplanetary ships. And even then, we could wander around for the rest of our lives without ever finding anyplace we could set foot on."

"Oh. Yeah, I guess you're right." Colt sighed deeply, feeling a little deflated.

Taz lifted his head and twisted around to meet Colt's eyes. "Don't look like that," he said softly, resting a hand on Colt's cheek. "I'll think of something."

Colt couldn't bring himself to smile. "Like what?"

Taz didn't say anything. His eyes burned into Colt's. They moved at the same time, Taz rising to his knees astride Colt's lap, their mouths meeting in a deep, hungry kiss. Colt crushed Taz against him, hands roaming over the wiry body that he knew so well. Taz grunted and pressed even closer, his erection digging into Colt's ribs through the butter-soft material of his pants.

Colt let out a moan. It sounded as desperate as he felt. That same desperation rolled in waves from Taz. Colt wormed a hand between their bodies and started undoing the buttons on Taz's vest. "Taz," he whispered, his voice rough with rising excitement. "Need you."

Taz pulled back with a visible effort. His blue eyes were heavy-lidded and bright with need. "Upstairs. There's a bed." He scrambled to his feet, one hand linking with Colt's. "Come on."

Colt let Taz tug him to his feet and lead him up the stairs. At the top of the steps, Taz turned right down a narrow, dingy hallway. He opened the last door on the left and pulled Colt into a tiny one-room apartment. Motes of dust turned lazily in the dim light that filtered through the single small, grimy window. The room was completely empty except for a narrow bed tucked into the far corner. Even the food synthesizer was missing, broken bits of wire and smashed electronics trailing from a gaping hole in the wall.

"This place is filthy," Colt observed.

"You got a better spot in mind, Princess?" Taz shoved him onto the bed and plopped down on top of him. "Quit bitching and get your fucking clothes off."

Home would be better, Colt thought mournfully, but didn't say it. He obediently began the process of undressing. It wasn't easy with Taz still on top of him, kissing him and generally getting in the way, but he didn't care. He was used to having to get them both naked while they were tangled together. Once Taz got started, there was no stopping him. He was all hands and lips and tongue, aggressive and demanding, and Colt wouldn't have changed that for anything.

Several minutes later, their clothes discarded in a heap on the floor, Colt pulled Taz up to straddle his hips, responding to Taz's silent signals. Taz's slightest sound or movement held worlds of meaning for Colt. He knew instantly what Taz wanted, always, and right now Taz wanted to be taken. To ride Colt like one of the extinct creatures he was named after. Colt was more than happy to oblige.

"We don't have any lube," Colt said in a lust-tight voice, petting Taz's hair as they kissed.

"Use spit." Taz bit Colt's bottom lip, then sat up, hands brace on his chest. "Hurry."

"I don't want to hurt you."

"You won't." Taz cradled Colt's face between his palms. "Please, Colt. I need you inside me tonight."

Colt's chest went tight. Taz's eyes were wide and hot and wanting, all the barriers gone, and Colt wanted to cry at the raw emotion he saw in that beautiful but usually mask-like face.

"Taz..." Colt stroked Taz's arms, longing to give voice to everything he felt but afraid of doing it. "Why?"

He didn't know how to articulate what exactly he wanted to know, but Taz seemed to understand. He leaned down and rested his forehead against Colt's, his delicate fingers smoothing the shaggy dark hair away from Colt's face.

"If this is our last time," Taz whispered, "I want it to be special. For you. For both of us."

Colt didn't know what to say. It was the closest Taz had ever come to telling Colt how he felt, and it was the only time Colt had ever heard him admit to the possibility of defeat. It made him feel warm and cold at the same time. Lacking the vocabulary to say the things he ached to say, Colt answered the only way he knew how— with kisses and touches and the heat of his body. Taz responded in kind, and Colt knew that they understood one another.

Despite Taz's frantic hurry, Colt took his time getting Taz ready. Taz's words had crystallized in his mind the possibility that they might not make it out of this alive. If it was to be their last night together, Colt wanted it to be perfect.

Taz threw his head back and gasped when Colt wormed a fourth finger inside him. "Fuck, Colt. Now. C'mon."

Colt reached through the V of Taz's thighs to grasp his own cock, holding it upright. Taz spit into his palm, slicked Colt's cock and impaled himself in one stroke. Colt's body arched up, his hands reaching to hold Taz's slim hips. Taz drew a deep, shaking breath. Then he began to move, and Colt's world shrank down to heat and sweat and the smell of sex.

They fucked silently, harsh panting breaths and the slap of skin on skin the only sounds. They kept it slow and unhurried by unspoken agreement. By the time Colt felt the orgasm coiling in his belly, his body was wet with sweat, all his limbs shaking.

Taz was close too. Colt could tell by the way his breath hitched, his thighs tightening around Colt's hips and his shaft swelling in Colt's hand. "Colt," Taz panted, fingers digging painfully into Colt's chest. "Now. Now."

Colt bent his knees and dug his heels into the mattress, hips snapping up and down, slamming himself as hard as he could into Taz's body. A few thrusts later, Taz went perfectly still. A drop of sweat rolled off the end of his nose and dripped onto Colt's cheek.

"Oh..." Taz breathed, and came, coating Colt's fingers and belly with semen. His eyes stayed open, locked with Colt's, and the depth of feeling there sent Colt tumbling over the edge. He came deep inside Taz, staring into those eyes that he loved so much.

Taz lifted up, letting Colt's softening prick slip out of him. Colt drew Taz silently into his arms, and Taz went without hesitation, resting his head on Colt's chest and slinging a slender leg over his thighs. Colt didn't care that they were both sticky with spunk and sweat. He'd watched Taz come undone, something no other human being had ever witnessed, and now his love lay warm and sated in his arms. He smiled, blissfully happy in this one perfect moment.

"Mars," Taz mumbled, tucking an arm around Colt's waist.

"Hm?" Colt stroked Taz's bare back, fingertips following the crisscrossing pattern of whip scars. "What about Mars?"

"We can go there." Taz wriggled a little, tucking his head under Colt's chin and planting a soft kiss on his throat. "The newsfeed said they're growing crops there now. There's families and towns and stuff. Plenty of room to disappear."

Mars. The first planet to be terraformed. Colt had seen pictures on the newsfeed. It looked like paradise, green and blue and alive. So different from Hell's End where he'd spent the past decade of his life, or the domes on Pluto where he'd been born and spent his early childhood. What would it be like, he wondered, to breathe air that hadn't been recycled a thousand times? To feel the sunshine on your face and the free wind in your hair?

"Okay," Colt said, leaving for the moment the question of how they were to get there. "We'll go to Mars."

Taz hummed and curled tighter around Colt, his body already relaxing into sleep. Colt kissed Taz's hair and let his eyes drift closed. Whatever tomorrow held for them, at least they had this. Right then, he couldn't bring himself to care about anything else.

* * * * *

Colt jolted awake. He lay staring at the ceiling, every sense on alert. Someone's here, he thought. He tried to scan the room without letting on that he was awake. Maybe he could take the intruder by surprise.

The stealthy scuff of a soft-soled boot sounded from the inky shadows beside the door. A piece of darkness detached itself and slinked toward the bed, and with a shock of fear Colt knew that Sorensen's people had come for them.

Taz didn't make a sound, but Colt felt him wake. As carefully as he could, Colt squeezed Taz's hand where it lay across his chest. Taz tapped Colt's palm once with his index finger, paused, then tapped twice. The signal meant that Taz would take out the person stalking toward them in the dark, and Colt would be ready to take down any others.

Colt squeezed Taz's hand again, indicating that he understood.

The shadow crept closer. Colt watched from under barely-opened lids. A black-clad arm reached out, and Taz struck. Quicker than thought, he clamped a hand onto the person's wrist, using the leverage to pull his would-be attacker down and kick them in the throat. The intruder gurgled and collapsed, writhing on the floor, and all hell broke loose.

The door burst open, letting in the dim light from the hallway. Easily a dozen people in black poured into the room. Colt growled and surged to his feet. Their attackers had clearly wanted to take them by surprise. Kill them in their sleep. Colt smiled grimly as his fist connected with someone's jaw. They clearly knew nothing at all about Taz if they'd thought they'd take him — or Colt — that easily.

They fought grimly, but they were naked, unarmed and outnumbered. There was only one way it could end. Colt knew it and he knew Taz knew it. A strange sort of peace seeped into Colt's mind. So this is how we die, he mused. It could be worse.

"Oh, what, you assholes want some of this?" Taz shouted. "Not even if you paid me!"

Colt glanced over and was stunned to see two men and one of the women from before lunging at Taz, trying to lay hands on him. They appeared to be attempting not to kill him, but to capture him. Colt blinked, then turned just in time to kick a stunner out of the hand of the man behind him.

A gasp and a sudden stillness from Taz's direction made Colt turn around again, just in time to see Taz pull a small dart out of his neck. Taz staggered, shook his head and collapsed into the arms of one of the women as Colt watched.

"Taz!" Colt easily threw off the man who'd grabbed him from

behind and leapt to Taz's side. He ignored the people seething around him, all trying to take him down. All he could see anymore was Taz's white face and limp body, carelessly slung over the woman's massive shoulder. Taz's lips were tinged blue, and for a heart-stopping second Colt thought he was dead.

Everything went still and silent. Colt forgot to breathe in the horror of that moment. Then Taz's chest hitched in the slightest of breaths, and the world started to move again.

Colt lunged and grabbed the woman's arm in an iron grip as she turned to leave. A pop and whistle sounded to his left, but he ignored it, all his energy focused on stopping the bitch who was trying to take Taz from him.

"Don't you fucking touch him," Colt growled, putting every bit of menace he could summon into the command.

The woman didn't answer. Hands grabbed at Colt, pulling him away. He struggled free, lunged for the woman's retreating figure, staggered and fell. It wasn't until that moment that he noticed the bright, aching pain in his left thigh and realized he'd been shot.

He started to push to his feet and run after the woman who was carrying Taz out the door. Then inspiration struck. He rolled his eyes back and let his body go limp, dropping to the floor.

Feet shuffled toward him. He concentrated, forcing his heartbeat and breathing to slow to a crawl the way Taz had taught him.

"Is he dead?" a voice asked.

Someone's fingers pressed against his neck. Not long enough, thankfully. "Yeah. Must've been a heart attack or something, your shot only hit his leg." The fingers went away, and Colt felt the person rise. "Let's go. The boss is getting impatient."

A rough laugh to Colt's right. "The twins better thank their lucky stars that L'arisian didn't want this one anymore. He's gonna be like nothing they've ever had. Those two ain't used to having a toy with any spirit left."

"I don't want to fucking know," a woman's voice growled. "They give me the creeps."

"Let's get the fuck out of here!" The man sounded half panicked. "We'll get the whip or worse if we're not back soon. If the Ortegas don't catch us first, that is."

Colt heard the scurrying of boots across the floor, then the door slammed and silence descended.

Colt let his heartbeat and breathing return to normal, scrambled rather unsteadily to his feet and immediately started pulling his clothes on. A sense of urgency like he'd never known prodded him. Etienne L'arisian had betrayed them. He'd sold Taz to Lorena Sorensen's sadistic twin children, and given her people license to kill Colt.

He couldn't find it in himself to care that he'd had been so expendable. All he could think of was getting Taz back before the twins got hold of him. He'd seen one of their victims once, when he was twelve. The vision of the body, horribly tortured and mutilated, had haunted his dreams for years. The twins had only been seventeen at the time.

Colt pulled his boots on and headed for the door. Then stopped. He knelt on the floor and searched through Taz's clothes until he found Taz's knife and the little syringe of poison. He pocketed both weapons, stepped over the still body of the man Taz had killed and slipped silently out the door.

* * * * *

He wasn't sure how long he followed the people who'd taken Taz. He trailed them all the way back down to level five, keeping to the shadows, his feet sure and silent. The wound in his leg didn't appear to be serious, but the injury to the muscle slowed him down and he'd lost a fair amount of blood. By the time the group entered a huge, forbidding structure that had to be the Sorensen mansion, Colt's heart was racing and his breath coming short.

Crouching in the shelter of a grotesque statue outside the building, Colt considered his options. Every cell in his body screamed at him to charge inside, snatch Taz and run like hell. But he knew that to do so would be hopeless. If he could have taken on all of them, he would have done it back in the apartment. He couldn't. There were too many of them. He'd have to use stealth instead of muscle.

Reaching into the back pocket of his pants, Colt drew out the small pair of multi-purpose lenses . He slipped them on and adjusted the magnification. A tiny blue light beside the front door told him what sort of system protected the mansion. Colt swore under his breath. Lorena Sorensen had always seemed too megalomaniacal to invest in the most high-tech, foolproof security system available.

Doesn't matter, Colt thought with grim determination. I'll find a way in. I'll die before I'll leave him there.

Sweeping the imposing face of the structure with his lenses, Colt found himself hoping that he managed to live long enough to get Taz out.

* * * * *

Nearly twelve hours later, having investigated every possible way in, Colt leaned wearily against the station wall behind the mansion. He'd been hoping to find a window that he could open by disabling the security system, or simply break, but that hope had been quickly dashed. The windows were made of the latest glass-plastic hybrid, a perfectly transparent compound with the tensile strength of steel. Nothing could break them. The ones that actually opened, as well as all of the doors, required a DNA sample scraped from the skin plus a voice scan and a password.

He might be able to overpower someone for the DNA sample, but he knew he'd never be able to force Sorensen's staff and slaves to give the voice command or the password. They were far more afraid of their mistress than they'd ever be of him.

Colt eyed the small, unassuming door that opened onto the back alley where he crouched behind a discarded box. He'd seen several people leave in the time he'd been watching the door. So far, no one had entered that way, but the faintly glowing touchpad beside the door combined with the number of staff who clearly used that entrance made him suspect that this was the weak point in Sorensen's defenses.

As he watched, a group of girls in crisp white uniforms approached the door from the other end of the alley. One of the girls pressed her thumb to the touchpad. A dull red beam shot out from an aperture above the pad, directly into the girl's eye. A moment later, the door slid open and the girl entered. The other staff members went through the same process each in turn.

Colt grinned as the last girl went inside and the door closed behind her. This door worked on a combination of thumbprint and retinal scan. He wouldn't need a conscious or cooperative victim to get in. All he had to do was wait.

That turned out to be more difficult than he'd ever imagined. Having finally found his way in, Colt practically vibrated with impatience. The need to find his lover was so intense it hurt. With nothing to do but wait for someone to approach the door alone, Colt couldn't help imagining the things Taz might be enduring. The Sorensen twins, Lorelei and Orlando, had a reputation for cruelty surpassing even that of their mother. Colt's hands twitched, aching for action.

Colt was on the verge of charging the door and trying to break it down with brute strength when he heard whistling. He went still, concentrating all his energy on the sound. A second later, a young man appeared, strolling toward the door. With a shock, Colt recognized one of the men who'd taken Taz.

Colt didn't wait any longer. He slid along the wall, keeping to the shadows. Just as the young man reached for the touchpad, Colt leapt on him. He wrapped one muscular arm around the young man's throat and held both his wrists in the other hand, immobilizing him.

"You brought a man in here earlier today," Colt said softly. "You were taking him to the twins. Where is he?"

The boy's throat worked against Colt's arm as he swallowed. "I don't know," he gasped.

Colt tightened his grip. "You're lying. I saw you there when you took him. Tell me where he is, or I'll kill you." The threat rolled easily off of Colt's tongue. He didn't want to consider whether or not he actually meant it.

To his surprise, the boy laughed, the sound tight and wheezing. "If I tell you, she'll give me to the twins."

Colt took a deep breath, forcing himself to stay calm and think. He knew the young man was right. What was more, he'd no doubt get the same answer from anyone else he managed to catch. And time was running out. The longer he stood here, the more chance he had of being caught himself. Which left him with very little choice.

He was going to have to be scarier than Lorena Sorensen and the twins, something he would've never thought possible.

Summoning every ounce of menace he possessed, Colt shoved the tip of Taz's knife into the young man's groin. The razor-sharp weapon sliced through the synthetic leather like it wasn't even there. Colt felt the change in texture and resistance when metal met flesh. He tried not to flinch when his captive yelped and jerked in his grip.

"Tell me where he is," Colt demanded in his coldest voice, "or I'll cut your fucking balls off."

In a startlingly quick move, the young man twisted out of Colt's grip and scampered out of reach. Time seemed to slow down. Colt watched with a detached calm as the man lunged toward the door. Clearly he hadn't believed Colt's threats, and with that, Colt had only once choice left. There was no room for doubt, no time to mourn the loss of the last hoarded piece of his innocence. Taz's life was on the line, and Colt would stop at nothing to save him.

When Colt threw Taz's knife, embedding it in his enemy's throat, his only regret was that he still didn't know where to find Taz.

Colt caught the young man before he hit the ground. Resting the back of the dying man's head against his own forehead, he took a still-twitching hand in his and pressed the thumb against the touchpad. He shut his eyes and held his breath, hoping that the man's eyes would stay open until the retinal scan finished.

A soft chime sounded and the door slid quietly open. Colt shuffled inside, dragging his victim with him. The young man's weak struggling and tortured gurgles had stopped altogether by the time Colt got them away from the door and around the corner into what looked like a storage room.

He yanked Taz's knife free and dropped the body on the floor. A moment's searching turned up a towel, which he used to clean the knife. He refused to look at the dead man's face as he left the room and went to find Taz.

The task of finding his lover kept him from brooding over his first deliberate kill. The place was huge, a vast maze of zigzagging hallways leading to unexpected places: a tiny, bare bedroom, a luxurious meeting area, a training room full of weapons. So many others that they soon began to blur together, and every one of them empty. Colt was glad of it, but the brooding quiet unnerved him.

He first heard the murmur of voices as he crept up the stairs to the third floor. A man's voice, followed by a high-pitched female laugh that sent cold chills shooting down Colt's spine.

The twins.

Moving quickly yet silently, Colt followed the voices down a short corridor to a black metal door which stood partway open. His heart thundered against his ribs, the blood coursing hot and fierce through his veins. The pain in his injured thigh faded to a dull ache, lost in the sudden surge of adrenaline. He sidled up to the metal door and peered inside.

He'd expected it, but nothing could have truly prepared him. Taz hung by his wrists from chains set in the ceiling, his toes barely touching the floor. He was naked, his slight body limp in his bonds. Blood trickled down the insides of his thighs, shockingly bright against his pale skin. Numerous tiny cuts covered his chest and stomach. They were an ugly purple-red and badly swollen. Telltale white crystals told Colt that the wounds had been rubbed with salt.

Pocketing the knife, Colt rushed forward and lifted Taz gently in his arms. Taz's eyes shot open, his body tensing. He went perfectly still when he focused on Colt.

"Colt?" he whispered. "What... how did you..."

"You didn't think I'd leave you here, did you?" Colt pressed a kiss to Taz's lips. "Where are the twins? I heard voices."

"There's another room back there." Taz nodded toward a closed door in the back of the room. "They went in there to rest and eat. If you'd shown up a few seconds earlier, they would've caught you too."

Colt ran his gaze over the length of sturdy chain, now puddling on Taz's belly. "How do I get these things off you?"

Taz lifted his bound hands. "The cuffs have a clip that attaches to the chain. I think they were afraid to unchain my hands long enough to move me anywhere." He glanced toward the closed door, then back to Colt. "Hurry."

"Can you stand up?" Colt tried not to see the flinching horror hiding behind Taz's cold eyes. He couldn't focus on that right now, or they'd never get out.

Taz nodded. "Yeah. Just... just let me lean on you for a minute, okay?"

Colt swallowed. As gently as he could, he set Taz on his feet. Taz sucked in a breath, but held his own weight. He leaned against Colt's chest, his sweat-matted curls resting on Colt's shoulder. He lifted his cuffed wrists without a word. Colt found the clip, flipped it open and let the chain drop.

"What about the cuffs?" Colt wondered.

"Key's hanging on the wall there," Taz answered, eyes darting between the room where the twins lurked and the open door of his prison.

Taking Taz with him, Colt shuffled across the room, snagged the key and unlocked the cuffs. Taz tossed them aside as if they burned him.

"Come on," Taz said, rubbing his red and swollen wrists. "Let's get the fuck out of here."

"Oh, but you've only just arrived," a feminine voice lilted. "And we have another guest, how lovely!"

Colt turned toward the door in the back of the room. Lorelei and Orlando Sorensen stood there, masculine and feminine mirror images, tall and beautiful and terrifying.

Instantly, Taz sprang away from Colt and into a fighting stance. He radiated cold, confident menace, but Colt knew better. He'd felt the fine tremor in Taz's body, seen the fear glaze his eyes. That, more than anything else, sent anger flooding like a red tide through Colt's brain. These two spoiled, sadistic little bastards — literally, if the rumors were true — couldn't be allowed to put that look in Taz's eyes and live. For the first time in his life, the thought of killing made him glad.

"I'll kill you both," Taz said, very softly.

Forbidden Love: Bad Boys

Lorelei's bell-like laughter rang through the room. "Of course you will. You and your lover." She turned her ice-blue gaze to Colt, smiling appreciatively as she looked him up and down. "Did you kill Ross? Mother called us just now and said one of the downstairs staff found him in the pantry. She thought we did it."

Orlando's lips curved into a sadistic smile. "As if we'd use such unrefined methods."

"Or stoop to using Mother's goons when we have such a nice new plaything." Lorelei shook her head sadly. "Pity. We were training Ross in the art of torture. He was coming along nicely."

Taz shot a quick, shocked look at Colt. "Colt?"

He nodded. "Had to."

"Oh. Fuck." Sorrow flashed through Taz's eyes, swiftly replaced by a fine, hot fury. Deadly gaze fixed on the twins, Taz held his hand out. Colt knew instantly what Taz wanted. He slapped the knife handle into Taz's outstretched palm. Taz threw the weapon with a quick flick of his wrist, and it hit its mark with a thunk. Lorelei gasped and dropped to her knees, fingers closing over the knife handle sticking out of her chest. Orlando let out a wail and rushed at Taz. Colt met him halfway, caught his wrist and threw the smaller man to the ground. He knelt on Orlando's back, twisting his arm behind him. The bones broke with a loud crack. Orlando shrieked, writhing under Colt's weight.

Taz leapt forward and grabbed Lorelei by the hair, pulling her head back to expose a long expanse of graceful white neck. He wrestled his knife from between her ribs and pressed it beneath her chin. Blood trickled from under the point, winding down to join the red river pulsing from the hole in her chest.

Colt barely heard Taz when he spoke, but he knew what Taz was saying. Those blue eyes held his, wide open and blazing with all the things they never said to each other.

"This," Taz murmured in Lorelei's ear as he slowly slit her throat, "is for Colt. For what he had to do to rescue me." Lorelei clawed at her throat, eyes impossibly wide. Taz didn't even blink as the blade dug deeper, sending a red geyser spraying across the floor. "I wish there was a hell, so you could suffer forever the way you deserve."

A horrible gurgling whistle filled the room. Colt's stomach rolled, but he refused to look away. Not this time. Not ever again. Lorelei thrashed for a few more seconds, then went still. Colt watched the spark go out of her eyes, and was glad. Under Colt's leg, Orlando had stopped squirming and lay crying silently. Colt shook his head, disgusted. The man was nothing but a coward.

"Give me the knife," Colt said as Taz staggered toward him.

Taz's eyes flicked to Orlando's face, then back up to meet Colt's gaze. When he spoke, his voice held an unfamiliar note of tenderness. "You don't have to."

"I want to," Colt answered, and meant it. He let go of Orlando's broken arm and held his hand out. "Give me the knife."

Taz stared at him. Colt stared back, letting Taz see his resolve. Everything had changed now. There was no going back, and no point in regrets. After a long, still moment, Taz laid the knife in Colt's hand.

"I'm sorry, Colt," he whispered.

"Don't be." Colt yanked Orlando's head up by the hair and held the knife poised over his neck. He bent down, putting his mouth near Orlando's ear.

"Your sister died for me," he said in a calm, measured voice. "You're dying for Taz. To pay for making him look like that."

"What?" Orlando whimpered. "Look like what?"

Haunted, Colt thought. Hurt. Afraid. Like he'll wake up screaming every night for the rest of his life. But he couldn't say it, not with Taz right there, shaking and bleeding and trying so hard to hold onto his icy, pitiless mask.

"You're not fit to breathe the same air as Taz," Colt said, and killed Orlando with a swift slice of the knife.

Orlando gurgled and went limp in his grasp. Blood spilled hot and thick over his hand, the smell of it mixing with the sudden sharp tang of urine as Orlando's bladder let go. He wiped his hand on Orlando's shirt, then cleaned the knife as best he could with an unstained corner of cloth.

He rose to his feet and stood contemplating his handiwork. His second murder in less than an hour. He thought he should feel something about that, pain or regret or... something. Anything. But he didn't. All he felt was relief that Taz was still alive, and a fierce, grim joy that his tormenters weren't.

"Colt?"

He raised his head to meet Taz's gaze. Taz's face was paper white, his eyes just a little too wide. Without a word, Colt reached out and pulled Taz into his arms. Taz pressed his cheek to Colt's chest and let Colt hold him. His skin felt cool and damp under Colt's hands.

"Let's get out of here," Colt said. "We have to find someplace safe and find a doctor or something. Maybe one of the girls down at Miss

Forbidden Love: Bad Boys

Mary's knows somebody who can help, the spacers are always knocking 'em around after they're done, they can—"

"No," Taz said sharply. "No doctors."

"But you're hurt." Colt ran his hands carefully down Taz's bare back. Taz hissed and went tense when Colt's fingers gently stroked his buttocks. Colt fought down a surge of pain and sorrow and pure blind anger. "Fuck, Taz, what'd they do to you?"

A violent shudder ran through Taz's body. His fingers clutched Colt's shirt. "Don't ask me that. Just... just clean the wounds and don't ask. Please."

"Okay," Colt promised, though it hurt to say it. "C'mon, let's find you some clothes and get the fuck out of here."

Taz let go of Colt and stood gazing up at him as if he wanted to say something and didn't know how. He shook his head, took his knife from Colt's hand, and walked a bit unsteadily toward the back room where the twins had been before. Colt followed him, one eye on the other door.

The room was small but plush, furnished with a huge bed, an old-fashioned wardrobe, and an overstuffed sofa. Taz opened the wardrobe, rummaged around for a moment and pulled out a pair of soft red leather pants and a long-sleeved black shirt. He pulled them on. The bottoms of the pants dragged the floor and the shirt sleeves hung several inches past his fingers, but he was no longer naked and his injuries were covered. They could walk around in public without drawing undue attention, which was all that really mattered.

Taking Colt's hand in his, Taz led the way through the torture chamber and out into the hallway. Colt kept his eyes moving, expecting at any moment to be greeted by Lorena Sorensen or some of her muscle. But as before, the place was eerily empty and silent. Colt couldn't help wondering where the girls in the crisp white uniforms had gone.

They made it all the way to the back door where Colt had entered without seeing a soul. They glanced at each other and ran to the door. Taz thumbed it open. On the other side stood the two women who'd nearly gotten them in the Inferno, another lifetime ago.

Colt whirled around, Taz's hand still in his, ready to run for the front door. Lorena Sorensen stood there, smiling beatifically at him, and he felt his last hope die.

"Surely you didn't think you could simply waltz in here, kill my children, steal their toy, and waltz right back out again?" She swayed towards him, still smiling. Her eyes gleamed with a mad light.

Colt didn't need to turn around to know that the two women behind him were preparing to take him and Taz both. He steeled himself for a fight, however hopeless it might be.

Then he remembered the syringe.

In a flash, Colt had moved behind Lorena Sorensen and grabbed her around the throat with one hand while pulling the syringe out of his pocket with the other. She struggled, but he was bigger and stronger and absolutely determined. He pulled the cap off the syringe with his teeth and plunged the needle into the side of her neck.

"Back the fuck off, now!" he bellowed at Sorensen's women. "Or I shoot your boss full of poison!"

The two women stopped, wide eyes flitting between Colt and their mistress. "Do as he says," Lorena said, sounding remarkably calm. She didn't believe he'd kill her. Fine with him. She'd find out.

"We're going," Colt growled. "And we're taking this piece of shit with us. You two are gonna wait one hour, then come to the Inferno. She'll be there. Got it?"

The two women glanced at each other, then turned identical questioning gazes to their boss.

"Do it," Lorena said, and the two moved aside.

Colt smiled grimly to himself as he dragged Lorena through the door. Lorena's people were obviously afraid to move a muscle without their mistress's say-so. Perfect.

Taz took the lead once they were out of the house. Flitting from one bit of cover to the next, he led them across the level to a rarely-used lift. They rode in silence, going up. They stepped out into a noisy crowd on level twenty-seven, the one just below the Star Dome. Thankfully, none of the throng seemed to take any notice of the strange trio, most of them too high on Rapture or homemade liquor to care.

"This way," Taz said, motioning Colt forward through the crowd. "I know a place we can go."

"But... but the Inferno!" Lorena gasped. Her face was grayish and beaded with sweat. "You said..."

"Shut up," Colt ordered, pushing the needle deeper into her neck.

She shut up. Colt hauled her bodily along, following Taz into the narrow space behind a public toilet. Dark stains covered the walls and floor, and the air reeked of urine and worse things.

"You have to take me to the Inferno!" Lorena insisted, sounding panicked now.

Taz fixed her with a cold look. "You didn't believe we'd kill you.

That was a mistake." His eyes met Colt's. "Colt?"

He knew what Taz was asking. But he no longer needed Taz to protect him. He didn't know how to feel about that, and he didn't want to think about it.

"I'm okay," he said.

Taz nodded, accepting Colt's decision. Still looking into Taz's eyes, Colt pushed down the plunger. Lorena keened and struggled in his grip. Colt dropped her onto the dirty ground, yanked the syringe out of her neck and tossed it behind a pile of trash a few feet away.

"You have five minutes," he told her. "I hope it fucking hurts."

They left the filthy alleyway hand in hand, without looking back. They didn't talk; there was nothing to say.

Colt followed Taz without asking where they were going. He thought he could guess. When the docks came into view, Colt knew he was right.

"How do we get on board?" he asked, staring through the huge viewports at the enormous starship hovering on the other side of the airlock.

"The chief engineer owes me one. I saved her ass in a bar fight once."

"You're sure she'll help us?"

"She'll help." Taz turned his intense blue gaze to Colt. "We're going to Mars, Colt. We'll never have to see this fucking place again." Colt had daydreamed for years of going into the Black. But in the end, it was only a vague dream of escape. Mars was a whole new life. A chance to start over. It sounded good.

"We'll get work there," Colt said softly. "Save up some money. Buy us a little place somewhere, out where there are trees and rivers and not another soul for miles around. Grow our own food. Live off the land."

"We don't know how to grow stuff, Colt. We don't know how to do anything."

"Doesn't matter. We'll learn."

Taz laughed, and Colt wondered if he'd ever heard that note of childlike excitement in Taz's voice before. Rising on tiptoe, Taz wound his arms around Colt's neck and lifted his face.

The kiss was soft and sweet and full of promise. Colt cradled the back of Taz's head in one palm, keeping the other hand protectively around his waist. When they pulled apart, Taz sagged in Colt's arms, pain creasing his brow.

"Let's go find your engineer friend," Colt said. "I want to get you on board and settled. I need to see how badly you're hurt."

"It's not so bad," Taz said softly. "They'd barely gotten started on the torture. They'd been spending most of their time trying to scare me. Wanted me to beg for my life or something, I guess."

"Did it work?" Colt asked, knowing the answer already.

Taz arched an eyebrow. "What do you think?"

"I think you probably pissed them off pretty bad by not breaking down the way they wanted you to." Colt ran a finger down Taz's cheek. "I think it's a good thing I found you when I did."

"I think you're right."

Colt gazed at the starship, then turned a thunderous look toward the interior of the station. "L'arisian fucked us over, Taz. Sold you to those monsters, and told them to kill me. We can't let him get away with that."

Taz took both Colt's hands in his, lacing their fingers together. "I'd love to rip his guts out and feed them to him. But we can't. If we go back now, we'll die there. It's not worth it."

"Not worth it?" Colt gaped at him. "After what he did to you?"

"I don't want to die, Colt. I don't want you to die. I want us to leave Hell's End, together, and start over."

Colt's anger at Etienne L'arisian burned in his belly, but he knew Taz was right. They couldn't have both their revenge and their new life. There was a choice to be made, and they both knew what the right choice was.

"Okay," Colt said, stroking the backs of Taz's hands with his thumbs. "You're right. We'll go to Mars, and forget all this."

Taz stared up at him with a solemn expression. "Colt, I know I've never said so, but... but I...."

He trailed off, but Colt understood. The unspoken truth shone bright as starlight in Taz's eyes. Colt leaned down and kissed him.

"I know," Colt whispered. "I know."

About the Author

Ally Blue used to be a good girl. Really. Married for twenty years, two lovely children, house, dogs, picket fence, the whole deal. Then one day she discovered slash fan fiction. She wrote her first fan fiction story a couple of months later and has since slid merrily into the abyss. She has had several short stories published in the erotic e-zine Ruthie's Club, and is a regular contributor to the original slash e-zine Forbidden Fruit. Her books are available through Loose Id and Samhain Publishing.

Ally's website: http://allyblue.com/

Ally's LJ blog: http://www.livejournal.com/users/ally_blue/

Ally's Yahoo! Group: http://groups.yahoo.com/group/loveisblue/

Soul Seduction

Soul Seduction
By Sapphire Phelan

Dedication:

I dedicate to my husband, Bill, for encouraging me in my writing endevors, to my son, Chris, to the writers' groups I'm with who have helped me, and to my good friends who were my first fans.

I've been alone in this forsaken park in the middle of this damn human-scum city without even having seen any of my kind since . . . damned, had it really been just a little over a hundred years?

A hundred years worth of human filth--feces left by homeless drunks and flea-bitten mutts to gum and trash dropped by human brats. The double-damned park reeked of human piss and unwashed bodies. All day long, as I hid in my prison I would hear the screams and yells of those disgusting human brats as they played on the swings and jungle gym and even worse, the shared laughter between lovers as they walked hand-in-hand on the park's trails. Moreover, at night, the only company I had was from drug dealers, the occasional jogger and lovers fucking, the sounds of their groping and moans loud in the still night air. So, just because I'm a mean sonofabitch, I would magick some angry fire ants to sting those lovers or with a click of my fingers, cause some sweet-faced child to tumble from his/her swing and break a leg. Still, it didn't relieve me of my hatred for this place. It didn't help me break free of it. It didn't lessen the madness a hundred years of this park brought to me. Instead, it intensified it.

Worse, there was no one to relieve me of my loneliness, or my needs. The one, terrible thing the bitch Queen of the Seelie Court could truly do to punish me--no fucking sex. Maybe that makes me selfish, but hey, I'm a fey! When did any member of the Fairy court have a conscious? Besides, I'm the Love Talker. Selfishness is my middle name and my own needs, my game.

Things began to look up though, when Alicia Turner came here for the first time. She was five years old, and so cute as a button, so cute that it made me want to puke. Her parents had just divorced and her father had her for the weekend. They picked up burgers and fries for a picnic at the park. They fed the leftover crumbs from the hamburger buns to the pigeons that clustered around their bench and Alicia's father said that though her mother and he were no longer married, he'd always be there for her and the divorce wasn't her fault, that he'd always love her. Afterwards, Alicia played on the weathered jungle gym set nearby while her father watched. Whether from the heat of the sun or maybe he was just tired, her father's eyes closed and his head lolled against the back of the bench, his snores harsh music on the summer breeze.

Bored, I came out of hiding and had been about to use magic to make her fall--maybe she'd break a leg or something--when something gave me pause. She laughed, a gay, carefree laugh that starts from your toes and soars up to burst out from your mouth like a wild bird escaping its cage. How like a member of the Seelie Court she seemed then. Her hair shone like a newly minted gold doubloon and the wind caught the long locks and played with them, tossing them here and there. Her green eyes sparkled with life, bright and inquisitive, more like a Fey's than a human's. She jumped from the top and landed feet first in the sand, then plopped down on her butt and began playing with her doll.

A strange feeling came over me and I felt a need to get closer to her. I slipped out of the fairy ring that was both home and prison to me and darted over.

"Hello," I said, squatting down outside the sandbox.

She looked up and smiled. "Hi! My name's Alicia, what's yours?"

"I have many names, but you can call me Bran."

"Bran? That's a funny name to have--like cereal, or something." Her brow furrowed, lines indenting on her forehead.

I reached out and grabbed a strand of her hair, lifting it up to inspect it. It felt soft, like the newfound down of a baby bird and I leaned over and sniffed. An odor like roses drifted off her hair, invading my nostrils. An innocent human child, something fairies have always had the urge to steal, leaving a changeling in their place. I've wondered why anyone would ever want one of the mortal's brats to raise and finally I understood. It was that special aura about them, innocence and mortality that drew the jaded immortals. A need to get close to death. We could not die.

"Alicia," I said with deep persuasion. "Look into my eyes."

She stopped playing with her doll and glanced up. Her eyes glazed over and her mouth hung open slightly. I smiled, and held out a hand.

"Come with me, Alicia."

"Hey, what are you doing with my kid?"

I looked up to find Alicia's father giving me a threatening glare as he leaped to his feet. I bolted back to the safety of my fairy ring. From there I watched as he grabbed his daughter and her doll and carried both away.

He never brought Alicia back to the park after that.

That pissed me off, of course. Being a fey of the Unseelie Court I was a dark soul, normally used to doing all sorts of nasty things, especially to humans. However, I couldn't do anything to him, especially since he never came back. It didn't mean that I couldn't take it out on others though. That year more people than normal were either hurt or killed in the park. Boredom and the forgetful mind of a fey finally halted the bad things. Except, I never forgot Alicia. She had done something to me, inside of me, made me dream and wonder, both in my sleeping and waking moments.

I saw her again, thirteen years later, when she turned eighteen. Tall, slim and beautiful, a glow of innocence like a shining cloak that she wore, she came to the park. Dressed simply in a pair of blue jeans and a T-shirt, she had brought a sandwich and soda, along with a book.

Hecate's blood, maybe she didn't have the unearthly beauty of a fey woman, but she sure would give the Seelie and Unseelie Queens themselves a run for their money. She was an immortal's dream made flesh. Soft, succulent; I could almost taste the salt on her skin and breathed in a hint of the sweet smell that wafted off her like soft summer grass. Like a breath of fresh air that managed to break through the rancidness that filled this place. I grew hard with want.

She sat down on a park bench not far from my fairy ring. The bench had once been brown, but had weathered down to a gray color. She ate her lunch and read the book, oblivious to everything around her.

I slipped out of the ring and strolled up to her, using my glamour to make sure she didn't recognize me from years before. It wouldn't do to have my prey bolt before I had captured her.

"Is it okay if I sit next to you?"

She looked up.

Damn, I remembered those lovely green eyes, haunting like a Fey's. Something tore inside me, unusual in that I had never felt anything like it before.

She glanced aside. "Sure. I don't own this bench."

I sat down. "What are you reading?"

"A book called *Fairies and Other Supernatural Beings*."

I grinned. "Oh, so you're interested in the Fey."

Strange warmth invaded me that she would be reading up on my kind, and I realized that it was pleasure. My grin faded in the knowledge that I would feel anything so simple, so good..

She closed the book and laid it in her lap.

"I don't know why, but ever since I was five years old I've felt compelled to know about fairies. It all began with a visit to this park with my father, actually." Her gaze swept around the park. "I know it's an unlikely place to begin an urge to want to know about beings like that. But I think it was because of this strange and extremely tall man I met that day. There was something about his eyes." Her gaze found mine. "Whoever he was he sure scared the hell out of my father. Guess Daddy thought he was a child molester or something like that. But I always thought he was a fairy--he didn't seem human, not of this world."

She shivered and held out her hand. "Enough of that, though. I'm Alicia Turner. And your name is. . ."

I gave her what I knew was my most devastating smile. "Branigan Darkman."

"That's a strange name. You know, I swear I've heard it before."

She looked down at the book in her lap, her brows knitted together. Worried that she would guess I grabbed her chin in my hand and turned her gaze to meet mine. With a snap of my fingers on my other hand the book vanished.

I stared into her eyes, holding her gaze tight. "Really? Now where would that be?"

I made the skies suddenly dark with storm clouds and caused a wind to whip up, scattering trash in mini whirlwinds across the park.

Alicia broke free of my gaze and stood up. An uneasy expression crossed her face.

"It looks like rain--I got to go." She made as if to run off, but I jumped up and grabbed her by her arm. She stared at me, reminding me of a deer when the wolf had it cornered, unable to escape.

I breathed in her fear, growing harder.

"I have a place near here that'll get us out of the storm." I used my most persuasive voice, full of artful seduction.

I heard the doubt in her voice. "Where?"

"Come on, I'll show you." Keeping a tight hold on her arm I led her to the fairy ring, using my glamour that could make any mortal do anything.

The wind worsened, whipping tree branches and ripping leaves from them, tossing them into a wild dance. The whole park had become storm-ridden, except for my fairy ring and its surrounding area.

Alicia noticed. "This is so weird. The wind is everywhere in the park, except in this clearing." She saw the fairy ring. "What's that? It looks like some kind of ring of stones and flowers."

I stood behind her and reached around with my hand, covering her left breast. I whispered into her ear, nibbling on its flesh, "Alicia, it's been so long since I've made love to a woman. My sweet, little golden one." My lips left her ear and traveled down the side of her long neck, using them like the loaded weapon I knew they were.

She leaned back against me and shivered. I kept up the kissing; lingering at her neck, and then sunk two sharp canines in the tender flesh there. Blood welled up. I sipped at the rich, salty liquid, before I broke off the bloody kiss and using my magic, sealed up both holes, leaving a love mark there. I felt the connection between us, a new and fragile invisible line, but beginning to grow stronger with each second nevertheless.

She moaned and wavered on her feet.

I kissed her ear again and whispered, "Now, you're mine. Your father stopped me from stealing you the last time, but this time there's no stopping me from taking you. You're an adult now and ready to become mine in all the ways possible. Ready for immortality and endless pleasure."

We moved toward the fairy ring. Alicia danced drunkenly in my arms as we drew nearer. Foolishly, I didn't use the glamour again, thinking that our connection from the blood I took was enough of a hold over her. Just as we were about to step into the circle her body tensed and she broke free of my arms and lurched away.

She swung around and faced me. I stood halfway in, one foot just planted on the inside of the circle, the other one outside. The stance gave some relief to my cock, for it had hardened from the taste of her mortal blood and the knowledge that no matter what she soon would be mine. Her eyes widened with shock and maybe with just a bit of terror.

"You!" she hissed, drawing back in fear. "You're that stranger I met when my father brought me to the park! How can that be?"

My lust had caused the glamour to wear off and I stood there in my true form. The same form I used when she was a little girl.

"Who are you?" she asked, wariness evident in her eyes. "You're a fairy, aren't you? That's the only way you could have fooled me."

I shrugged. "Some call me the Love Talker. There are other, older forms of being that I am, but most importantly I'm an Unseelie Slaugh Sidhe, cursed to be imprisoned in this place of human slime. The Queen of the Seelie Court placed me here a century ago, when she caught me fucking her daughter."

I inched closer, until I felt the heat from her body. "Come, Alicia, and let me make you mine. I can grant you immortality. You'll never grow old and I can promise you, I'm one hell of a lover. Relieve me of my miserable existence."

She shook her head, her eyes wide with fear. "No, stay away from me."

I bared my teeth in a smile, a cold, nasty one, suddenly too tired to care anymore about hiding my true self to her. "The bitch Queen's daughter wanted it and enjoyed being filled by me, but Mama was angry and so here I am, caught in this place. I can never leave it, surrounded by all the nasty odors and thoughts of humankind." I edged nearer, reaching out to her. "Alone, do you understand what it is like to be all alone, with no contact with your kind for over a hundred years? And it's not just the sex, though I sure as hell miss that, but there's no one to talk to or be with in the closeness of warmth and companionship. That Seelie bitch queen knew exactly that this would be the worse kind of punishment she could do to me!"

She turned and ran. I chased her through the park and was about to use magic to block her from escaping me but something stopped me. Inside my head I heard the bitch Queen's laughter and I knew why. So I ran after Alicia, but couldn't go beyond the invisible barrier of Seelie magic that kept me here when she left the park's confines.

If we fey could feel, then that day my heart was torn into two pieces, broken like china dashed to the ground. The storm raged around me, tearing the park up. I used the taste of the blood connection I had done to her soul when I drank from her neck, calling her, but she never answered my call. Full of agony, I howled, my voice rising with the fury of the storm.

* * * * *

Ten years flew by; a drop in the bucket of a fey's life. Endless throngs of people came to and left the park. Each day at noon and each night at midnight, I sent out my call to Alicia, trying to draw her back. However, it seemed her soul was stronger than my magic.

Finally though, I had won. Our connection had proved stronger than her soul and force of will.

Alicia stood next to the fairy ring at midnight, her head sunk down between her shoulders in broken submission.

"I'm here, Bran." A wealth of pain colored her voice.

I magicked myself from my place and appeared next to her. "Alicia."

The light of the full moon lit up the area. I saw she had grown older, a few lines painting her face. Tiredness filled her eyes, fading them from the sparkle that I remembered.

I sniffed the air about her. "You're still pure, I see. Good."

"I tried to give myself to several guys that I dated, but something wouldn't let me." She reached up with her hand and touched the side of my face. "It was you I kept seeing and I just couldn't do it. You cursed me as much as that fairy queen cursed you to this park."

107

I lifted her up into my arms and stepped into the circle. We vanished from human sight and entered my home. My prison.

Once inside, I loosened my hold and slid her body slowly to the ground against mine. I molded her against me, letting her feel the hardness between my thighs. With a click of my fingers, the room lit up with a million tiny lights that glittered like stars. I moved away and stalked over to an extra-large bed that dominated the room. I sat down on the edge and with a smile, gestured to Alicia.

"Join me."

Her hands knotted together, she swept her eyes around the room, lighting momentarily on the armoire, the table with two chairs and the Roman bath.

I laughed, sounding bitter. "As you can see, I have all the amenities of home and comfort. Queen Anu did give me that, at least."

I stood up and went over to Alicia, trying to draw her toward the bed. "Now, I have the companionship that I've been denied all these years."

She stood in my arms and I bent my head, whispering into her ear. "Let me show you why they call me the Love Talker. Let's talk about the sensuality of the flesh, mortal and immortal." I kissed her. "Let's talk about the eternal dance of passion. How I will relieve you of your innocence and show you such erotic things you can't even begin to imagine."

I captured her mouth. Soft like velvet, and I drank in her unique, sexy taste. I moaned.

It had been so long. . .

My tongue parted her lips, sliding in to caress and dance with hers. I grazed the sensitive walls of her mouth and she moaned. I swallowed the sound, enjoying the flavor of her innocent passion. My kissing changed, going from gentle to a hard, demanding one. I didn't give her time to breathe; instead I drank the air from her lungs, not caring what it did to her, but that I satisfy the hunger that burned inside me.

My hands flittered over her clothing and with deftness and dexterity, I tore them off, exposing naked flesh to my hands, lips, and tongue. I left her mouth and traveled from her cheek to her neck, where my mark from ten years before still bruised the flesh, looking like a strange, light birthmark. I bit into it and blood beaded up, and I sucked greedily, wanting that special taste of her mortality. This inflamed her and she cried out, trying to get closer to me. Feeling the constriction of my own clothing I magicked them away, baring my own naked flesh to the air and her hands.

She stroked my skin, touching me in various places and ending up at the nest of curls between my legs where my cock reared like a sword in a velvet sheath. Her hand touched the tip and with a hiss, I watched as a single wet bead pearled there and stained her fingers.

I whispered, "Taste it." I took her hand and brought it up to her lips. "Taste me."

Her tongue flicked out and licked the wetness off. My lust heightened and I shook with need.

Alicia's eyes found mine. "You taste like sin, chocolate and creamy 2% milk."

I laughed. "There's nothing fat free about me, sweetheart."

I walked her backwards the short distance to my bed and laid her down on it. Her white skin shone pale against the black velvet of the cover.

"I'm glad you don't worship the sun like so many of the other stupid humans do," I said. "Your skin is so perfect, so pale. It'll be light against my darkness."

I lay down next to her and leaned over, taking the nipple of the breast nearest into my mouth. "Mmmmm. . .nice," I growled, my tongue flicking it as I sucked on the tight little bead.

She cried out and arched her back, filling my mouth full of her delectable flesh.

With regret though I left that breast and moved over to the other one, caressing and tantalizing it in equal pleasure. With my sharp canines I nibbled on the nipple, taking care not to hurt her.

Alicia moaned and arched it into my mouth, offering it like a sacrifice to a god. I accepted her offering, paying special attention to both it and the other one, sucking and laving them with my tongue.

Hecate's blood, but her innocence had the most seductive flavor I had never before tasted. I had heard from other fairies that sex with a mortal virgin was the greatest aphrodisiac, but I hadn't believed them.

I took her hand and curled it around my shaft, showing her the movement I preferred. Soon her hand stroked up and down, sliding down to the balls and cupping them, then streaking back up to my head and palming its shape. I shook and roared, grabbing her hand and drawing it away.

"Keep that up and I'll spend what I plan to put inside you," I warned her.

"Please," she cried out.

I stilled. "Please, what?"

"Take me, make me yours," she begged, her eyes shining with unshed tears.

I warned her of the consequences. "Once I make you mine, there's no going back. Do you understand? I'll never let any other male, mortal or immortal have you." A hard undercurrent ran in my voice, hovering not far from complete darkness.

She shivered, both from the fear and need that rose off her in the stink of her sweat.

"I understand." Her answer came in a soft whisper.

I began to kiss her again, feeding from the sweetness of her mouth with both my teeth and tongue. Then I kissed my way down, going from cheek to throat, pausing at her breasts, and then continuing my assault down to her softly rounded belly, my tongue dipping into her belly button. She cried out, shuddering, and with a dark smile I maneuvered down to her nest of honey-blonde curls that promised me delectable delights beneath. My nose pressed against the mound, I breathe in her particular smell. Then I swept past it and ducked underneath, parting her legs wide enough to tuck my head between them. My nose and mouth hesitated at her entrance, and her intoxicating arousal wafted to my nostrils. I stuck my tongue in, tasting how moist and delicious she was. She tasted of light and everything innocent.

Everything I wasn't.

Deep inside me, a tiny voice snickered, saying that I would be the first to know her. And that once we fucked, she would be mine till the end of days. I hesitated. The Love Talker and one woman? And not even a fairy woman, but a mortal one? Then her sweet odor found me again, and my mind forgot everything except need. My need for her.

I moved a tentative finger forward and slid it into her sex. Alicia moaned and arched her back off mattress, her hands fisting both the cover and sheets.

Oh Hecate, this mortal female was almost ready for my invasion.

I probed with a second finger, realizing that I wanted to increase her pleasure, and found her tight, too tight for my size. I closed my eyes and ran my second fingertip through her slickness. My tongue found her precious little button and I suckled it, as I continued to play her with both fingers. Her breath caught and I paused, my smile pressed against her. Resuming my administrations, I stroked and tasted, until she crashed over the edge and let out a scream. I backed away and kneeled between her thighs.

"I've got to have you," I said, my gaze catching hers. "Now."

I laid on her, and grabbing my organ, rubbed the tip against her, mixing my fluids with hers. Then with one hand tucked under one soft cheek of her ass to hold her secure, I pressed forward. She stiffened as I drove in, meeting resistance from her virginity.

"It hurts," she whimpered, her hands pushing at my shoulders.

"Shhhh," I replied. "It hurts for the first time, or so I heard." I shrugged. "I never had a virgin before. But love and lust has always been a combination of pain and pleasure, least that's how I found it to be."

With one hard push, I jabbed through the barrier and then stilled, letting her grow use to my fullness. Then slowly, I moved, pulling back out, letting my length brushed against her clit, then easing back in. In and out, I kept it slow until the pain became pleasure and she urged me to go faster.

I lowered my mouth to hers and again tasted her unique flavor. I withdrew my sex and slammed it back in as her hands slid into my long hair, tangling her fingers in it. She pressed her hips into me and I drew her legs up and around me. My breath caught as without any prodding she deepened our kiss.

Yeah, baby, that's it. Hecate's blood, but you're a fast learner.

Her pace increased, catching up to mine. Suddenly, she flew past, her breath hitching, her eyes glazed. She grabbed my ass and rocked, her fingers digging in deep.

Hecate!

She shattered then; screaming my name, her back arched, her legs stiffened, and her nails raking deep into my hips as she pivoted to the stars.

Waiting for the final spasm to pass, I growled and began to rock into her fully. Once, twice, and then I exploded into her warm moistness as I had never done so before in my long, immortal life.

Panting, I opened my eyes, shocked. I saw wonder glowing in her eyes and in her lovely features. I didn't dare let her know how deeply our coming together had affected me so I closed my eyes.

Any other male, mortal or immortal, could be like this, but not the Love Talker. Never the Love Talker. It'd be like taming the tiger and turning it into a common house cat.

I felt her run a tentative finger along my lower lip. "That was truly wonderful, truly. Can we do it again?"

I laughed, keeping my eyes shut and rolled onto my back with her clutched to my chest. I whispered, "Maybe later, but just go to sleep for now and rest. Give yourself time to heal."

Her smile pressed against my chest, she drifted off to sleep as I reopened my eyes. I stayed awake, holding her close to me and stared off into the darkness, uneasy.

* * * * *

Finally I freed Alicia and she snuggled against my side, her mouth opened and admitted little snores. Easing myself away, I got off the bed and padded naked to the other side of the room. A snap of my fingers and I magicked myself out of there. I stood within the fairy ring, my gaze tight on the surrounding trees. The night wind moaned through their leaves, its insidious whisper telling me what I refused to face.

The Love Talker has finally fallen and his beloved is/was a mortal innocent.

The wind whistled away, laughter in its wake.

I shook my fist, snarling, "That's not true! All she's good to me is to ease my loneliness, to give me something to fuck."

But the wind tossed my words back to me, mocking me.

Hecate's blood, forget the wind, my own inner voice was laughing at me.

I dropped to my knees, head bowed. Something wet flowed from my eyes and I touched it, my fingers coming away with water.

Tears?

But only mortals cried, never fairies.

I stared down at the wet fingertips. I licked them, discovering the taste to be salty. Shock filled me, for tears meant you could feel and that you could be hurt. Oh, did it ever hurt. I closed my eyes, trying to keep the tears from leaking out further.

"So the Love Talker has truly succumbed to that mortal disease called love."

The feminine voice held a trill of mocking laughter. I looked up and into the dark green eyes of the Seelie bitch Queen herself. Anu wore a simple pink skirt that the wind caught by the hem and played with, and a white top molded like a second skin over her taut breasts. Even with my newly found need for Alicia, this being almost caused me to lick my lips in longing.

"Come to gloat over me?" I asked, refusing to look away.

"Stand, Branigan Darkman." Her voice, though soft, held iron authority in it.

I stood up. My legs apart, I refused to be cowed by her eyes roving over my naked form, pausing at my cock. With pleasure I realized that her glance didn't cause me to grow hard with desire. Something I'm sure that Anu never faced before from any Fey male.

Her gaze found mine. "Your mortal has got you by the balls, Darkman."

She twirled around, the hem of her skirt fluttering in the wind. "Unfortunately, she cannot stay with you."

Fear stopped my heart, but I kept it out of my voice. "What do you mean?"

She paused, a smile on her face that didn't look pleasant. "I sent her away. She will not remember you or how you dallied with her in your bed."

Frightened, I rushed back to my chamber on the wings of magic, Anu's laughter following me.

The bed was empty, it's wrinkled, tossed bedclothes the only proof that Alicia had been there with me.

I felt numb and hid how bereft I was deep inside me. My knees wobbled and I felt the urge to drop to them, but I forced myself not to, not wanting the bitch Queen to even know how I truly felt. Instead, I shook my fist and curse her. "How dare you take away my convenient piece of ass. Now I have to go back to hand jobs."

* * * * *

Whether because she felt sorry for me, or more likely, to keep probing my agony, Anu allowed me to view Alicia in a mirror she offered as a present to me. I never left the fairy ring now, but would stare into the reflection of the mirror, watching the daily life of the mortal I now admitted to myself that I loved. To all intents and purposes she had truly forgotten me and our coupling. Until one day Anu's little punishment caught up with the fairy queen.

Our lovemaking had borne fruit. Alicia was pregnant with my child.

Hecate's blood, she carried my child! Pleasure ran rampant in me, at the knowledge my love for Alicia was growing inside her, developing arms and legs and intelligence. Would it look like me in my true form, or would it be more like Alicia?

I paced back and forth before the mirror like a caged tiger, as she had found out the news from her doctor. I watched as she denied knowing any man, that she was a virgin.

Unfortunately, the doctor proved to her that she had lost that precious treasure and that no, she would not have a virginal birth. Her belly grew and she cried alone at night in her bed. My fingers pressed against the glass, I called out to her, sending out waves of love and comfort, praying that she would receive it.

She called out in her sleep. "Bran?" She awoke and sat up, her eyes staring into the darkness. "Oh God," she said, "I remember." Her hands rested on her rounded stomach.

"I remember."

Tears welled up in her eyes and they tumbled out.

A golden light formed in one corner of my chamber, small as a ball and dim at first, but growing larger and brighter. It flashed, vanishing. Anu stood there; dress in a long, filmy gown, a crown of tiny white starflowers and red berries upon her head. Her long, hair flowed loose to her waist, a mixture of reds, gold and autumn browns. She moved to stand behind me.

"I see the mortal remembers you, Love Talker,:" she said with malice. "Do you love this mortal? Would you give up all for her? Change your arrogant ways for her? Even though she's only a mere mortal."

Not looking at her, I replied with a shrug, "I'm just grateful that you didn't saddle me with one woman for eternity, much less a baby to boot."

She reached down and caressed the top of my head, playing with my hair.

"So you wouldn't give up your immortality even for her?" She gave a shrug of her shoulders and laughed. "My answer, the Love Talker? Give up your immortality for some pitiful mortal female? And yet, you still watch her in that mirror. No, I think the both of you are better apart. Your punishment has not been enough for me to offer you this small crumb."

Obviously, she would never forgive me for her daughter. I remembered the old mortal saying, when you play you pay. Well, no doubt Anu believed in me paying for my playing with a vengeance.

I glanced down at the floor, narrowed my eyes, and thought hard. If I said I wanted Alicia, then I would never see her or my child. Anu would take away the mirror and then I wouldn't even have that comfort. But if I pretended that I didn't love her or wanted to be with her, then she might take it into her arrogant head to give me Alicia as further punishment. To shackle her to me like a 'ball and chain', so to speak. Fairies are so arrogant, that most times we can't see past our own noses. However if I'm wrong, then I would never see Alicia ever again. Pain wrapped itself around my heart as I thought of never holding her in my arms again, of endless existence without her love. Immortality can be a real bitch, especially when you finally knew what true love really meant. And though it would hurt, I had to make Anu believe that I still was the Love Talker, unrepentant.

Once again, I gave a shrug of indifference.

"She's just another pussy for the Love Talker to fuck." I turned to look at Anu with an amused grin. "Like your daughter was. Both were equally pretty pathetic in bed. My own hand gives me more satisfaction."

She grabbed me by my hair and gave a vicious tug. I forced myself not to feel the pain or worse, reveal the one I felt deep in my heart from the lie I had just uttered. I stared back at her, keeping my face blank of any emotion.

"So be it." She slapped my face hard, stinging it. I felt sure a red handprint would show up on the skin.

The glow returned and enveloped me. Uncertain, I felt its warmth wash through me, cleansing me of what I was. Then sharp pain lanced through me and I doubled over, wrapping my arms around my body.

By Hecate's blood, what was the Seelie bitch Queen doing to me now? Had I outsmarted myself in the long run? Had she stripped me of my immortality and then brought death on me?

The pain receded. I opened my eyes and found myself in bed, just not my bed. I swept my gaze around the strange room and locked onto another pair of green eyes. Alicia was next to me in the bed, her eyes wide with disbelief.

"Bran?"

She touched my shoulder, as if maybe to convince herself that it was really me.

I shuddered, enjoying her soft hand on my naked skin.

"Alicia," I said with a smile. "I love you."

Her puzzlement became wonder as I opened my arms and she fell into them. She snuggled against me, her hand dipping beneath the covers and finding me. I moaned as she stroked my length. It grew longer and thickened as want broke hot through me. I took her lips with mine, my tongue thrusting inside her mouth to waltz with hers.

"Not even a second as a mortal, and already you and she are going at it like rabbits.

How disgusting."

Anu!

Alicia tried to break away but I wouldn't let her, just kept my grip on her tight. I glared at Anu as she stood at the foot of the bed. I wondered how long she had been watching us.

"What do you mean by mortal?" I demanded.

"I decided to grant you the mantle of mortality. You have a soul, just like she does.

Now you and she can be together, until death do you part." She shrugged. "Just think, you'll grow old and die, like all mortals. So pathetic, and such a perfect way to finally punish you, Love Talker. Spending what is left of your life making love to just one woman."

With flash of bright light, she disappeared.

Alicia took my face between her hands. "Oh, Bran, you're mortal like me now. I'm so very sorry."

I withdrew from her grasp and kissed her. "You have nothing to be sorry for. If Anu meant to punish me by taking my immortality away and giving me a soul, I can handle that, as long as we're together. I want to be with you and our child. I found that living forever can be an empty life, but that only a few years with someone you truly love is true immortality. With my own soul now, I understand even more fully that love is the ultimate seduction game."

I kissed her again, pushing her down to the mattress.

A devilish urge made me grin. "I have a lot of lovemaking to catch up on." I bent my head and caressed one of her breasts. She cried out with ecstasy as I showed her exactly why I was once called the Love Talker.

About the Author

Sapphire Phelan grew up, always writing stories. Finally at age 17 she published some poetry to a poetry magazine. Getting paid for a few measley lines and being in a magazine was cool to a teenage girl. It tooks years later, but as of couple years ago she began to have pher short stories published, under Sapphire Phelan, and her other pen name, Pamela K. Kinney. Sapphire writes the erotic paranormals, while Pamela does the horror, fantasy, science fiction and is also writing a nonfiction Haunted Richmond, Virginia book too.

You can find out more about Sapphire at:

http://FantasticDreams.50megs.com

or at her blog, Sapphire Phelan's passion Corner at:

http://SapphirePhelansPassionCorner.blogspot.com

or her MySpace at:

http://www.myspace.com/PamelaKKinney

Forbidden Love Issue 3 Sacred Bands:
Recommended for mature readers only.
Thebes, 4th C BC.
The elite fighting force, inspired by Plato's Symposium, consists of 150
homosexual couples, the fiercest force of their day. Forbidden Love, 21st C AD.
In deference to the Sacred Bands of the Thebes elite, this collection is all M/M
couples, facing darkness and danger as a working team. Matched male lovers
willing to face death itself in the name of love. A collection of stories written
by some of the best names in M/M romance brought to you by Under the Moon
Publishing.

Master of the Night

Master of the Night
by ASTRID COOPER

Tonight, come to me! Be mine!
Faucon breathed his sex-scent over the lure.

Smiling to himself, he carefully arranged the black pearl necklace on the red velvet cushion. It would draw a woman with the darkness of soul, and with the passion of fire. He enjoyed the allegory of necklace and cushion, but few of his kind went to such trouble.

To have the deepest hunger assuaged required a finesse that he had honed over centuries. He was master of the night. Among his kin he was admired and hated—thus, why he hunted alone, and never shared the spoils.

It was a rare Hunter who truly appreciated the subtleties of the chase; that it was easy to prey upon a woman. In his experience, the Hunter always prevailed, but where was the challenge in that certainty?

Faucon leaned into the display window, and set the cushion against the glass. Exhaling over the necklace, he bathed the bait with his own redolence.

He closed the shop at the usual time and retreated to his private rooms, pampering himself in a long, deep bath with scented oils. Climbing from the tub, he lightly dried himself, then massaged patchouli lotion into his skin, and combed it through his long hair. The scent invaded his senses, coiling deep, igniting tensions and memories.

Images swirled in his mind's eye: naked men and women, bodies entwined, priceless fragrances burning in braziers, but dominant, the musky sex-aroma.

Who had taught him the use of perfume to augment sexual attraction?

Had it been in Rome or Babylon? The comb stalled as he frowned at his reflection, remembering...

No, it had been in the Court of Cleopatra. He smiled to himself, the memory bittersweet. Now, *there* was a woman of contrasts and subtleties! He hadn't bedded her, preferring instead the intercourse of shared intellect. He had mourned her death; few mortals had touched him so deeply.

Faucon shrugged aside his melancholy as he shrugged himself into a black silk robe, loosely tying the sash around his waist.

He had been too long without a woman and as a result, his life force was at its lowest ebb. He would have to be careful this night, else his hunger would destroy the object of his lust.

Lust, but never love: his kind could not afford the luxury of commitment or promises. And in that there was a tinge of regret he swiftly suppressed. Hunter could not allow such sentimentality of soul. If his kind had a soul and there were some who said not.

Taking up a carafe of brandy and a crystal glass, he reclined on the black velvet *chaise*, his easy repose at odds with the tension ache within his body.

Faucon savored the eighty-year old cognac as he savored the thrill-sensation of the hunt-to-come. He would have the woman in all ways, bring her to peak and let her scream over him; through him. He would drink deep and fuck deeper. Maybe biting and bruising, if she demanded it. Blood and pain only heightened the moment, making it exquisite and intense.

How would he first mount her? His gaze swept around the room, lighting on the round antique table. It presented interesting possibilities. He would place her upon it, her naked body spread wide; he would feast between her thighs, delve a tongue into her secret recesses. Taste her secret perfume...*Ah,* **that** *taste*!

He groaned. Anticipation heightened his sex-scent, his blood crashed through his veins, a tempest reaching its crescendo at his groin. He gave into the exquisite pleasure of his hand.

Was it hours or minutes later, he had no way of knowing, lost in his dark delirium, but his hunter's instinct alerted him.

She was here!

His nostrils flared. He caught her scent, musk-rose, tinged with woman—neither reluctance nor enthusiasm. A challenge, she presented: a woman to be seduced, coerced; a contest to be played, but no doubt as to the victor—no doubt at all!

His heart pounded against his ribs.

She had entered the shop silently—so silently he had not heard her, or sensed her...

Great Ashur, I am so hungry!

He analyzed her scent: a woman of deep passion, but ... He frowned. He could not read her fully and that was a surprise, and an enticement. Le Faucon enjoyed a mystery, especially if that mystery was a woman!

He placed his glass on the table and standing up, moved stealthily across the room, his bare feet caressed by the thick rug. Caressed. He would soon caress and be caressed. His cock throbbed in anticipation.

He paused in mid-stride, alerted to the danger, the depth of his desire…

An ache spread out from the pit of his stomach, traveling upwards, along nerves, through veins and arteries. His arousal engulfed him, his every cell pulsing, scalding with the need to have her, taste her, feel her and…possess her soul—the greatest prize! He relished the awakening, adding to it, building it so that his body vibrated, sex coiling like a cobra ready to strike, ready to fuck her senseless; to allow himself to assuage his deepest hunger. His cock and balls tightened, hard and hungry. Abstinence had made him dangerous. He would have to be careful, not drink too deep, too hard and thereby destroy her.

Faucon drew in a slow breath, held it, struggling to restrain hunger. He was Master of the Night; master of his passion, of his desire! Master! His nails bit into his palms, the pain diverting his craving. For the moment.

Faucon lurched across the floor and paused. He leaned against the door frame, arms folded, watching in the shadows as she moved towards the window.

His eyes widened in surprise.

He almost laughed at the irony, for hers was a pale beauty: silver blonde hair caught up in a chignon, skin like fine porcelain. She wore a cream linen suit, low heeled shoes and pearls at throat and lobe. This was her disguise—as much to deceive herself as the outside world: for Faucon knew the depth of her passion. She would be a goth at heart: he liked Goths—the historical and the modern: both were unpredictable, wild, uninhibited. He craved all this and more in his prey.

Her right hand stretched out to the necklace, while her left hand curled around the window ledge, anchoring her slender body as she tried to reach the lure.

He studied the spectacle: her tight round derrière and the slender legs, complete with tiny waist. She was dainty, fragile. Perhaps too delicate for him? It would not matter, he would have her, he would just be more careful—in the beginning.

Faucon drew in her sex-perfume, letting it coil inside his body. He tasted her strength. She would be a worthy mate! He exhaled and their essences of patchouli and rose combined to fill the room.

He saw her shiver and heard the breath catch in the back of her throat. A flush raced through her body and muscles tightened: acceptance of him.

Good.

He never forced, but he coerced unmercifully. Rape might be the province of others, never his.

"Is there something I can do for you?" he asked gently, the low timbre of his voice seductively smooth and deep.

She let out a cry and spun around, almost losing her balance. She retreated a step.

His senses probed and he heard and felt the blood swirling in her veins, the fast heartbeat from fear and sex combined. Ah, her reaction, so deep, so potent! He drew in a breath. Her awakening to him was full of promise.

"I—I saw the necklace. How much is it?"

He emerged from the shadows and she retreated another step, her blue-green eyes wide with fright.

He halted. Women did not fear him; he made certain they did not. He smiled, a well-rehearsed smile to engage, to charm.

She regarded him, all of him, her gaze sweeping from his head to his heels and every place in between, lingering on his naked skin.

He inclined his head, a silent acknowledgement of her intimate, interested attention. Faucon liked to have his women *interested.*

"The necklace will be yours. The price is something I am sure you will be prepared to give." Faucon smiled. "Why are you afraid? You were the one sneaking into my shop. A thief, perhaps? Should I call the police?"

"I am not a thief."

"No?"

"No!" She lifted her chin. "I don't want the necklace. Good night." She made a dash for the door.

"Ah, it *will* be a good night, you have my promise!" Faucon said, leaping to block her escape.

"What do you mean?" Amid the quaver in her voice was a throb of recognition, a desire for what his *double entendre* offered.

"Just this." He leaned forward, his mouth taking hers in a kiss fleeting and gentle, but suggesting much more.

Beneath his lips, hers trembled.

She tasted of honey and rose and sex. Faucon lifted her against him and plundered her mouth, plunging his tongue inside, seeking and finding her own.

"No!" she moaned into his mouth.

He raised his head. "No? I rather thought your body said yes."

"I can't. I don't know you."

He smiled. "What is to know, but that you want me, I want you.

What else is there?"

She put a restraining hand against his chest, pushing him away. The warmth of her fingers burnt through the silk to his skin, to his bones.

"I don't do this sort of thing."

"What sort of thing?" he demanded, now highly amused. She was playing the innocent with him and innocent she was not. He read that in the fire in her eyes and in the heat of her blood.

"You want me to ... want me to ..."

"I want to fuck you, yes!" he said. "And you want me to."

"I do not!"

He ran a finger over her mouth. "How easily the lie flows from your lips. What is your name? If I'm to seduce you, then I ought to know your name."

"You aren't going to seduce me," she said, folding her arms over her chest.

"Sweetheart, I already have!" Faucon laughed. Her hand arced through the air and he caught it, a fraction from his cheek.

She gasped, the pupils of her eyes dilating. Faucon sensed the struggle within her.

Carnal desire would triumph, suppressing her reticence, but it would be amusing to play with her awhile, to scandalize.

"If you want to slap me, be my guest, but there are other places on my body where I prefer to be smacked."

"How can you stand there and admit that you enjoy pain?"

Laughing, he raised her fingers to his lips and sucked. She tried to pull free, but once ensnared, no one ever escaped until he was good and done. And good and done took a very, very long time.

"I don't enjoy pain," Faucon said, "but I like rough handling."

"There's a difference?"

"Assuredly. The finesse with which the blows are delivered marks amateur from expert. De Sade knew it, and I shall teach you the subtlety of—"

"You aren't teaching me anything! Let me go. If you don't, I'll scream."

"Of course you'll scream because that's half the fun. Besides, I get pleasure from a woman's screams."

Terror spiraled out from her. "What...what?"

Facuon—you fool! He was moving too fast for her. He spread his hands, to placate. "Sweetheart, I'm not going to hurt you; I will do nothing you don't beg of me. I promise."

"Then let me go."

Faucon sighed and retreated. He waved his hand theatrically at the door. "Go then, if that's what you want."

She raced forward, her hand fastening on the door knob. Faucon exhaled over her.

"Taste me, touch me, feel me," he whispered.

She turned to look up at him. She really was small, fragile—her delicacy frightened him.

His mind touched hers in a subtle intrusion of which she was unaware. His thoughts became hers; her vision was his.

Terror, desire, shame and…curiosity. Who was this man? So tall, so strong? With shining blue-black hair to his waist, the black eyes, the fine chiseled features. The strong jaw, the mouth…a man beyond handsome—beautiful, like a god.

He smiled at that. He had been worshipped as a god, once.

Her gaze, her thoughts roved over him. *I can't do this! I must not! But I want him! I want him to*…her mind slammed shut and Faucon reeled backwards as if she had struck him. It took a moment to orientate himself.

"Taste me, touch me, feel me!" he said.

"What did you say?" she asked.

Faucon shook his head. "You had best go, because if you stay, I will fuck you in every way I can—in ways you cannot imagine—dare not imagine."

Her narrowed gaze impaled him. How he wanted to impale her with his cock. He would entice, seduce and enflame, but she must choose to stay; this was the nature of his game, the thrill of the chase that heightened the sex to come.

"Go!" He stepped backwards, the rustle of his silk gown the only sound in the utter silence between them, in the utter silence of hunter and hunted: a measuring beyond measure.

She again reached for the door knob, then paused.

"What did you say your name was?" she asked.

"I didn't." He paused. "Faucon. Or rather, in your language, Falcon."

"I prefer the French. What sort of name is Faucon?"

"Le Faucon is my *nom de guerre*." Given to him five hundred years ago at Agincourt when he had fought for the French. *Le Faucon*— the Falcon. A memory invaded his consciousness: of arriving at the battlefield, the *bar sinister* across his shield to denote his bastard status. But by the end of the day he had become the confidant of the dauphin and elevated to knighthood, the black falcon device emblazoned over his shield and hauberk. By the Prince's decree he was Le Faucon, because he had swept into the camp like a bird of prey, out-diced lords and taken their gold and seduced more than one lady to his bed... That had amused the Prince of France, so Faucon was born that day and he had maintained the name ever since, as a mark of respect to the friends and foes who had fallen in battle. He was, if nothing else, sentimental.

"The Falcon, your war name? I don't understand."

"You speak French?"

"Yes and Latin."

Now he was hooked. Damned if he would let her go, whatever her protestations! The last time he had spoken Latin...the Roman beauty writhing atop him...what was her name? He frowned. She had been Caesar's sister and insatiable and cruel.

"It's rare, these days, for anyone to speak Latin," Faucon said.

"I'm a Librarian."

Faucon caught his smile as he saw the challenge in the tilt of her chin. He'd never fucked a librarian before; this would be a first! He grinned.

"What's so funny about being a librarian?"

He shook his head. "What is your name?"

"Fleur."

"Ah, flower." His gaze raked her body. "An apt name for you."

She snorted, another flash to her eyes and a flush to her cheeks. "I'd rather—" she pursed her lips.

"You'd rather?" he prompted. "Another name? More suited to your true nature?" He studied her intently "Circe."

"I am no oracle; no seductress."

"But you want to be, deep inside, as you want me deep inside."

"Don't be ridiculous!"

He laughed. "Circe."

She slapped him then and he caught her hand and pressed the palm to his mouth, his tongue playing over her skin, the delicate wrist, feeling the pulse beat against his lips. He blew onto her skin and then suckled her wrist.

"Oh," she whispered.

"Oh? Or rather—*oooooh*?" He mimicked a woman's moan of pleasure.

She laughed and the sound coiled itself deep within his essence.

"I can give you pleasure, Circe. Let me. Do not be afraid of me, or yourself. Give in to the desire."

She studied him. "But I don't know you."

"You will know enough of me. I offer you a gift." His hand slid over her wrist, drawing her closer. "Accept me. Now." He sent the first sliver of pleasure-energy into her.

She swayed on her feet and he enfolded her against him.

His mouth took hers swiftly deeply, opening her wide with his tongue, as he would open her nether lips wide to forage, before his cock went deep, spreading her wide.

He groaned against her mouth.

"You're in pain?" she demanded.

"The ultimate pain, Circe." He set her back on her feet. "Do you want to undress for me, or do I act as valet?"

Her breath came in short gasps. She reached for the chignon and released the clasp, shaking her hair free. He caught strands of hair between his fingers and rubbed, raising them to his lips. Strands of pure silver, silken, fragrant and utterly compelling—would she be as soft and as malleable as the hair between his fingers?

His hands strayed into her jacket, parting it, pulling it down and away. The silk blouse with its tiny seed pearl buttons proved a challenge for his hands that were for once incompetent. Laughing, she pushed him away, and slipped out of the blouse, letting it flutter to the floor.

Faucon smiled, studying her pert breasts with their rosy-pink nipples.

Her hands went to her waistband and in moments the skirt slithered to her ankles.

He saw black silk panties and groaned. A porcelain doll, this woman, whose eyes were fire and her spirit obdurate. Contrasts that he craved; all his kind craved.

Faucon stepped to her and lifted her against him. He kissed her again, deeply, intensely, while his right hand quested, fingers finding the space between skin and silk; he slipped into her pussy, finding it warm, moist. Her fragrant liquescence spilled over his flesh. He probed, pushing against the inner muscles clenched around him.

He groaned, she groaned, their tongues meeting in a fever-union.

He finger-fucked her, carefully, gently, until her body relaxed. He teased more fingers into her, scrolling, revolving. Her heat scalded his flesh as her scent seared his every cell.

Faucon drew in her essence, his body hungrily feeding. She arched against him, lifting one of her legs around the back of his waist.

"More," she whispered, grabbing a fistful of his hair, dragging his mouth to hers. Her hand quested between the folds of his silk gown and fastened on his cock.

Faucon moaned as her fingers curled around him, pumping.

"No," he said, pulling her hand away. "No. Too soon. I want you, all of you, first."

She stared up at him. "I've done something wrong?"

"No, sweetheart. No! It's just that I want more before..."

"Before?" she demanded.

"Let me show you, I can't explain." He carried her to the chaise and set her upon it. Lifting her legs onto his shoulders, he crouched before her. The first hint of panic tinged her as he lowered his mouth. Her hand in his hair held him at bay.

"No."

"You've never done this before?" Faucon was shocked and delighted. "Sit back and enjoy the ride."

"I can't."

"Yes, you can. I'm going to do it, Circe."

"I'm Fleur, not Circe."

"No longer the flower, *chèrie*."

Faucon leaned into her and his mouth captured her mound, drawing in flesh that no other man had sampled. That thought brought a painful contraction of his balls. His tongue probed and suckled and dipped into her, as far as he could go, then retreated to kiss.

"The gods call it ambrosia," Faucon said. "This woman's wine, intoxicating." He lapped.

She moaned and shivered.

He edged her legs apart with his shoulders and settled into her nest. Moments later he felt her legs wrap around his neck, her ankles at the back of his neck.

He found her clit and probed it with his tongue tip.

"Aaaah!" she lifted off the lounge.

"You like this?" He smiled against her flesh. "And this?" His teeth grazed.

She climaxed, and he drank deeper, hungrily transmuting her juice. His nerves thrummed as her heat, her sexual energy invaded his body. He continued his plundering, unrelenting, unmerciful, unheeding to her calls to stop, *please stop!*

Again, she came, and he granted her a respite as his life-force was energized. He leaned upwards and kissed her mouth.

"Do you like the taste of my kiss?" he asked. "We are combined."

"You are shocking."

"I hope so." He kissed her again and her mouth was hungry for him.

Faucon stood up and shrugged off the silk robe. He shook his head, his hair flying around him like a dark cape.

"Stand up, Circe," he said, holding out his hand.

"I don't think I can," she said and laughed.

He pulled her to her feet and raised her against his body. He turned and sat upon the chaise, bringing her onto his lap.

"I want to see your face when I fuck you." He scrolled the tip of his cock over her pussy, dipping in to the cleft, retreating to her clit.

She squirmed above him, trying to capture his erection. "You're teasing me."

"Of course." He entered her a fraction, then withdrew, returning a moment later to seek a new depth, before retreating. Over and over he played his subtle game of slide and seek.

"Stop it!" she said and pinched his thigh.

Faucon laughed. "That hurts. Do it again! Harder, Circe."

"You want pain?"

"When it is you who inflicts it."

"I bet you say that to all the girls."

He smiled. "Not often."

She pinched him hard, scraping her nails over his flesh. He gasped and closed his eyes with sweet delirium. Gods almighty—this woman...!

Circe gripped his hair with one hand and with the other, she fisted his cock and then plunged downward taking his length in one swift, stroke.

She cried out and Faucon paused in cold realization.

Virgin.

Her essence combined with virgin blood was a heady brew and it coursed into his flesh, his every cell fervent.

He held her buttocks, stopping her motion upon him. "No, sweetheart, slowly, gently. I'll hurt you."

"I don't care. I want you, I want you all of you. No matter the cost."

"So be it!"

She controlled the depth and speed and more blood entered him; more life. His own blood sang, his senses sang; light and warmth coruscated his body.

Faucon enfolded her to him, his mantle of energy soothing, as her mantle enflamed.

He contained his first climax-ripple, his eyes screwed shut; exalting in the moment, bringing it to a deeper level, the energy imploding, rather than exploding. The pressure built, the aching need, now like a thousand knives slicing his flesh from inside out—he could hold back no longer and he released into her, a sudden hard, upwards thrust. She screamed, a release of her own borne of pain and passion: of pleasure and agony.

Minutes later, both shivering they withdrew to regard one another.

Faucon ran fingers through her hair.

She smiled. "Again!"

Shock washed through him. She was asking for him again, so soon. "I will hurt you."

"I hope so."

Faucon shook his head, but acquiesced. "This time, on the floor, on your hands and knees, Circe."

"Like this?" she asked, crouching, looking back at him over her shoulder.

Faucon groaned, and dropping to his knees plunged into her.

The shop became their testing ground, their hunting ground and every surface accommodated a style and quest for a deeper, daring passion.

Faucon's body was pounding, alive, never had he felt so alive. Never had he tasted virgin's blood, but he did so that night and his sex swelled.

"I have saved the best until last, Circe," he said, lifting her into his arms. He carried her into the back of the shop, to his bed, the black velvet coverlet adorned with red embroidery—the sacred scrolls and glyphs of his race.

He set her in the middle of the bed, kneeling between her splayed legs. He licked her from head to toe, gently nibbling and biting every inch of flesh, finger-fucking her until she was screaming. Then, he plunged his engorged cock into her and paused, deep and hard within her hot, hungry shroud.

His hunter-mantle covered her, gently smothering, gently taking more of her quintessence. Circe moaned and struggled, panting in the cloying heat.

"Who are you?" she whispered.

"Faucon," he said.

"But there is more. Tell me."

"I cannot. All I can tell you is this," he said, flexing his cock inside her. "All you know is this." He withdrew and returned, giving her a taste of the sex-energy transmuted from his body. It brought her to climax and beyond, a deeper existence, beyond the human realm.

His gift to her, he allowed her the taste of the incubus.

It was mid-afternoon and she slept as if one of the undead.

He stroked her cheek and teased back hair from her face as he stared down at her. She moved her cheek into his palm, caressing him with her face. Gasping, Faucon stepped away.

This woman was danger; never in his life had he experienced such from a mortal. If he stayed she would burn him with her innocence, her insatiable innocence.

He turned and walked away, but then paused, for one last glance.

The envelope leaning against the bedside lamp was her payment: the title deeds to the shop and its contents, as was the black pearl necklace lying against her throat.

The Falcon's gift would allow her the freedom to pursue a life away from the library.

Gone was the librarian, and soon she would emerge, like a chrysalis to another reality, become the woman she was meant to be. No longer Fleur, but Circe: seductress in her own right.

She sighed and opened her eyes, raising herself on an elbow.

"You're leaving me?" she demanded.

Faucon frowned. She should be asleep; he'd put the magic on her to keep her asleep... "I have to go."

"Faucon by name and Faucon by nature? Swooping in on the prey, then flying away after the mating—typical!"

He spread his hands. "As you see."

"I want you to stay."

"Impossible," he said. "Sleep, now, Circe. Sleep and dream and one day I will return, because I am not finished with you. Look over your shoulder, for I shall be there; sleep and in your dreams, I shall be there. I am always in you. Always—in all ways, Circe!"

"But—"

"The letter, take it to my lawyer; his address is inside. He will explain."

"I'd rather you did."

Faucon smiled and shook his head. "I make no apologies, no promises. Now sleep, Circe." He breathed out the magic and saw her struggle against its potency. Her strength amazed him; almost she resisted, but finally she succumbed. He left the shop without a backward glance, and thrust his hands into his jacket pockets.

Who had been the hunted, and who had been the hunter in this encounter? He neither knew, nor cared. His body was assuaged and he must move on. But he would return to her—one day, sweep into her life, into her body, take and be taken. *Oh yes*!

Faucon by name and Falcon by nature.

To Moscow with Bony: An alternate history of a world without Waterloo, where Napoleon and Wellington march to Moscow.

Follow what might have been if Napoleon's offer to work with the English and journey into Russia had been accepted. Told from the viewpoint of a Sergeant from Liverpool this Alternative History novel blends adventure, humor and military action in one tempting package.

Night Wolfing

Night Wolfing
by Brenda Williamson

At the stench from the rancid alley, Etta wrinkled her nose. She tried not to gag on fumes of old food rising from the dumpster near her. Horrid odors of dog feces and urine blended with the stink of garbage. Wet newspaper had the worse kind of smell when mixed with food scraps.

The wind chilled her limbs and she shivered. Her fingers clutched at her jacket, keeping it closed tight to her neck. She loved the autumn but the cold snap of winter fast approaching gave her another shudder. Her nipples tightened into knots in protest. Mindlessly she rubbed a comforting hand over them.

Footsteps tapped the pavement in sync with hers. She spun around with her heart pounding to the suddenness of someone following. Again, with a quick pirouette, she looked back, but couldn't see anyone. The fog surrounding her had an odd, thick shape as the mist rolled in off the bay, layering the streets with a hazy screen.

A storm would come before the night ended and the pale glow from streetlights produced shadows she watched carefully. A voice, softer than a whisper caressed her ear as the wind lifted a lock of her hair. Her pace quickened, however, not by much as high heels hindered outright running.

When she went another block and reached another dark alley, she slipped into the alcove of a narrow doorway, and she waited. His movements stopped when hers did, and she wondered if it weren't echoes she heard from her own shoes.

She thumped a hand to her chest to slow the panting arousal of fear.

Then she heard the shuffling of his shoes against a concrete sidewalk, a coarse brushing of hard soles on pavement, scratchy, quick, but almost silent. She peered around the corner of the alcove and saw the outline of a man. He acted lost, turning, walking, and observing. His head cocked in her direction. She leaned back against the wall. The hand she placed on the door touched something sticky as she pressed herself into the weather-roughened wood. A small groan rumbled in her chest. She didn't want to think what she might have touched.

Her heart pounded hard when the sounds of someone walking came closer. Soon, if he were a stalker, he'd reach the alley and he'd find her easily, if he looked.

Oh please, she thought. *Oh please, oh please, oh please, let him pass me.*

Forbidden Love: Bad Boys

She'd felt his presence from the minute she left work. She took a different route, turned at corners she didn't usually turn at, and practically circled back the way she came, determined to prove her mind worked overtime.

Why me? She closed her eyes as if not seeing him would make her invisible.

Etta watched the shadowy figure glide past her with a soundless stalking pace she didn't like. She waited a minute and eased out of the niche. She would go back the way she had come, and head on her regular route home when the coast was clear. Taking a deep breath, she turned out of the alley and bumped an old tin can. It clanked and clinked against the pavement.

She froze.

By the time she heard the steps of the shadow running toward her, someone else grabbed her around the waist and a scream formed in her lungs. The trapped air gurgled in her throat, unable to erupt into a sound.

"Run," the man holding her commanded.

He spun her away and released so the momentum threw her balance off, and she stumbled into a wall. A hard, dull wham of two things colliding in the dark behind drew her attention.

No moon, no stars, and a dim streetlamp across the road didn't let her observe much, but then she didn't need much to see that two bodies fought. Their wrestling hold of each other took them farther into the alley and out of her line of sight.

When growls echoed from the depths of the alley, she backed away. The frightening inhuman reverberations affected her worse than a bad dream. She'd had nightmares of such sounds. For as long as she could remember, she sensed she was different from most people. Not only by seeing at night, but by the way she experienced the feelings of others. She did research on the internet and the best explanation she found, labeled her with psychic empathy.

Etta wasn't sure how long she stood listening, waiting, and shaking hard enough to make her skin feel loose. The man said run and her ridiculously strange urge to stay prevented her flight. The pain from one, or both of them, captured her soul in a battle with self-preservation. She waited and when one body emerged from the black passage, he came in a rush.

His long fingers gripped her arm tight. "I told you to run," he growled low, towing her from the place. "You could have been hurt."

No sound came out of her open mouth to protest. An instinctive trust developed in light of his comment.

"Where do you live?" He tugged her along the sidewalk.

She gasped when she looked up at him. The light from another streetlight illuminated his face.

Blood smeared his mouth and his chin. It seemed he read her thoughts when his sleeved arm wiped over his lips. White teeth, long, pointy, and dangerous continued to drip blood from the corners of his lips.

Etta swallowed hard. Something about him attracted her and that confused her more than it scared her. The blood should have frightened her and it didn't. His fanged teeth struck a different nerve. Not wary, but curious. She tried not to think of vampires, only the legends of such creatures interested her. She would never consider herself a believer in supernatural beings, but still, an eternal existence did hold a small intrigue.

"Who are you?" She managed to voice her first of many questions. Oddly, she felt connected to him by more than his heroic qualities, yet she still didn't know what he had fought in the alley.

"Sloan."

"That's it, just Sloan?"

"Dimitri Sloan."

"And what are you?" The question popped out rather abruptly. Long teeth had a way of suggesting there was something strangely different about this particular man.

His continued restraint frustrated her, except she didn't feel threatened by him. The emotions he emitted warmed her insides. Just as if he spoke them, she felt his concern, and remarkably, it was for her.

"Well I'm sure as hell not him." His head jerked back toward the alley.

"Doesn't answer my question," she said, a little forcefully, finding him irritatingly handsome.

"A blood wolf."

"A...a blood wolf?" She tried not to stammer or show emotions he need not know about. "What is that, some scary story to keep kids in at night?"

"I'm a scary man."

"Are you?" A smile tugged at the corners of her mouth.

Her insides churned by an amazing sensation she absorbed from his desire of her, she tried focusing on facts instead of what his mouth would feel like against hers or what his hands might do if they were under her clothes.

"And what's that creature in the alley?"

"A blood wolf."

"You're crazy, if you think I believe you." Etta twisted her arm, wrenched it free of his loosened grip, and started to walk away. She believed him and didn't want to. She had never heard of blood wolves, and she didn't want to now.

"Wait." He grabbed her hand.

She looked up at him towering over her. Her heart skipped a nervous beat. His fingers were slippery as if wet and before panic rose, he let go of her. He backed up, leaned on the glass display window of a greeting card shop, and bent forward. She felt his pain while watching him put his hand inside his long, black leather coat. He brought it out covered in blood.

"You're hurt." She looked at the blood he left on her hand.

"Damn." Dimitri dropped his head back, hitting the glass window hard.

"What should I do?" She reached her hand toward him and drew it back. The blood fascinated her. The sweet smell, the slickness, she held a finger up wanting to lick it, but Dimitri grabbed her hand. He jerked it from in front of her face as if it were important to stop her.

"It's not all mine." His comment didn't make sense.

She stared at him, feeling his concern, sensing his blend of emotions as if she were a closer part of the night's events.

"Etta, if I pass out, you've got to get inside a building until daylight."

"How do you know my name?"

His silky voice spellbound her by the mystery.

"I've been connected to you for months."

"The dreams I have?" She didn't think he'd answer.

"I've had them too." His gaze locked to hers.

She shuddered. A sexual tension mesmerized her and she didn't notice the move of his hand folding around her hip until it glided up under her jacket. His thumb followed over the curve of her breast.

For two months, she woke each night, exhausted by dreams. In the fervor of an unknown terror a man made love to her with more passion than she ever experienced in life. Her empathetic senses reached out and connected to him as if she'd always known his touch.

"Why? How? No, not how, that would be like me trying to explain my abilities."

"You don't know, do you?" He cocked his head slightly, and the streetlight allowed her to see his face better.

"Know what? Why you would help me, how would I?" A noise from the alley startled her.

Dimitri pushed away from the glass window, and his hand dropped from the heated place on her ribs. He grabbed her elbow and pulled her into a hurried walk.

"Can't we slow down?" She tripped over an up-heaved part of the sidewalk.

"No." He steadied her with a second hand taking a firm hold on her shoulder.

"Where are we going?" She stumbled along with him.

"Away from the night wolfing."

Footsteps followed them and he picked up the pace. Etta glanced back into the dark, aware that in the void of blackness, an evil lurked.

"What is night wolfing?"

"Blood wolves feast heaviest on the night of the full moon."

"On what?"

"Blood, naturally."

"Oh, of course, naturally," she muttered sarcastically.

Dimitri stopped and pulled her near. Her hand went inside the lapels of the open coat to his chest and she felt his heart, beating fast like hers. It beckoned her closer.

"Why have we stopped?" She looked around hoping there wasn't going to be another problem.

"So I can protect you." Points of his fanged teeth showed when he talked.

Etta watched him push up his sleeve, exposing his thick wrist. He lifted his arm and her eyes widened in surprise. He sunk the gleaming white teeth into his skin.

"What are you doing?" She made a worse noise than he did for the pain he suffered.

He didn't answer. His face lifted and his fingers claimed her jaw. With his grip firm, he held her steady and pressed his mouth to hers. Liquid spurted onto her tongue and the sweet warmth trickled down her throat. She swallowed the blood without a choice.

She thought, yuck, except it tasted delicious. When young, she recalled times that she cut her finger with a knife, or her lip from licking an envelope. The taste of her blood hadn't repulsed her then either.

"It'll help protect you." He rubbed the slightly rough pad of his thumb over her lips, further deviling her senses with his emotions of desire.

"It's sweet." She licked the traces from his finger, sucking his thumb into her mouth.

He pushed her tongue back and rubbed her upper teeth, circling over her incisors, and arousing her with the slow actions. The unusual attraction did not stop her from enjoying the sensations coursing through her.

She forgot about the blood on her hand until he licked her fingers and tickled her palm with his wet suckling. Mesmerized by his detailed wash between each finger, she breathed heavier.

When Dimitri pulled her up against him, she went eagerly.

"Now what?" She already anticipated his next move. The empathy allowed her to feel all his emotions. The strong sexual ones emitted heat and the burning lust flowed between them.

His head lowered and his mouth sealed over hers. She slumped against him and let the breath he captured from her sigh, swirl inside their locked mouths. The kiss deepened. Powerless to resist, she held onto him. Her fingers curled and grasped the lapels of the leather. Etta didn't want to release the man she had searched for in the shadows of her dreams.

His hands slid down her back and gripped her bottom. He tugged her tight into the firmness of his erection. They were strangers in the night, and she gave into the passion instead of the fight most women would put up. He rocked her harder against his pants, his moans unleashed indescribable feelings of need within her. His teeth pressed into her lips, cutting the flesh, and she liked it.

"Etta," he murmured, sucking her lips into his mouth, devouring her fervid gasps.

She reached up and wove her fingers into his long, dark hair, holding him to her greedy kiss. His soft lips caressed hers equally as anxious.

Without warning, he pushed her against the brick wall. Her eyes squeezed shut from the hard impact and flew open at the lift of her arms above her head. He manacled her wrists in one hand. She twisted against him in surprise, and then his free hand covered her breast. He moved it tentatively in circling strokes, caressing, and taunting her plump, unyielding hard nipple.

Her moan hummed in the cavern of his mouth as the ache he

created followed an invisible thread to a point between her legs.

A sudden sound jerked him free, leaving her panting and out of breath.

"We need to take this off the street." He held her face. "I don't think we'll have any more encounters tonight, but I can't take a chance losing you."

She nodded not wanting to be lost from him either. Their meeting had been a long time in coming and she needed the dreams to end so her life could begin.

Etta hurried to show Dimitri where she lived. She continued to run her tongue around her lips, enjoying the sweet remembrance of his blood and actually wanting to taste more. His hand already wrapping hers in a possessive hold, intermittently squeezed tighter reminding her he'd been hurt.

"Is it bad?" She tried to look, but he kept her walking.

"It'll get better once we get to your place."

A couple blocks later, Etta led Dimitri up the steps to her apartment. Her stomach rumbled with a nervous flutter. She kept imaging all sorts of things about him and couldn't decide if she should discuss her dreams with him even though he said he had similar ones. She wondered if his interrupted sleep came with the rough animalistic passion she craved.

"I'll get something to clean your wound." She left Dimitri in the living room and went to her bathroom.

"Gauze, tape...oh where the hell is the antiseptic," she grumbled.

"None of that is necessary," he called from the other room.

"You'll get an infection or some...thing." She carried the stuff from the bathroom.

Etta froze in the doorway.

Slone stood naked.

With his head bent in examination of the gash in his side, she couldn't see his eyes so nothing stopped her from looking at the length of him. Dark-skinned, with dark black hair, she felt like a ghost in comparison.

"This is how you wanted to see me, isn't it?" His gaze lifted and she detected a hint of playfulness.

Etta gulped and nodded in agreement. "You read minds?"

"It's our empathic connection." He rubbed his hand over the sealed wound on his side. "It's almost gone.

"Our connection?" She hoped not, at least not until she had a chance to touch him. In their brief closeness, the feelings strengthened.

"I meant the wound."

"Oh."

Dimitri walked toward her. His semi-erect cock swayed. Her insides throbbed in eager anticipation of connecting with him. He made it clear he hadn't shed his clothes because he liked to walk around nude.

He grabbed the hair at the back of her head, and dragged her to him. She thought his devilish grin answered her unspoken assumption they would have sex. She already had tremors stimulating her with a small orgasm.

"First we feast." His announcement shocked her.

"Dimitri!" Etta jerked with a tremor of fear.

His mouth opened and the lamplight glinted off the white of his fangs.

"Accept." His long fingers dug into her hair against her scalp. "Relax, Etta."

His voice touched her with a magical soothing. She let herself listen to him with her heart instead of the empathy. He stroked her cheek and she closed her eyes, letting him tilt her head to the side.

She shuddered at the pressure of his teeth cutting into her neck. He sucked hard, drawing blood through her veins, making her pulse quicken.

"Dimitri," she moaned softly at the pleasurable pain.

The next thing she knew, she heard his voice pulling her from a tunnel of darkness. The cadence of his heart, beating in tempo with hers, calmed her nerves. When he drew back his head and aimed for her mouth, she accepted the spit of blood. The sweetness touched her taste buds and she swallowed the trickling of warm liquid.

She slurped up the small traces on his lips and let the sweet fluid intoxicate her.

Dimitri eased his grip on her hair and allowed her to move. He put a finger to her incisors and rubbed them with the same arousing moves he used before.

"Bite." He commanded, dragging her face toward his skin

She put her mouth against his shoulder and with an uncontrollable urge for what he suggested she tried to bite into the heated damp flesh. Her teeth didn't cut and she looked up at him. The willingness and the ability confused her.

"Start small." He held his wrist up.

She touched his arm. He sunk his teeth into her shoulder,

puncturing a vein. Blood raced to the point he sucked. She wrapped her lips over the pre-existing hole in his wrist and sucked. She felt an odd sensation when her teeth lengthened letting her press them deeper into the gash. She never thirsted or hungered in her life for the way the taste of Dimitri's blood made her tongue cling to him, as if he were a delicious dessert.

Questions abounded and she couldn't form them. When she pulled his arm from her mouth, she twisted and planted her teeth into his chest. The more she drank, the more she desired. She kissed and licked his flesh, delighting in every sleek curve to his muscled torso.

Dimitri pulled her back from him and his mouth pulled her lips into his kiss. His tongue circled and wet her with affectionate licks. He ventured away from kissing her breath to her cheek, her chin, and down her neck.

He jerked her blouse open and buttons ripped from the fabric.

"Dimitri." She dug her fingers into his arms.

If it weren't for the front fasteners on her bra, he would never have gotten to her aching breasts so quickly. He dragged his tongue over one nipple and then bit into her flesh.

She cried out with an endurable pain and bit into the back of his shoulder.

Dimitri grunted. His mouth latched onto her breast and the pain faded under the teasing strokes of his tongue.

Meanwhile, his hands unfastened her skirt. He slid the clothing down her legs, letting it land on her feet. Beneath the elastic of her panties, he pushed his fingers into place where he massaged both cheeks of her ass. She shuddered to the parting of her flesh and his finger gliding over her anus. She compressed herself to him when he inserted his finger. He removed it and with a hard tug, he ripped the seam of her panties. The torn bit of cloth dropped on top of the skirt.

"I want you in me," she moaned.

His fingers retraced the path to her bottom and gripped the fleshy cheeks.

"And I want in you."

He hoisted her up and guided her onto his rigid cock. He fit snug but without trouble since her insides were dripping wet. From the tremors of climaxes each time she drank blood from his hot flesh, her orgasms saturated her with a natural lubricant.

"You taste so good," she groaned, scraping her fangs in long scratches on him wherever she could reach.

Forbidden Love: Bad Boys

His finger rubbed her bottom, stimulating her with a new sensation. She rocked her hips to suck him in deeper. The hot flesh of his shaft throbbed as it stroked her vaginal walls.

Their biting each other ended, and deeply endearing kisses kept them busy. Dimitri pushed her back against a wall and thrust into her with rhythmic flexes of his hips. It seemed they went for hours utilizing every piece of furniture in the room for various positions.

Eventually, the tension of their climaxes rose to new levels and her teeth grew sharper on his flesh and bone. Blood appeared minimal since they didn't waste what precious ounces they extracted. When her body met with the depletion of energy and physical strength, she closed her eyes.

Dimitri had different plans. She felt his cravings intensify. While he let her rest, face down on the bed, he took her from behind. He held her hips in the grip of his firm fingers and rammed his cock into her cunt. Fast and brutal, he drove deep, jerking her up and down. She reveled in the quick climax and the amazingly volatile orgasm. Before her insides finished clenching, he flipped her to her back. He swung a leg over her body and his cock slid over her face.

He parted her legs with the push of his hands. She whined with uncontrollable clarity in her eagerness and yet he made her wait. Caressing the inside of her thigh, he kissed her belly.

"Dimitri, please." She raked her fingers over his ass.

He sucked on the sensitive skin close to her pussy. The flat of his tongue wiped her shaved slick skin and she squirmed with pleasure.

Without guidance, he put his cock into her mouth. The dripping wet sperm had as similar a sweet taste as his blood. She grasped his ass and pulled him down hard. Her throat muscles squeezed on him with every swallow she took.

The very emotional fibers in his soul melded with hers. His orgasm was hers, physically as well as mentally. Her mind exploded with a rainbow of sensations she couldn't begin to understand, but she appreciated for the passion.

He wanted an unrestricted access with a pressure and pain.

Etta dug her hold into the soft downy skin of his buttocks and brought him into her deep-throated swallow.

"Oh God, yes, take it all." He plunged to her urging.

Etta didn't think her waning climax had a chance at revival until Dimitri's mouth settled over her cunt. He licked her clit and brought her an ecstasy that made the bed dance. He bit her at the height of orgasm and she bit him. Blood mixed with his hot semen and she drank with joyous excitement. Her tremors escalated, entwined with his as if they were made of one soul.

When he gathered her into his embrace, they both panted for a long time without words. Speech wasn't necessary with the emotional surges of their blended gifts. She snuggled into the enveloping damp heat of him.

"Sloan?"

"Huh?" His hand rubbed over her.

"Do we...should we..."

"It was beautiful, Etta, and any other words would be wasted trying to describe the feelings we shared."

His fingers turned rough over her breasts. She arched in surprise when he pinched her nipple, twisting it hard, and letting go. He wanted her again. The beat of his heart on the palm of her hand went faster. His breath heaved with an exciting renewal of energy and she read the signs.

He jerked her close and sipped at her lips.

"You'll know every time I want you."

"Yes," she groaned at the slap of his hand on her ass.

She felt it would be no less often, than she would want him.

* * * * *

Morning came in the form of a bright room. Etta lifted her tired eyes and looked at Dimitri laying along side her. He made an impressive sight stretched out on the bed. She sat up and with apprehension, touched every place he tore her skin.

"It's all healed." He rolled over and cupped her face.

"I ache all over." She rubbed her breasts. "It wasn't a dream, was it?"

"No dream." His warm hands slid around her and pulled her down to him. "You were a dormant blood wolf."

"That's crazy."

"You don't believe me, even after last night?"

"I'm working on it." She leaned on his chest and let her fingers pet the short black hairs swirled around one of his deliciously hard nipples.

"You bit me." She lowered her head while lifting her lashes and looking at the sultry droop to his eyes.

Sticking out her tongue, she circled the brown nub and then took it between her teeth.

"You got in a few good bites of your own," he softly moaned.

"You acted as if that were bad when that other blood wolf followed me." She moved to his other nipple and tugged it with her teeth.

"There are bad guys in every culture." He made another sound, deeper, like a feral growl of a beast. "Last night, that blood wolf wouldn't have cared to let you get used to the lusting. If you didn't know what you were doing, you'd have provoked the animal in him, and that could get you killed."

"You gave me your blood and said it would protect me." She rubbed her finger over her lip remembering how he spit that first delightfully sweet taste into her mouth.

He lifted his head and kissed her nose. "The blood acts as an aphrodisiac and sedative. I did that to prevent you from provoking me into killing you."

"So you're no different than that other one?" She drew her head back to get a good look into his beautiful golden brown eyes.

"I told you the difference." His resonance came fringed with an anger she didn't understand. "I didn't want you getting hurt."

"Why?" She suddenly felt used.

"The connection we have."

"Why?" She felt like a five year old with her questions. "What is this connection other than a little sexual chemistry?"

She closed her eyes and tried to bring back the memories of the night. The profound lusting—had she confused that with love?

"Chemistry means a whole lot where we're concerned." He smiled and put a hand on her cheek.

Etta opened her eyes and looked at him. She didn't want a bonding made of physical attributes. Her emotions, while in a tangled mess, were rooted to endearments.

"Blood wolves mate forever." He rubbed her bottom lip with the pad of his thumb. "Some go a lifetime looking for the right female."

"You say that as if men were the only ones doing the looking."

"That's pretty much the way it works. Females, like you, don't always know they're a blood wolf unless they were brought up knowing."

"I'm an orphan."

"I sort of figured that might be the case."

"If there's only one mate per male, than why did that other one want me."

"There are circumstances where more than one male can feel the connection. It's not always perfect and they rush into the feasting, mating impulsively."

"Like us." The situation seemed to get worse the further he

explained.

"There was nothing impulsive about this for me. I told you, I've been watching you for a long time. I wanted you to be the one my life is tied to forever."

Etta got up and slid off the bed.

"Let me get this straight." She picked up a robe and put it on. "You chose me, but I impulsively had sex with you, therefore I'm stuck with you?"

She tried not to inhale with a sharp excitement when Dimitri got off the bed, but how did she ignore his gorgeous physique or the enormity of his erection. The sunlight streaming through the window made his cock appear much larger than it did in the dim lamplight the night before.

His strides brought him to her. He gripped her arms. She hadn't tied the sash to the robe yet, and it fell open. His gaze went from her face to the opening of the garment. Her thoughts were screaming for him to tell her the feelings were real that she sensed from him.

"You're mine, Etta. Let another man touch you and I'll kill him." The seriousness of his tone frightened her.

He jerked the robe down her arms and used it as a bind against her arms. He bowed his head and tried to kiss her, except she turned her face away. She wanted his human emotions expressed in more than a sexual way and it frustrated her to know she couldn't ask him if he loved her. She didn't even think the affectionate way she felt toward him, could actually be construed as a concrete sentiment.

"You have no right to dictate what I do. We just met."

She didn't struggle when he kissed her neck. The threads of sexual memories immobilized her body.

"Dimitri, I don't want you like this. I want..."

He kissed lower. His teeth raked the tip of her breast. She waited for the puncture of his fangs with mixed emotions. Instead, he took her nipple in his mouth and sucked it. He did the other one with an equally long stimulation.

"Stop." She pushed him away.

Dimitri stumbled back, obviously not expecting her to say no to his seduction. His eyes, at first, wide with shock, narrowed. His mouth pinched in anger.

She wrapped the robe around herself and walked in heated strides to the living room. She sensed her needs in him and looked to force him to confess the connection between them had more to do with the responses to their empathic senses.

"I want you to leave." She kept her back to the sound of him moving behind her.

He didn't say anything. When she glanced over her shoulder, she saw him putting on his clothes. He didn't argue with her and she felt a slight disappointment in that fact. He had on everything, including his long leather coat. The heart-stopping sight of the gorgeous man caused her a bit of confusion. She wanted him to go, but only out of frustration. She needed him to stay, because everything about him aroused her.

She dropped her awe stuck gaze to the floor and stared at his boots. He had big feet...large hands...and what they said of men with those attributes, were right, he had an exceedingly healthy sized cock.

Her insides clenched as he neared. Her pussy tensed hard on the nothingness.

"I have some errands. I'll be back tonight." He lifted her face with his fingers beneath her chin.

She readied for his kiss, instead his cocky grin infuriated her. She turned her head letting his soft moist lips graze her jaw and his breath, heat her ear.

"You will miss me." He emphasized will as if he really knew.

"What are you afraid of, Dimitri? It's not just last night, either. I feel it buried beneath your hardened exterior. You hide a secret bound to a painful part of your life."

"That's not for you to worry about."

"It is, if you think we're soul-mates." She frowned when he left her without an answer.

Etta slammed the door shut and shuddered at the impact. It irritated her that her vulnerability with loneliness could cause her to have a blonde moment where an attractive man was concerned. She rushed into bed with a hunk and it served her right to find out he was crazy.

Determined not to become a slave to emotion or to Dimitri, she dressed for work with the intention of researching blood wolves. As much as she wanted to deny they existed, she couldn't shake the memories of her night. The biting, the blood, and the ecstasy were real. He wanted the closeness of their bodies enmeshed with passion and she needed their minds to forge the same kinship.

Sequestered deep in her heart she felt the bond he mentioned. To save her sanity, she should find a way to break the physiological hypnosis, if only she hadn't felt his deeper feelings of wanting her so damn much.

* * * * *

Etta went all day sitting at her computer, surfing the web for tidbits of info on blood wolves. A few scattered myths, but nothing with any basis for fact. Believed to be werewolves, much of their characteristics fell heavily in the line of something similar to a vampire. Their appearance didn't change other than growing long fanged teeth. With their teeth, they extracted blood during fights, mating, and pleasure, yet they didn't require blood to live.

When she looked at the time on the wall clock, it was quite late, and well past dark outside. A whole day spent on research and she had learned virtually no more than what she knew from being with Dimitri.

She turned off the computer and hurried up the steps leading out of the basement office. The only information left to learn would have to come from Dimitri Sloan. He said he would be at her apartment; waiting to touch her, wanting to sting her with the erotic pleasure of his bite.

She admitted it to herself—she did miss him.

Outside, Etta tugged her denim jacket tighter. A chilling air swept around her and she looked behind at the empty sidewalk.

"I've been waiting for you." Dimitri's voice came from the dark ahead.

She took a deep breath. "We need to talk." She exhaled.

"Later." He came forward and grabbed her hand. "After I've tasted every inch of you—inside and out."

Breathless with desire, she went into his arms. His mouth fastened over hers. Oddly, he tasted different, but she put it off as something he ate.

His scorching wet kisses alternated with the scrape of his teeth, teasing her skin. He maneuvered her back against the crates. She protested weakly, she felt powerless to stop herself, let alone him.

"Turn around." He twisted her.

His hands slid under her blouse, bunching up her bra.

"I don't understand this," she whimpered. "I don't know why I can't refuse you."

He didn't say anything. She squirmed against the thrill he gave. His long fingers kneaded her breasts, plucking her skin, and driving her ache for him, into a deeper craving.

"I can't believe I'm going to say this, but I've missed you." She shuddered at how fast his hands grasped her skirt and jerked it up.

Dimitri's deep, sinister laugh almost disturbed her enough to stop

150

his fondling. Even the sensations he created between their minds, had a dark and dangerous quality to them.

Her hips bounced at his tugs on her panties. The elastic cut into her skin with his hard yanks. Then the seams ripped and his rough-skinned palm pinched the lips of her pussy.

"Don't make me wait," she gasped.

His fingers jammed into her and she threw her head back on his firm chest. Her climax, started long before his touch, began peaking. Her muscles went rigid, all except for her fingers clutching his wrist.

His teeth plunged into her shoulder and she involuntarily thrashed. He didn't let loose and a flood of memories couldn't explain the pain of his bite.

"Let go." She wiggled to get out of his embrace.

He shoved her forward and his teeth scraped her back. Her blouse tore and hung like a rag from her arms.

Within the mixture of her scream and his growl, a roar broke them apart. She grabbed her clothing and turned to see a duplicate of Dimitri. His eyes were black with rage and he rushed the Dimitri next to her.

"She's mine, Deiter," he said.

The low threatening rumble from his chest seethed from him in a continuous flood of terrifying sounds. She stepped back, unsure what to do. Crossing her arms over her chest, covering her naked breasts, she watched the men stalk each other.

"I found her first," the man near her, replied.

"Dimitri?" She looked from the new arrival to the man she had let touch her. The difference between them couldn't have been more obvious in hindsight.

"Come over here." Dimitri commanded.

Deiter grabbed her arm as she moved to go. "She's now mine, Dimitri."

"I got to her first, Deiter. She has my scent all over her."

"Dimitri?" She tugged her arm and Deiter tightened his grip.

"He's my twin, Etta. He's the one that followed you last night." Dimitri explained.

She cringed when Deiter jerked her in front of him. His teeth gleamed in the moonlight. He grabbed her hair and yanked her head at an angle.

"Leave her to me, Dimitri, or I kill her."

Deiter's face came close to hers. The heat of his breath wafted over her cheek and he panted near her jugular. She sensed he had a killer's lust and she didn't mean anything to him.

"You wouldn't. Females don't come that often for us to mate." Dimitri worked his way closer in small, unnoticeable steps by shifting from one foot to the other.

"Well then, I guess you can be the one to go looking for another bitch."

"Excuse me!" Etta elbowed Deiter and wrenched free of his hold, surprising herself and Deiter. "I'm no man's bitch."

His hand swung to grab her and she dove out of the way.

He came at her and his fingernails raked her face. She cried out in stunned pain. Dimitri was already charging and she tried to get out of the way.

"Not so fast." Deiter's arm circled her waist and hauled her back.

Etta twisted away and Deiter's teeth ripped a jagged slash into her neck. Dimitri jerked her to him and his touch went to the wound.

"You'll be all right." He put her hand over the gush of tepid blood. "Hold it tight."

He released her then and the brothers clashed—two bodies thudding together had no perilous sound. She gathered her jacket from the alley and slipped her arms in the sleeves while running. A wise thing to do, and yet she couldn't keep going without knowing the outcome. Like the night before, a compelling energy kept her from leaving Dimitri.

Etta's heart raced blood through her veins, giving her a high, not unlike the one she had drinking the blood. She imagined animals held the same survival instincts and the funny correlation of her as an animal, turned serious when a howl ripped from one man's throat.

"Dimitri?" Her foot taped nervously on the walk.

She stood in the alcove of a side doorway of a store and watched the two men battle. They were a blur of dark clothing clashing and separating, repeatedly. Oddly, they didn't appear to punch each other as much as they aimed to bite.

Mindlessly, she rubbed her mouth until she took notice of the fang teeth pinching her lower lip. The scent of sweet blood mesmerized her with an erotic lusting for a taste. The growls and grunts echoing in the alley enveloped her thoughts. She felt pain, but whose. The link she formed with Deiter seemed no different then the one she felt with Dimitri, except the length of time she spent with Dimitri. The one night together made emotions stronger and more committed between them.

She held her fingers over her mouth and clicked a fingernail on one of her long fang teeth, while the aroma of blood made her dizzy with her thirst. It seemed funny the way her acceptance of what she was came easier the longer she was around Dimitri. The way her empathy picked his emotions from a world of people, had forged a special kinship making him a part of her.

She moved her hand from the laceration and dabbed it to find the flow of blood stopped. She licked her fingers clean while she waited for the battle between brothers to end.

Her heart lurched to each horrible sound laced with the pain she felt the men inflicted on each other.

Etta wanted one man to win, but she dreaded the guilt. The confrontation between brothers was solely because of her. It disheartened her to be the cause of any closeness the two may have shared.

Suddenly a heart-wrenching wail dragged her from the doorway. The jolt of pain catapulted her lungs into her throat. With one man standing, and one man down, she ran right into Dimitri's arms, relieved he was all right.

"You're hurt?" She rubbed her hand over air, afraid to touch him where blood oozed the greatest.

"It'll heal."

She put her head against his chest and hugged him. "Is he dead?"

"Does it matter?" He gripped her hair and bent her head back. "I told you what would happen if you let another man touch you."

"You bastard." She hit his arm. "You should have told me, explained, given me more information."

"You didn't answer me." His fingers tightened in her hair.

"Yes, it matters."

He let go and she stumbled back. His emotions were out of control and still, she berated him.

"He's your brother and it should mean something to you as well."

"It does."

"But you killed him anyway."

"No, I tore him up pretty good, but I couldn't kill him, not even to win you."

"Win me? You don't have to win me, Dimitri. This being a blood wolf is new for me and the two of you have such powerful emotions regarding me, I have the two of you confused as one person in my mind. However, knowing you have a twin now helps me separate my mixed feelings. I knew there was something different in the way I felt about your brother, but I ignored it, because I thought he was you."

"I understand, Etta. Hard as it is for me to accept immediately, I sensed your feelings before you acknowledged them. It's hard to trust you could want only one of us when we're two men that have more in common than most."

"He doesn't have your kindness."

Dimitri laughed. "No one ever said I was kind."

"And then there's your tenderness. It's a very attractive quality."

"Am I tender enough...with you?" His hand swirled around the side of her face and held her chin.

Her heart could burst with joy and melt under his heated gaze. She snaked her arms around his waist.

"Did you know how I wished I didn't live in the city or how I don't particularly like my job?' She put her head on his chest and listened to the way the thump of his heart slowed.

"Crowded areas aren't places a blood wolf likes to hang out." He rubbed his jaw against the side of her head. "I have a house in the country, deep in the woods."

"I've always wished I could live in a forest." She lifted her face and invited his kiss.

"All blood wolves like to live in the woods."

His mouth moved against hers for a minute and then she went in hunt of the blood. She couldn't help the way the sweet taste intoxicated her.

"You are a rapacious beast, my love." He held her face and kissed her hard. "Let us take our lusting off the streets."

"And you'll tell me more about being a blood wolf?"

"Right after I feast on every inch of your delicious soul." His hand slipped inside her jacket, beneath the torn blouse, and cupped her bare breast.

"I like the sound of that." She smiled against his kiss.

"It might be a while." His warm fingers rolled the tip of her nipple into a sensitive knot.

"I can wait." She dropped her head back allowing his teeth to scrape her neck.

He pulled her in close. His hands roamed the areas he would eventually pleasure with kisses. His teeth pressed dangerously hard against her jugular and she shuddered.

He let go and kissed the pulse beneath her ear.

"Trust me?" he whispered.

Etta nodded. Until Dimitri came into her life like a storm, she didn't know sex could be as electrifying as a thunderbolt.

She pushed her hand down to the front of his trousers and caressed his rigid cock. The strokes upon his erection aroused her into an orgasm. Her legs dampened.

"Weren't we headed home?" She brushed her lips over the prickly stubble of his whiskered jaw.

"As soon as I've tasted you."

He let her signal when she was ready for his bite. Not by the way she squeezed and massaged his solid arousal, but by the free flowing emotions in her mind.

His teeth sunk into the throbbing vein and she sighed with the carnal delight to the start of their night wolfing.

About the Author

Brenda Williamson was born in the state of New Jersey, in the United States. She is married, has one son, and a house full off cats. Writing full-time, one would think she has a hobby to get away from the many hours of writing, but writing is her hobby, too. She writes in all genres of romance, generally with erotic elements; historical, suspense, paranormal, and contemporary. She is a member of Romance Writer's of America and several of the RWA special interest chapters.
Brenda's Publishers with available & coming soon titles ~

Samhain Publishing Sword of Rhoswen * Wolverton Blood * Devil's Kiss * A Beautiful Surrender * One Bashful Lady * A Desperate Longing **http://samhainpublishing.com/authors/brenda-williamson**

Whiskey Creek Press Range War Bride * The Witch Stone * Torrid Teasers, Vol. 6 * Summer Sizzlers Anthology * Lust Anthology * Celtic Love Knots **http://www.whiskeycreekpresstorrid.com/authors/Brenda_Williamson.shtml**

Venus Press Morgandy's Lover * Gypsy Wolves **http://www.venuspress.com/catalog/authors/brendawilliamson.htm**

Aspen Mountain Press Babes in Toyland Anthology **http://aspenmountainpress.com/new-releases/babes-in-toyland/prod_25.html**

Lady Aibel Press His Lady Vampire **http://www.ladyaibell.com/product_info.php?manufacturers_id=64&products_id=124&osCsid=d44f460nangh0k4nvf9e0k9c74**

Midnight Showcase Fiachra's Kiss **http://www.romps.midnightshowcase.com/fiachraskiss.html**

eXtasy Books – Indigo Winds **http://www.extasybooks.com/mm5/merchant.mvc?Screen=PROD&Store_Code=EB&Product_Code=10&Category_Code=**

Amorous Authors - Tales of Love & Lust **http://www.amorousauthors.com/**

Links for Brenda Williamson ~
Website: http://www.BrendaWilliamson.com
Newsletter: http://www.BrendaWilliamson.com/Newsletter.htm
Chat Group: http://groups.yahoo.com/group/BrendaWilliamsonRomanceParty/
My Space: http://www.myspace.com/BrendaWilliamson
Email: Brenda@BrendaWilliamson.com

Forbidden Love: Bad Boys
Crimson Promise
By
Sapphire Phelan

Available Now from Lady Aibell Press

Two lonely people: Victor and Na'lesa find love, sex and blood, and not necessarily in that order.
Victor has escaped to another planet in the future to survive, for Earth is now poison to the Undead. He is the last vampire from Earth that still exists.
Na'lesa has been alive for eons, the last of her species. She has been changed thanks to a virus invented by the scientists of her race and has become a being who must feed on blood.
One night, they run into each other over some prey and discovered an attraction to each other.

This erotic science fiction vampire e-book can be purchase at Lady Aibell Press or at Fictionwise.com.

Coming in 2007 from Lady Aibell Press: *Iridescent Invasion* by Sapphire Phelan: What do you do when aliens invade your planet? Why, fall in love, have hot sex with one of them and save the world! What else can a girl do?

I REMEMBER
by Phylis Sullivan

I remember
how the
sound of
my name
upon your lips.
Touched me
deep inside.
I remember
how your
breath
whispered
across my lips.
Making them
part in
anticipation.
I remember
how the touch
of your cool
fingers along
my fevered body.
Sent flames
zipping along
my nerves.
I remember
how you
felt as
I clasped
you in my hand.
Your moan
as I caressed
your cool
hardness.
And Oh...
I remember
how it felt
as you
slid so
slowly in.

Your name
a sigh
from my lips.
I remember
how our
bodies
fit perfectly
as we joined.
Your growl
as our
passion
climbed higher.
I remember
how your eyes
blazed gold
with desire
and hunger.
The fear
behind
the gold.
I remember
how my
finger caressed
your fangs
and the
doubt left
your eyes.
116
The sharp pain
of your
fangs sliding
into my flesh.
I remember
how the sweet
ecstasy as
you drank
flooded my
body.
Our cries
echoed

in the night.
I remember
how our
bodies
shuddered
in release.
As we
reached
the peak.
I remember
how I felt
such a part
of you.
And how
alone I feel
now that
you are
gone.
I remember.
June 2006

About the Poet

Having enjoyed reading since a young age, Phylis Sullivan at age 45, is now beginning to explore the other side of books.

That of developing and exploring stories of her own. At this time, she has been devoting quite a bit of time to writing poetry with the hopes of one day publishing a poetry book on vampires.

A mother of twins who are quickly approaching the teenage years, Phylis has been happily married for 18 years and lives in Nebraska. She has won a couple of awards for entries in the genre of fanfiction as well as second place in The Nebraska Mothers Association 2005 Literature Contest for her poem *"The Sound of Children"*.

Before Dawn

Before Dawn
by Terri Pray

Dedication

To Sam, thank you now and always. Without you I'd still be hiding my scribbles from others.

"Are you sure about this?" Alexandria inquired, her voice filled with an almost believable concern. "It's not the wisest course of action. Everyone knows Turos wants nothing to do with women unless they are slaves. He hates women of our rank."

Juliana looked over her shoulder at her sister as she dropped the shawl down on the back of the chair. "Which is why this plan will work out just fine. I seriously doubt that any woman of our number would dare risk such a thing to spend some time with the man. No, they would try to bribe or force him, or simply attempt a clumsy move to seduce him. I've thought all this through from start to finish so have the courtesy of maintaining a little faith in me." She could still taste it, the scent of the arena, that powerful mix of blood, sweat, and death. The way the sun had played along his oiled muscles, and the look of dark lust in his eyes all combined to form a powerful image that left her thighs pressing tightly together.

"Oh, you've thought everything through have you? What about the consequences if you're caught. You know what they'll do. If you're caught you might end up being stripped of rank and sold off." Alexandria shook her head, a scowl forming over her otherwise perfect features. "Think about this Juliana. Do you really want to take that risk just for one night with him? He's just a man, nothing more and nothing less."

"Yes." Silly question. What red blooded woman would not want to spend that time with the man? How many had he killed in on the sands of the coliseum? Men like him were rare, even amongst the gladiators. Just one look at him sent a shiver through her body like no other man had ever caused before or since. She set down the silver backed hairbrush before turning to look at the older woman. "Have you seen him? I mean taken a real look at him?"

"Yes, I guess." Her sister shrugged, and pushed back a stray lock of black hair from her pale face. "I mean he's attractive, very much so, but not worth risking my freedom for. No man is worth that. Gods above woman, don't you value your freedom at all? Just think what the shock would do to our father. The scandal if this got out. The Plebs would have a field day with the gossip you could start by doing this."

A scandal, so what? It was not as though there weren't a dozen such scandal's being carried by the gossip mongers of the city every day. Besides, some men were worth the risk. She only had to close her eyes to see him. His flesh glistening in the sunlight, oil and sweat coating his form, blood on the sword he held in his hand. Perhaps a body at his feet, another gladiator, or a criminal being put to death. His gaze would move over those in the stands as he sought out the sign for the man to live or die at his hands.

No longer a man at that moment but a living god.

One she planned to spend some time with, no matter what the outcome.

"You're insane." Alexandria sat down hard on the lounging couch. "Our father has gone to great lengths to provide for us, so we don't have to be married off to some local swine herder, or worse. We have our pick of men, as long as we stay within the correct social status, and you want to throw that all away."

"No, just determined." Throw what away? The chance to be married off to a man based on his wealth? Or political position just to help out their father? There had never been the risk of a low placed marriage and not one of the men she had been introduced to sparked the fire in her soul the way Turos could with a single glance. "Did you know he sold himself into the hands of a trainer?"

Her question must have caught her sister off guard as it took her a few moments before she gave the habitual dismissive shrug before answering. "Yes, so what? He's not the first to have done so and won't be the last."

"Well, he must have had a good reason. He's not married. No debts to speak of that I have been able to discover. So why did he do it? I'm told he was even of a good family, not a Pleb. He had rank, power and position all coming his way and he threw it to one side. There has to be a reason he did that."

A woman? The rumors had been mangled at best, but one kept surfacing. A woman of the Patricians had been behind his decision. Just what she had done, or why it had affected him in such a way, no one knew, but at least it also explained why he hated women of Juliana's rank.

"You're obsessed." Her sister growled. "Who cares why the man did it? He's a slave now. He sold himself into slavery, don't you get that. He's nothing more than a Gladiator no matter what he was in his previous life."

"Right, so why then is the sweat of a Gladiator sold as an aphrodisiac? Why do women fight for the right to see him? Or others like him? Come on, you know what he is like. He's handsome, rugged, strong, determined. He could have been spawned by Mars himself." How much did the sweat of a gladiator sell for these days? More than many could afford, and it had become one of the most sought after ingredients for love potions in Rome. And her sister was forgetting that slaves could buy their freedom, including gladiators, once they had earned enough money. Even a slave had access to some sources of funds. Men and women alike sent gladiators gifts, prizes for their performances in the arena.

"It's a trend and nothing more." Her sister shrugged, dismissing the comment. Had Alexandria forgotten that she, like so many women amongst the Patricians had purchased gladiator sweat for her private potions? "Something made up to amuse the Plebs."

"Most of those who buy the potions are women of rank, not mere Plebs. Where do you think a Pleb would get the money from? They have to fight to keep their position and cannot risk their money being wasted on such frivolities. Sometimes I think it would be better if they were kept to their parts of the city and never permitted to mingle with us."

"You really don't like them, do you?"

"Plebs?"

"Yes, the plebs." Just what had gotten into her sister? The dislike of the common classes in Rome had grown to an amazing level where Alexandria was concerned. If there was a reason beyond basic snobbery then Juliana had not been made aware of it.

"No, why would I. Most of them are not worth the time of day." Her sister shrugged, toying with one stray lock of hair. "They smell."

"It's called sweat, comes from an honest days work. Not something you would know about. You're a snob, you know that. If it were not for the plebs Rome would crumble. Our wealth is built on their backs. Our soldiers come from their ranks. So perhaps you should think twice before acting in such a manner." Juliana was wasting her time and knew it. No matter what she said about the plebs her sister would never change her mind. She was too much like the others of their ranks. Most cared nothing for the ordinary citizens of Rome. Oh there were rare exceptions to that, but for the most part the two sides seldom mixed unless it was to do with business.

"Bah, are you back on that track again. Perhaps you were born into the wrong family, sister dearest. Gods. Can't you be satisfied with your life and status? There are thousands of women who would kill for the position you have." Alexandria shook her head. "You're foolish. You've been touched by the gods and not in a good way. I think father should have the priests look at you, see if you have been cursed. Perhaps there is a way to cure you."

Forbidden Love: Bad Boys

"I don't need a cure." Not unless it came in the form of Turos. His hard body pressed against hers, his hands on her wrists as he slid into her willing sex. "I need a good hard cock between my thighs."

"Then use a slave. There are plenty with decent length cocks out there. We could buy you one today. I've no problem in taking a trip to the slave sales with you." Alexandria pushed up from the couch and walked across the room to her sister, taking her hands in both of hers. "Please. Listen to me. He's just a man, with a cock. Nothing special. I can buy you two, even three just like him. Please, come with me to the market place. We'll get this problem taken care of then you can move on with your life. With our lives and positions. Those are the important matters for women like us."

"It's not the same." Juliana growled. "I'm going through with this and no slave from the market place could take his place. Not in a thousand years. Not even if he were Jupiter himself."

* * * * *

"So this is the slave?" A gruff male voice broke through her thoughts. "Who is she a gift from again?"

Juliana glanced up from beneath the hood of her cloak at the soldier she had bribed to bring her to the quarters of the gladiators. Everything rested on him now. If he gave her up then she would be dragged back to her family home and thrown before her father before facing the worst punishment a member of the class of patricians could dream of. To be cast out from her family and sold as a common slave.

There were other risks as well. A fight over a slave, her companion distracted at the wrong moment and she could be mistaken as a runaway. No one would believe her protests if that happened. Forget being exposed, just one false move, a slip, a man unwilling to take no for an answer and she would become the very thing she now pretended to be.

A slave.

Marius. She had been careful in who she had picked out from amongst her fathers men. Out of all of them he was the most approachable. Like her sister he had tried to talk her out of this but in the end had backed down and agreed to the bribe in order to escort her to the house of gladiators.

"She is a gift of the evening from the house of Alexandrous." He tugged on the chain that had been locked about her throat. The chain. He had made it clear a slave needed to be chained for such a presentation. She had fought the idea, and craved the touch of the chain at the same time. Perhaps her sister had been right. She had been born in the wrong class. Did a part of her crave the touch of steel as much as she desired Turos?

Juliana shivered at the dangerous thought.

"She's a gift for the gladiator, Turos."

"Another one? He's had a few visitors of late, gifts of this nature. Even a few male slaves offered to him, though he wasn't that interested in those. No accounting for taste is there? Ah, well then let's have a look at the slut." The guard grabbed for the cloak, trying to yank it away from her body.

"No, she has been set aside for his use only." Marius acted quickly and slapped the guard's hand away. "I do not believe Alexandrous would be pleased if you trifled with his gift. He wishes the girl to please the gladiator, no one else. I might be forced to draw my sword in order to defend his wishes and that could get a little messy if you know what I mean."

"Ah, I see. But still what harm would there be in just taking a look?"

Juliana held her breath, taking a quick look at the man who blocked their entrance. Like most of the guards he had the appearance of a man willing to sell his life for the right price. Perhaps not as well trained as a soldier, or a gladiator but he still exuded pure masculinity.

What did he want of her?

A quick look?

To strip her off?

Perhaps a kiss?

What if he wanted more and Marius was forced to defend her? That would bring attention. Too much attention and that might lead to them being discovered. She would just have to comply with whatever he wanted. Her stomach knotted, thighs pressed tight together beneath the thin robe she had donned. Is this what slaves went through? Being open to be touched and stopped by any free man they walked past? She had never given it a thought before tonight, yet now she faced the stark reality of just what she had let herself into.

"Go ahead. But just a look mind you. She is to be fresh for Turos tonight and must be returned to the house of Alexandrous by dawn." Marius gestured with a growing impatience towards the still closed door. "Open up, time marches on and dawn waits for no man."

"Or woman." The guard tugged at her cloak. "Come on girl, strip it off. I want to see what that damn gladiator has been sent this time. You should see some of the delicious looking sluts he has been sent. Don't know why they are wasted on a slave, too good for the likes of him."

She froze, her breath caught in the back of her throat.

"You heard the order, slave. Take the cloak off."

Slowly she reached for the simple clasp at her neck, unhooking it before dropping the cloak to the floor. A thin robe covered her form, a light pale linen that clung to her form leaving little to the imagination, or so the look in the eyes of the guard told her.

"Nice. Very nice indeed. I don't suppose you'd like to share her? What her owner doesn't know won't hurt." The look in the guard's eye had her worried. If he pressed the matter then she would be at the mercy of Marius.

"And you think the girl wouldn't tell him?" Marius shot her a quick look, one that warned her to stay still, not protest and to let him handle the problem. At least she had picked a man who would work with her, protect her, and not betray her. Or so she hoped.

"Whose going to believe the whining of a slave?" The guard took a step closer, reaching out towards her covered breasts with one hand only to have that hand slapped away.

"I've got my orders. Don't get me wrong, I'd love to get my hands on this sweet piece of meat, but it's an honor thing. You understand." Marius settled his hand on her shoulder, giving Juliana a discreet squeeze. "I've been watching this chit for a while. She's a delicious thing, just not worth selling out my honor for."

The guard nodded and stepped back, rubbing the back of his stinging hand. "Maybe you'll have changed your mind after Turos has done with her."

"Don't count on it." The door closed behind them with a soft thud. "It's not too late to turn back, Juliana. I could have you safe at home before anyone could be the wiser."

"No, I have to go through with this." Or she would never have the courage to try again. "It's just something I have to do, Marius."

"It's your neck, girl."

Yes, it was.

His hand tightened on her shoulder for a moment before he pushed her gently down the corridor. Torches flickered along the wall, casting their smoky tinged glow across the stone walls. She had never stepped foot within the confines of the gladiators house before now, and had not known what to expect, but now it seemed more like a prison than a home to some of the most feared men in Rome.

Why were they kept like this? Locked up. Imprisoned. Like animals?

To add to their mystique?

"This is his cell."

"Cell?" She glanced back at Marius then at the heavy wooden door. "They really lock them up in cells?"

"Yes, where did you think a gladiator was kept?" Marius frowned then nodded towards the door. "They are slaves, just as you are. It's time lass."

Yes, it was time. She opened the door, or tried to. "It's locked."

Marius chuckled and unhooked the key from the side of the door, sliding it into the lock. "Turos, wake up. I have something for you."

The heavy door opened, a light flickering on the wall providing just enough illumination to allow Juliana to see into the room. It was a small cell barely large enough for his cot, a table and little more. A covered piss pot stood in the corner of the room, a candle sat on the barred window, and the torch on the wall. Not much. Not when she knew just how he was almost worshiped by those who saw him fight.

Did they know the simple life he led in the cell?

Of course not. To the women in the stands and most of the men, he was a god brought to life. One who dispensed justice with the swing of a blade and fulfilled the needs of the city with that same blade.

"A gift?" His voice was soft, more so than she had expected from a man like him. "What sort?"

"The female kind." Marius pushed her into the cell. "I will be collecting her before dawn. But until then the slave Lina is yours. A gift from the house of Alexandrous."

His dark gaze narrowed on her. "Interesting. And just why did the house of Alexandrous send me a gift? Not that I am objecting to their choice in such. Pretty little thing."

"I'm not privy to the reasons, just the outcome." Marius shrugged. "But if you don't want her I can return her to the house and the matter will be done."

"How do I know she is not some high bred chit trying something?" Turos growled. "I've had women do this before."

"She's a slave." Marius tugged on the chain about her throat. "No high bred lady would permit a mere guard to insist she stripped off her cloak in the middle of the street, which is what happened. However I can always strip her down here and now for you if needed."

"Do so."

Gods. She had not thought of this. Of him not believing her performance. The color drained from her skin as heat bloomed through her core. What would a slave actually do now?

Back away? Beg mercy? No. They would attempt to placate the men involved, wouldn't they?

How though?

Her mind raced as she tried to remember how she had seen slaves behave in the past, just what they did when those around them were angry, or disbelieved the words or purpose behind the presence of a slave.

"Please, Masters. I would be happy to strip off for you. My Master sent me with the sole purpose of pleasing the gladiator Turos and I would not wish for him to be disappointed." Trembling Juliana took a step into the cell, her hands moving to the simple ties on her robe, loosening them. With a soft whisper the linen fell around her feet, pooling there. Slowly she eased to her knees, lowering her head to his sandals and pressed her lips against them. "I am a slave, Master, of the house of Alexandrous. If I do not please you, beat me and send me from your feet."

She could feel the gazes of both men on her naked form as she kept her head to his sandals. Did Marius struggle not to pull her up to her feet and drag her out of the cell? Or did he now fight the desire he had feigned for the guard? She could not be sure how he was reacting. Not with how she kept her head down and her back to the soldier. This all rested on Turos. He had to believe her. No lady of Rome would debased herself in such a manner. Only a slave acted like this. Gods, please. He had to fall for this.

"Hm. Stand up slave. Let me get a good look at you."

A soft tremble worked through her body as she pressed her hands against the floor and pushed to her feet. Naked before both men she could feel the heat creep over her face, down across her full breasts to the crinkled tips of her coral touched nipples. All the time she had spent preparing herself for this moment was nothing compared to the time she now spent standing in front of the two men. Moments became hours, hours turned into days yet the candle had barely so much as flickered before he spoke again.

"What do you think? Would you turn such a luscious piece of ass away?" Turos looked over at Marius. The smile turned his face from stern into handsome, strong with a hint that he would not be denied if he took a full interest in her, or her body.

"Not unless I was already dead."

She glanced back at Marius. Any expectations she had retained that Marius might give her away faded under the intense gaze that played openly across her naked form. Had he been telling the truth to the guard? Her thighs tightened, pressing together as she tried to hide the warmth that throbbed between them.

"Indeed. Then I thank the house of Alexandrous for their gift, which I plan to enjoy until she screams in delight." The gladiator reached out, closing one hand on her wrist. "Or pain, which ever I find is going to bring me the most pleasure tonight."

"Nothing that leaves scars. The master was adamant on that, gladiator."

"Agreed, but there are a lot of pleasures that will not leave such a permanent mark on her pretty hide." His hand closed on her throat, pulling her close. She tensed under his touch, the dark glint in his eyes, the hunger she saw in his face. She had not counted on this type of reaction. The violence she had seen on the sands spilled over into his private desires.

No, she wasn't ready for that.

"You'll enjoy it too, slave. Or I will, which is what matters."

"Please, don't..."

"I will return before dawn." Marius turned, closing the door behind him, shutting out all hopes of rescue for her.

"You weren't expecting this, where you Lina? If that really is your name." His hand shifted from about her neck. "You don't have the look of a slave, but you're the first one to take the game to this level." His fingertips brushed over her cheek in a soft caress. "Or did you think I would believe your play acting? I know the difference between a real slave and someone pretending to be one."

Fear surged into life, clenching around her heart. "Will you expose me to the guards?"

"No, not yet. At least I don't think so."

"Why?" Juliana fought the urge to step back from him. "You frightened me."

"Yes, I know, I wanted to see how far you would take your game, Lina." He cupped her cheek, brushing one thumb over her cheek. "You're attractive. More so than I had expected. The last one looked as though she needed to be taken down a peg or two."

Juliana felt the heat rise across her cheeks. "And why will you not report me?"

"I have a need for a woman before I fight tomorrow." His hand moved slowly down her throat, over the smooth skin of her shoulder. "You're attractive, young, willing obviously or you would not be here. So tell me, Lina. Why me?"

Why him? She had asked herself the same question a dozen times over in the past few weeks. "I don't know. I've watched you from the stands for a year now. I don't miss a fight. I can't. I tried once, I felt as though a part of me had been cut off. Or that I had become ill. I don't understand why it happened or why I felt like that."

"Addicted."

"What?" She blinked, taking a step back from him. His fingers caressed a light path down her breast. A tingle controlled her body, tightening her nipples into hard peeks.

"You're addicted. Like a soldier who can't face the day without a cup or three of wine." He watched her closely, tracing a path from one nipple to the next. He circled each ripe nub of flesh with the tip of his finger, teasing a soft shiver into being. "I've seen it before in men and women. You need to come and see me, to watch me. It satisfies a hunger in you, doesn't it? Or it did. That hunger has now grown out of control, which is why you are now here, risking your freedom."

Juliana nodded, her cheeks flushed. "Yes. I didn't know what else to do. I knew if I just came to you, as I was, you would turn me away. You always turn women like me away."

His hands tightened on her waist, fingers digging into her flesh. "You're a member of the Patrician, not a Pleb?"

"Yes." She fought not to cry out in pain. "Please, don't send me away."

"Bitch." He growled, thrusting her away to the cold stone floor. "I should call out and have you whipped from the cell."

"Why don't you like us?" Juliana tried to stand back up, only to be forced back to the floor with a sharp shove. "I've done nothing to you. I've all but worshipped you for the past year. What have I done that is so wrong?"

"You're nothing but a stuck up slut, like all of your kind." He snarled, his eyes little more than pieces of coal. "I should have you dragged out of here naked by your hair, so that the entire city can see you for the creature you are. Maybe you'd be sold to the soldiers, turned into a common whore, but you might even like that. You're just like she was."

"She? I don't know who you're talking about but I'm nothing like her. I came here because I admire you. I've prayed for a way to meet you, risked everything to come here. Even my sister tried to stop me, but you, being with you is more important to me than either rank, or family."

He advanced on her, his eyes flashing. "You stupid little cunt. Do you really expect me to believe that?"

"Then toss me out, have the guards drag me through the streets to the market. Denounce me in front of all. Condemn me to a life as a slave. If you wish that fate for me I will gladly embrace that." The words spilled from her lips without thought. Where had they come from?

I believe them. By Jupiter, if he wanted this of me I would do it, willingly if it meant he would believe me.

"Why should I believe you at all?" He scowled down at her naked form, but even in his anger he could not hide the way his gaze lingered on her breasts, or played over the tight plane of her stomach. "Show me. Lower yourself before me."

Lower herself? She already had.

Juliana looked up at him, taking in the darkness in his gaze. Her breath caught in the back of her throat, heat rippled through her inner walls as she looked over him. Yes, she could do this. Slowly she rolled onto her stomach and crawled to his feet. "I want to be with you. To serve you, touch you, be touched by you. If you will permit me." Her lips pressed against his sandals, the tip of her tongue tracing across the leather straps.

For a long moment he did not speak, nor move, but left her with her lips against his feet. Her heart sank into the pit of her stomach, fear of what he would do if he did not find her pleasing only added to her growing discomfort. All it would take is a word from him and she would be marched away to her father.

"Crawl to my cot." He stepped away, pointing to the narrow cot. "Now." His voice was filled with a low growl, but one that no longer hinted at anger.

Juliana tried to fight the shaking that threatened to lay a claim to her body. With a long, slow breath she pushed up onto her hands and knees, glancing over at him through the soft veil of her own dark hair. Her breasts pulled towards the floor, her nipples crinkled points of coral, a damp heat throbbing between her thighs. It did not matter that he might toss her out to the guards once he had taken what pleasure he wanted from her body. It was worth it. He was worth it. A chance, she had been given a chance to please him.

"Now, before I see sense and change my mind."

With a slight nod she hurried across the floor to the narrow cot and knelt up at the side of it.

"Onto the cot." He cleared the distance between them, one hand tightening in her hair as he pulled her up onto the narrow bed. So unlike the soft mattress she had grown used to. No feathers filled this padding, basic straw and rough sacking for a covering. Luxuries were not a part of life for a gladiator. She turned on to her back, looking up at him.

Did he like what he saw?

"Pretty little chit, aren't you. Good skin, the best clothing, everything you've ever wanted has been handed to you on a platter, hasn't it. Until me. Then what did you do. Did you throw a fit, become angry when you tried the first time to get to me and were told no?"

"No, master. This is the first time I have tried." Unlike the others that must have come his way, she had tried to learn more about him first. Men like him deserved women who did not look on him as a right, but as a man who did the choosing. He was no longer just a piece of meat in the coliseum, he was a warrior, a god, a man that left her heart racing at the slightest thought of his glistening body.

His grip tightened in her long dark hair. "Why do you call me that?"

"Because for this night I am your slave, your property, is it not right for me to address you as master if I am your slave?" She tried to smile, meeting his gaze warily.

He tugged hard on her hair, forcing an arch into her neck and back. "You have the look of one willing to do anything I wish, is that true, or just another one of the tricks of your kind. She used to give me that look, but I learned all too well that it was a lie. A well practiced act."

"Not a lie, I swear it." Could he not see how she wanted to please him? She forced a deeper arch into her back, lifting her breasts towards him in offering. "I will do whatever you want!"

"And if it pleased me to see you roll beneath the bodies of every guard and gladiator in this place?"

"I'd do it, willingly."

"Slut." He growled. "You're nothing but another whore, like all of your kind."

"For you I would become one." She tried to press closer to him as he sat on the edge of the cot, turning enough that she could put her lips against his thigh. "If it would mean that you would look on me with some favor, that you might touch me, seek pleasure from me, then I would sell myself to the legions in order to gain that favor in your eyes."

What was it about this man that she would debase herself to

such a degree with him? Her sister had been right, there were others, just as handsome, just as well formed as he was, yet still, even now when he treated her as garbage, she was willing to give herself to him.

"Why?" He pushed her away from his thigh. "Why would you go that far for me?" He slid his fingers through her hair, gathering the long dark length in his grasp. "Women like you do not give up who you are they make demands, try to play men like me, or any man foolish enough to give you a moment of time."

"Give me the chance to show I am not like them, please." She turned onto her side, moving closer to him.

"You even look like her."

"Like who?"

"Atia." He all but snarled the name.

Atia. She knew that name but for the moment could not place it. "I'm not her, I swear it. Nor am I like her."

"Are you sure?" He pulled her closer to his thigh, urging her lips to press against his thigh. With little more than a soft whimper she pressed a dozen soft kisses along the smooth skin of his thigh. "Perhaps you will prove that to me, or not as the case may be."

Juliana wanted to prove it to him, that she could wipe away the memories of the other woman. The one that had set him on this path and into a life of death and glory, whoever the woman had been, this Atia, she was nothing like her. Or so she hoped. "Let me at least try to show you who I am Master and that I am nothing like that woman."

She whimpered, licking along his thigh softly, tasting the mix of sweat and oil on his body. How often had she dreamt of this moment, where she could actually touch and taste him? Fear should have taken control of the moment, but love or perhaps lust ruled her now. His grip eased from her hair enough that she could place a tender path of nibbling kisses over his thigh, down to his knee. Did he not see just how much she wanted this? How she needed this moment with him? She desired him so much more than he could ever understand.

"What do I have to do to prove to you that I am not like her, that I don't want to twist you to my desires?" She whispered against his leg. "I know, or I understand that you don't believe me, that she did something to you that left you jaded, but I am not that woman."

"I want to believe you, Gods above and below I want to believe you, if only so I can enjoy one night of pleasure before I fight tomorrow." He brushed over the back of her neck, tracing a light touch along her spine. "Perhaps I can do it, ignore what you represent and just take the moment of pleasure with you.”

She shivered in silence fighting back comments that she did not dare give life to in case they pushed his choice the wrong way. She had risked so much to come this far. Her skin tingled under the light touch, nipples hardening before she had the chance to so much as whimper. Softly his hand traveled down the length of her back until he cupped her cheeks.

“So soft, so tempting.” He leaned forward, growling the words against her neck. “One night wouldn’t be so wrong.” Passion pushed past his fears as he gripped her buttocks tightly, rolling onto her. The cot creaked beneath them, his weight pressed down on her body, trapping her against the thin mattress.

Juliana arched up against him, her fingers tightening into his sides, thighs parting at a single nudge from his knees. How she had wanted this, dreamed about this moment with him. So there were a few details that did not quite fit the image she had entertained. No soft sheets, or silken words, just his body, hers and the narrow cot.

Raw sexuality in the place of whispered love. Dreams of romance fled, perhaps never to be looked on again. The wrong type of person, gladiators and members of her class did not form relationships. They had occasional delights shared together. Nothing more. Like now.

He groaned into her neck, the simple wrap of cloth about his waist pulled to one side and dropped on the floor. She could feel it, the touch of his cock against her inner thighs, the heat that built between them despite the anger he still might have felt. Juliana whimpered, her thighs parting further as she wrapped her legs about his body.

If a few moments of passion was all they could share, then so be it.

The tip of his cock nudged against her damp lower lips. “It’s been so long, too long since I had a woman.” He mumbled into her neck, nibbling a path down from her throat to her breasts, capturing one ripe nipple between his lips. “My slave you say, for the night at least?”

“Yes, master.” Soft tingles of delight rushed through her breast, throbbing into the hardened nipple. “I’m yours until the coming of the dawn.” Any hesitation fled at the touch of his cock between her silken labia. His grip shifted, settling on her hips as he lifted them up from the cot.

“Then I will take you as a slave, not a high woman of Rome.” He growled, his fingers dug deeper into her flesh as he shifted back onto his knees, lifting her up to roughly thrust her face down onto the cot.

Without mercy he pulled her ass high up into the air before settling behind her. "As a slave on your hands and knees, nothing more than a pet to be used. That is what you wanted from me, and that is what you will get. I offer you no mercy, no love, no tender words, just the sweat coated mating of two slaves."

Fear gripped her stomach, yet this is what she had asked for; hoped for. Her fingers curled into the thin mat beneath, vision clouded by the veil of dark, silken tresses. She had no way out of this- even if she had wanted to find one.

"Please..."

"Please what, little slave? Take you slowly? To speak the whispered words of seduction more fitting for a high born lady of the Patricians? Ah but you're a slave, a slut for the taking by your own words." His breath caressed warm and dangerous against the back of her neck, the head of his cock pressed between her lower lips.

A soft shudder worked through her body, her vulva clenching at the images his words brought to life. Common sense screamed at her to fight her way free, break away from his touch, yet her soul craved his domination, the feel of his body against hers, skin on skin in the most intimate of ways.

She groaned, pressing back her hips against his body, thighs parting wider as she sought to welcome him into her heated walls. "Please master, let me serve you." She could almost feel it, the pressure of his erection parting her sex, filling her body to the depths of her rippling core. Yet he still had not moved.

"You move almost like a slave, a wanton slut, seeking the touch of a cock in that heated slit of yours." He leaned closer, growling against her back. She could almost feel his teeth. Would he bite her?

Gods she hoped so.

With a long low groan he rocked into her tight sex, forcing her walls to accept him. Her nails caught on the rough bedding, a low cry forced into life as her body shuddered in delight. Her nipples scraped against the cloth under them, the scent of sweat, straw, stale wine and leather mingled. Her heart pounded in her chest, blood racing through her veins until the only sounds that filtered past the raging torrent in her body were the low passion filled grunts that came from the man who held her against the mattress.

"You're like other sluts of your kind. I'm not the first, won't be the last." His words were meant to sting, but failed.

"I'm your slave Master, I never said that I was an untouched one."

Forbidden Love: Bad Boys

She moaned, arching back against him.

"Insolent wench." He groaned. He slid one hand up from her hip, stroking the length of her back until his strong fingers tangled in the long length of her raven hair. "It's about time someone brought you back down to earth and taught you your place."

"My place, for tonight, is serving you." Juliana looked back over her shoulder, her arching up to him, her walls tightening with each deep thrust into her willing body. Her stomach tightened, nails threatened to break with the tight grip she held on the bedding. She had never known such a brute passion, or dreamt at how his touch would bring this depth of fire to life in her body. Musings, day dreams, the random thoughts generated by each trip to the arena had been but pale shadows compared to how she now felt. "Tonight I am yours."

"And tomorrow?" He pulled on the handful of hair he held onto, forcing her to meet his gaze. "Tomorrow you will return to being the proud Patrician bitch. Looking down from the stands, cheering on at the blood I spill on the sands. Will you cheer just as loudly if it is my blood spilt?"

"You'll live, master. Live and remain glorious, proclaimed such by all of Rome." She gasped the words, shaken with each harsh thrust into her body. She needed him, the feel of his cock as it stretched her tight inner walls, slick delight coating them, a throbbing building from the depths of her soul, forced into being beyond anything she had dreamed of.

Pressure, pain, tingles akin to a hundred fingers played over the taut skin of her ass and thighs. His hand with that cruel grip in her hair, sweat coating her body, his skin slipping against her own, the friction urging her into a wave of delight she had no control over.

"Tonight I rule. Not you. Not Atia. Not your kind. Me!" His words were little more than guttural growls. All the hatred, the anger he felt towards Atia now spilled out in his use of the woman beneath him. "No words of love, no more lies. This is what you want, this is what you need Atia!"

She wasn't Atia, but even that could not shake her body from the depths of passion she had found herself locked in. It no longer mattered that he used her as only a source of release, or a moment of vengeance. She has walked into this of her own free will.

Thought fled at his roar of delight, her own body responding with a cry of passion. Heat washed through her core, wrapping about his throbbing erection as she bucked beneath him. Wanton, heated and as needful as any well trained and owned woman might have been.

His slave if only for the moment.

* * * * *

"You look different today," Alexandria frowned. "Did you not sleep well last night?"

"I slept well enough, sister." The stands beneath the boxes were crowded, more so than usual, but the noise no longer bothered her. Her gaze never shifted from the sands, the place where he would stand soon enough.

"Then why do you look so drained?"

"I retired perhaps a little later than I should have done, but you have my word I rested quite well." They both had. Once he had done, when they had both collapsed to the cot in exhaustion sleep had claimed them, if only for a while.

Turos. Cold hearted warrior, a bastard who used women and tossed them aside, had lived up to his image. He had sent her from the cell just as soon as he had regained his senses, without the slightest thought to her well being.

The hurried walk home, his sweat coating her body, mingling with hers, the scent of him that lingered right up until the moment she had bathed. Gods. If there had been a way to keep the feeling of him on her body, a way to avoid bathing without the entire household becoming privy to what she had done, then she would have found it.

Cold. His eyes had been so cold when he had slapped her on the ass, sending her naked from the cell. Yet she told herself there had been something in his gaze. A hint of softness, a warmth, something that thanked her for the risks she had taken to spend the night with him.

"They say Turos fights one of the best gladiators to ever be seen in Rome, this day."

Not love, but care. A hint of something more between them, she had seen it in the depths of his calculating gaze.

A lie worth believing in.

"Are you even listening to me?"

"Not really."

"Your precious Turos might well die today. I would have thought that you'd care. Perhaps it would be for the best, that way you might just stop mooning about him. I still can't believe you did it. If our father finds out..."

"He won't." Sunlight reflected from the edge of polished swords. Metal studded leather slapped against well toned thighs as the low cry welcomed the gladiators onto the sands.

"He might, you came home wrapped in nothing more than a soldiers cloak. Of course he could find out."

The woolen cloak, how strange that had felt against her still tingling skin. Marius had thrown it over her form before she had taken a dozen steps away from the cell. A growl, one that had radiated pleasure and anger combined, had rang in her ears, but no words had been exchanged until he had seen her safely home.

A foolish risk, he had said. Yet his gaze had lingered on the curves of her breasts, his hands clenched and unclenched with the need to touch her forbidden flesh.

A soldier. A warrior. Just like her Turos.

"I hope his blood soaks into the sands." Her sister spat.

"He won't die." She murmured, the movement across the sands claimed her full attention. For a moment his gaze turned her way a silent exchange between them, a claim of ownership that no other could see or feel. Another lie? Not that it mattered.

"Men like him never truly die."

No, men like him became gods, and lived forever in the memories of women like her.

Between Two Thieves

Between Two Thieves
By Rian Monaire

Dedication
To my husband and little girl.

Reven Drake -- at least that was the name on his current driver's license -- was ready to go to work. Nine-millimeter tucked neatly into his shoulder holster, he shut off the engine of his relatively unobtrusive grey Saab, tucking the keys under the seat. He wouldn't be using it again, and woe to the foolish light-fingered one who took it. He pressed a tiny metal switch on the device tucked under the seat. The slow-burning but extremely hot fuse attached would set the upholstery on fire in a matter of seconds once the two-hour timer went off -- not a pleasant place to find yourself.

The closest to hell you could get, in fact.

He unfolded the picture of the latest job. He was struck by her eyes -- they held a clarity he'd rarely seen, offset by a prim hairstyle that emphasized angular cheekbones. *Pity. A pretty young one. I hate having to do those. Such a waste.*

He tucked it into the pocket of his leather jacket and tugged open the car door, stepping out quickly and slamming it behind him. A few blocks to the apartment, a quick one-two, and off to the Islands he'd be for a long-awaited break before the next job.

He walked briskly, noting the area around him, but keeping his expression relaxed. Nothing exciting -- same old same old. Buildings once cleanly painted, now a wash-faded grey and pink, the one uniformity scabs of peeling paint and dried mud. Pavement like pockmarked flesh invited a stumble or twisted ankle. The occasional nicely kept condo or tree surrounded by chicken wire broke up the homely monotony.

The apartment he'd been looking for wasn't anything like what he'd expected when he'd cased it in preparation for this afternoon's festivities; a plain split-level house converted into four apartments. Nicer than most in the row, but the railings showed wear, and there was a faint odor of mold as he stepped onto the porch. *She must not be as good as the last one.*

Three of the apartments were vacant. Crossing the porch quietly, he stopped in front of the only occupied unit. Below the doorbell, *B. Lewis* was written in black marker on a strip of friction tape, just starting to fade.

He shifted the flower box he used as a prop and rang the bell. This was always the tough part—getting in.

"Coming," Her soft voice barely carried through the scuffed wooden door.

He steeled himself as the door slowly opened. No pause to check, no "who is it?" Trusting, or expecting someone. Probably the latter. She had called in sick today—easy enough to do when you're fucking the boss.

She looked a bit paler than her photo, as if she really was ill. Her long blonde hair, twisted into a professional chignon in the picture, lay in rumpled waves over her shoulders. Her grey-green eyes were fixed on the box in his hands as if she couldn't meet his own.

He cleared his throat. "Brandy Lewis?"

She nodded, raising her eyes to his.

He dropped the flower box and drew his gun. *Make it fast; she won't need to see it.*

But she reacted faster than he would have expected, whirling toward the open doorway behind her. His chance for a quick shot was lost. He fired, but missed. She screamed, dodging through the doorway and slamming the door.

Before she could lock it, he slammed his shoulder into it, slinging it open to crash into the far wall. She shrieked again, scrabbling for a weapon. He shot again, this time catching her in the chest. She fell, inhaling sharply and managing, "Why..."

He squeezed off another shot without answering, and she fell.

He took out his digital camera to record the completion of the job. It fell from his hands, clattering to the scratched hardwood floor as he suddenly fought his gorge, his belly roiling with nausea. What the fuck was wrong with him?

Breathe. Calm down. Must've had a bad burger or something.

He inhaled slowly and exhaled. After a bit, the sickness faded. With still-shaking hands, he scooped up the camera and lined up the shot. The job's eyes were still partially open, and glinted as he clicked the shutter. *Brandy's eyes.*

There was a left-field thought. Why had her name infiltrated his mind like that? The rule always had been they're not people, they're jobs. That mantra had been drilled in his head since he'd first started taking instruction — he'd repeated it endless times since his first job at seventeen. He'd been all right until he'd gotten home, then had thrown up. His father had walked in as he was finishing, and had hit him hard enough to make his nose bleed. Great family memories, but not everyone had a "Happy Days" kind of life...though his dad did look a bit like Fonzie.

He cued up the picture to check it. *Damn, blurred.* A creamy fog nearly obscured the job's features, and the wound couldn't be seen.

* * * * *

Brandy Lewis.

Goddamn it. That phantom voice again.

He'd never noticed the smell of pain and fear, of blood and death that lingered in the air before. The afterimages of a life snuffed out.

Fuck this. I'm done. Time to finish with the woman.

He gritted his teeth and took another shot. This one was usable. He shuddered with relief and bolted out of the room, tearing off his prosthetic mask as he ran. It, the gun and his jacket were all tossed in a nearby burning barrel after being wiped clean and unloaded. A little kerosene from a bottle in his hip pocket, and it whooshed into flame. He stepped back quickly, so as not to catch his sleeve, or add telltale smudges to his clothing from flying soot. Getting out without a trace meant more than just being able to move fast. Those CSI bastards were slick.

His dark hair had fallen over his eyes, clinging to his sweaty brow. He paused, tucking the camera under his arm, and passed a shaking hand through it, pushing it back. He checked his reflection in the dusty window of an abandoned store, taking out the contacts that turned his grey eyes to blue and tossing them into the gutter.

Clutching his camera, he strolled off to collect his fee, carefully controlling his pace. *Everything's normal, nothing to see here. That's the ticket.*

* * * * *

The red glow of the sun through the thin shield of his eyelids fascinated him, and he admired it for several minutes before finally opening them and locating his fresh beer, just delivered by the brunette waitress with the tight, curving ass. He pinched the lime, squeezing the tart fluid into the sweating neck of the bottle, then pressed in the wedge of fruit. Capping the bottle with his thumb, he turned it upside down and watched the green wedge rise.

Only by taking other people's lives in one form or another could someone retire at 32, and he had done so. After the last job.

Brandy Lewis .

Yes, okay, when he'd killed Brandy Lewis. He found he got the shakes and nausea every time he even considered taking another job, but he had made enough investments over the years that he wasn't in danger of starving. Time to just kick back and enjoy the benefits of all his hard work. There were plenty to take up his slack.

Was it hard work, really? Killer?

Just what he needed--voices in his head, like some insane Jiminy Cricket. That shit had to stop.

He had done a job that needed to be done, period. Somebody had to do it, and he was elected. Carrying on the family name. His father had made damn sure he had. He still carried the scar from the day he had told him he wanted to go straight and go to college. That was an idea he'd dropped very quickly, after his father's "incentive" to remain had been explained to him: stay or die. Over the years, it had gotten easier; then he'd just closed off.

The waitress lingered, eyeing him, then finally spoke. "Are you all right, sir?"

Oh, sweetie, you have no idea. He gave her an easy smile and a nod, and she finally moved away. She turned after a few feet and gave him another look, this one more appraising.

He returned the appraisal, and upgraded his smile to one more sensual. Maybe later. For now, it was all about the beer and sunshine. Though it had been a while since he'd sampled a lady's wares...

His attention drifted to the abundant display of local

beauties strolling casually past his beach chair. Every
shade and hue of skin and hair color graced the clear, pale
sand. The smooth skin tones were broken up only by the
brightness of bikinis and skin glitter. His senses drifted with
the stimuli, and his shaft stirred.

A flash of blonde hair caught his eye, and he squinted
idly in its direction, then tensed from head to toe. Who was
that?

A woman in a turquoise shift, just down the beach, her
back to him... The flood of windblown hair looked familiar,
as did the shyness of her pose. She turned slightly, and
the sun, just starting to drift below the horizon, backlit
her profile: the slightly upturned nose, the strong jaw and
smooth forehead.

Brandy?

He was appalled at his first emotion — not fear or self-
preservation, but relief. He hadn't killed her after all. Stupid
fucking thought.

Brandy was dead, all right. He had seen the
newspapers: Secretary of Lance Worthington brutally slain.
Rumored to have been his mistress.

Rumored. That was the word that bit at his soul. The
rumor had been wrong. Very wrong.

His connection had called with another job, but he had
turned it down. His contact wasn't prone to chitchat -- he
didn't even know the man's name -- but in that instance, he
had one more thing to say.

"Did you hear about your last job?"

Reven coughed. "What about her?"

A pause. "She wasn't his mistress."

"What?"

"Yeah, she had just started the job a few days earlier.
His mistress was off in Tahiti. I had to get another guy to do
the job. Take it easy." He hung up.

"Wait! I..." Too late. He clicked off his phone. The
slim plastic case slid from his suddenly nerveless hand and
clattered to the floor.

He had killed her for nothing?

He gripped both sides of his head, trying to contain the
sudden rush of pain. He had ended the lives of many people,

and never felt anything like this. Why did Brandy Lewis burn in his mind so strongly?

Everyone else had been guilty of one thing or another, even if by association. As far as he knew, Brandy had been the only victim of circumstance. He could justify all of his actions, but her... Was that why her wide eyes, so clear in that moment before he'd killed her , stayed in his mind's eye long after so many others barely made an impression?

He'd been doing this for so long. He didn't feel anything anymore. He was fine. He just needed a break, something he had known for a long time. Burnout was common in all stressful professions, and his certainly qualified.

Right?

He jerked himself out of his reverie. The blonde woman was moving closer, her shift blowing back, outlining slim legs. He leaned forward in his chair, trying to get a closer glimpse of her face before she noticed him.

She turned, smiled and waved. He flinched, then realized how intensely he was staring at her. Of course she'd wave. It didn't mean she knew him. Big bad killer jumping at shadows. Maybe he needed to get out of the sun.

Of course, just because you're paranoid doesn't mean they're not out to get you.

She was walking closer. Her resemblance to Brandy was enhanced with every swaying step, her silky hair caught by the wind. She paused in front of his chair. "Hi."

He took a swig of beer to moisten his suddenly dry throat. "Hi."

"I'm Kitty. I just got here." She pushed her hair out of her face, an exercise in futility; the wind teasingly tossed it back.

"Do you have a sister?" he blurted, then mentally kicked himself. *Way to come off normal, genius.*

She laughed. "Pleased to meet you, too. No, no sisters. I'm an only child."

He tried on a charming grin, and managed to get it to fit. "Hi, Kitty. I'm Reven, and I think I need to get inside soon."

"Me too. Care to share a table for dinner?"

Do I?

Sure. He'd already drawn attention to himself by staring and asking weird questions. Why not blow her off and add more?

"Sounds great. Let's go." He slowly rose, making sure on the way up that his legs would support him. The heat and beer. Yeah, that's the ticket. Seven Coronas and hundred-degree weather would make anyone see things.

Dinner was surprisingly pleasant. A few glasses of room temperature Perrier helped clear his head, and Kitty was wonderful company. Her quick wit and appealing self-deprecation led him to relax more than he thought he could.

Her beauty didn't hurt, either.

Kitty toyed with her wineglass. "So, you're staying here?"

Reven nodded. "Second floor."

Her toying fingers twisted a lock of hair. "You get an ocean view? I wanted one, but they were booked."

Oh, yes, he knew the game. "Beautiful, actually." He smiled. "You want to come up and share it? I could open a fresh bottle of wine."

She took a sip of her wine, running the tip of her tongue over her lips. "Sure. I think that would be just perfect."

The waiter interrupted the discussion. "Will you be wanting dessert this evening?"

Kitty's face clouded, and she rose. "No, actually, I'm suddenly pretty tired. I think I'll head up to my room. Do you mind?" Addressing Reven as she spoke the last.

Surprised by the sudden change in mood, he could only nod. She rose and left, skirt swirling around tanned thighs. He admired the sweet swing of her hips and the brush of her windblown hair against her sky-colored shift. Moody, but she stirred him in more ways than one. Maybe it was finally time to get to know more about a woman than her first name.

Was he supposed to follow her? He'd never been uncertain about any move he'd made before. In this case, discretion would have to be the better part of valor. There would be time for bed, perhaps tomorrow. He would sleep alone tonight.

However, he was having chocolate mousse first.

* * * * *

Reven stirred, for a moment not sure what had awakened him. Slowly, his senses reported back. Someone was in bed with him. Someone who carried the scent of sea spray and attar of roses, and wore no clothing.

Did I hire somebody for tonight?

He reacted swiftly, but carefully, slipping a hand under his pillow and wrapping it around the slick, cool metal of the nine-millimeter hidden there. "Who the hell are you, and what do you want?"

Moonlight streamed in the open balcony doors, illuminating the female shape now curved against his cool flesh, her head resting on his chest. Tightening his grip on the gun, he pushed back the waves of wild hair covering her face with his free hand, and she lifted her head obligingly to his perusal.

"I'm sorry I had to leave you so quickly," Kitty murmured. "I had something I had to do."

Reven couldn't speak. Her skin was warm, silken. He was already hardening against her belly, firmly pressed against his groin. "Kitty. I... How did you--"

"Shhhhh..." her moist exhalations, scented faintly with cinnamon, stirred the hair dusting his forehead as she pressed her lips just above his eyebrow. "Everything's fine."

She kissed lower, catching the bridge of his nose, the ridge of his cheekbone, then finally his lips. Releasing his grip on the weapon, his hands moved to the small of her back, stroking the curve of her spine and cupping her buttocks, his fingers learning the texture of her firm flesh.

Her lips parted, and her tongue darted in, tracing the ridge of his front teeth. He returned kiss for kiss, grinding his erection into her. She didn't shy away, pressing harder against him, then breaking the kiss. She moved upward, giving him access to her rigid nipples.

He drew one into his mouth, tasting the salt of her skin and tracing the ridged silk of the nub. Her moan announced her pleasure at his touch, and she pressed her breasts more fully against him. He cupped them, pressing

191

them together, then alternated light flicks of his tongue against each turgid nipple.

She locked her thighs around his hips, and he could feel her wetness tricking over his balls, her heat so close to his hard cock. He twisted upward, trying to thrust, to plunge into her , but she held him down easily, reaching between their bodies and trailing a fingernail across his tufted sac.

Gritting his teeth, he tried again to plunge inside her, without success. Determined to move things along, he released her breasts and his fingers found the moist wet velvet of her core, circling his thumb over her clit as two fingers plunged inside.

Her body tightened, arching upward and back until tickling strands of her long hair brushed his thighs, heightening his arousal. Her hips began to move against his hand, urging him deeper.

In a flash, he rolled her over with him, grasped her slim thighs, and plunged his face into her sweet pussy. Sliding two fingers in again, he gently tongued the soaking bulb of flesh while moving his fingers in and out, slowly. On the inward stroke, he curved them upward gently, searching for her G-spot.

Her vocalizations upgraded from constant moans to a wail, and he increased his efforts, plunging his fingers faster and suckling her rigid clit into his mouth, then running his tongue over it.

Her hips moved rapidly, out of control, her head thrashing from side to side on the pillow. Her nails dug into the sheet, crumpling the fabric in her fists. He ground his cock against the bed, hoping against hope that he would be able to hold on; her unabashed response was affecting him in a way he couldn't control.

Her entire body locked, and a cry that put all previous sounds to shame forced its way from her throat. He could feel the pulse of her clit and the tighten and flex of her pussy walls in the wake of an orgasm. He waited, and as her spasms began to quieten, dove up her body, thrusting his cock inside her in one smooth move.

Her thighs locked around him, her body moving with him. Sweat beaded, then trickled down their bodies, slickening their flesh and increasing the wet sounds they made together.

Shit, I can't hold on…fuck, fuck, fuck, I can't…oh, God…

His orgasm flew through his body, out of control. The pressure that had been building in his balls since he first woke to sense her finally released, flowing from his shaft in what seemed like a never-ending flood. Too late, he realized he hadn't put on a condom. He tried to pull back, to pull out, but she only tightened her legs around him and locked her arms around his neck, catching his mouth with hers.

What the fuck?

He felt…weird. True, he had never had an orgasm this intense, but he felt like he was blacking out.

He tried again to break free, but she held on with amazing strength for such a delicate-looking woman. He couldn't breathe, couldn't get free, couldn't move.

This is insane. He renewed his struggles, trying at the very least to pull his lips from hers and catch a snatch of air. As he went silently into blackness, he could taste cinnamon.

* * * * *

Reven opened his eyes slowly, squinted against the light of the sun.

The light…

Was coming from the wrong side.

He sat up, ignoring his throbbing head, and turned. No, he wasn't mistaken. The balcony doors were supposed to be to the left of the bed, with an ocean view. These were on the right, and faced the tennis courts. Had he gone back to Kitty's room?

He looked down for evidence of last night's encounter, and froze.

He was looking down at a female body instead of his own. A familiar *female* body.

He grabbed a handful of his hair and tugged. Long, tangled and blonde. He pulled harder, until it hurt. He stayed female, and the hair remained blonde. His hands moved over his strangely soft skin. What the hell was he doing in a female body? Whose body was it, and where was she?

His fingers touched his groin, finding only smooth

folds and an opening he was intimately familiar with, just not quite so personally. He wasn't privy to how the fairer sex felt after a night of rousing carnal activity, but he was sure there should be some evidence...pain, wetness, something. He was pretty sure this body hadn't had sex. But if not Kitty, who?

The door banged open, and a huge, dark-haired man entered, shutting it quickly. "Kitty Wells?"

Reven cleared his throat. "No, of course not." Damn, even his voice sounded like hers. But whoever he was now, it couldn't be her.

The man's thick brows nearly met as his brown eyes narrowed to slits. "Nice try, sweetie." He slid a hand under his grey.

Reven reacted instinctively, rolling off to put the bed between them. The man moved quickly across the room, a shock of dark hair falling over his forehead. As Reven rolled, the man gripped one of his legs, causing him to fall forward onto one knee. His head struck the edge of the nightstand, and he started to fade out. As the world went dark, he saw the railing of the balcony as the man dragged him to it...and then over.

* * * * *

"It's done. It looks like a suicide."

"Thank you. I'll wire your payment." Kitty clicked off the phone, dialed again and smiled with Reven's lips as she keyed in the account numbers.

Kitty had indeed had a sister, and had loved her very much, as only an identical twin could. Even being adopted by different families couldn't break that bond, though she had only recently found her, shortly before her death.

Kitty's grin widened, and she moved toward the restroom. God, this was going to take some getting used to... how did guys walk right with these things? She eyed her new face in the mirror. The only difference was the addition of her own grey-green eyes, a match to Brandy's. From Kitty's lashes, a tear traced down Reven's cheek.

She inhaled deeply, them smiled at a sudden thought.

Even a killer can be made to regret. You just have to get into his head.

194

Forbidden Love: Bad Boys
    Literally.

About the Author

    Rian Monaire is the dark side of Stefani Kelsey, editor. They frequently battle for dominance. Both reside in Virginia with their husband and six-year-old daughter. Rian has many titles coming soon to Mojocastle Press.
    Stephanie Kelsey
    Writing As Rian Monaire

Eternity

Eternity
by Terri Pray

Dedication

To Sam, thank you now and always. Without you I'd still be hiding my scribbles from others.

You could say that I'm not the type to give up easily. Especially when I've decided that someone belongs to me and she is mine. Body, heart, mind and soul, even if she doesn't fully understand that yet.

Maybe that's why I stick around?

Golden hair, blue eyes, the body and face of an angel and I can recall each sweet sound she made when I claimed her. Her breasts are still young, firm, her nipples ripe tender little buds that beg for my touch, her sweet hips flare beneath the gown and I alone amongst men have seen the treasures that lie beneath.

Doctors don't count. Unless they are the twisted sort that take a sick pleasure in the way they get to look upon women in a vulnerable state. The sort of man I would have been if I had indeed had the patience to study for such a craft.

Melissa.

My sweet innocent angel or at least she was until that night.

She can't see me.

She barely remembers me as anything more than a bad dream. The beast that took her prized possession then left her to deal with the consequences.

Yet I've never left her side for more than a few moments in the past five years.

Oh, her father had other ideas. He saw me for what I am. A rogue. A despoiler of virgins. A man who would use a woman for anything and everything possible. He was right about that. More than he could ever imagine. I've worked my way through close to fifty women. Yet not one of them was like her.

A prize, a virgin with the passion of a whore, how could I leave such a prize as Melissa. Oh, please don't think I'm in love with her, I'm not. Love doesn't enter the picture for men like me. She's a way of earning money, a key to the estate, more than that something I can put up in a card game.

She'd pay the stakes to.

I know that. I've seen it, the hunger to know more that glowed within her soft eyes. That little whimper as I pushed her further into the darkness that I loved even then. The darkness that holds me now.

Gods, even the thought of that night makes my cock throb. She whimpered beneath me, her lips parted in that cross between a plea for mercy and a cry for more. Fear and need mingled in her eyes in a way that left me unable to hold back. I had to sate myself in her flesh, to take her maidenhead and to know that I was the first.

One time wasn't enough. Normally when I tumble a woman I'm gone. I'll take off, but she offered so much more than a simple turn in the barn.

Her lips, tongue, the way she wrapped them about my cock. Gods, she had been born with the need of a hundred women and I knew how to use it.

Is that the real problem her father saw? Not my hunger for his daughter but the hidden desires that simmer beneath her lily white breast?

Did he know that I would be the one, or fear that I would be the first of a hundred?

He watched us like a hawk but still we managed to creep off together, to find that time where I could plunder his families treasure. How he raged when he found us entwined and my smile, that knowing smug look, only enraged him further.

Mind you he's dead now.

We both are.

Not that it puts a halt on my plans. She's mine. She always will be.

Even dead I can still feel her fingernails clawing their path down my back, her teeth buried in my shoulder. Those cries she tried so hard to stifle yet tore their way free regardless.

I can smell her. She's learned how to pleasure herself yet it's still not enough. That soft linen nightgown clings to her form, her breasts brush against it, nipples hard, begging for the touch of a man.

Without thinking I try to reach out for her, my fingers sliding through her body, unnoticed by anyone save me. I can almost feel her. The way her skin heats beneath my touch but she doesn't even know I'm here.

Every now and then her mother tries to find a man to take her, to marry her off and keep her from taking that step into the dark side. That delicious wicked part of her being that I introduced her to and now she can never go back to the woman she once thought herself to be.

They don't stay for very long. No matter how hungry the mere sight of her makes them. She can't see me, they can't, but I can do things. Influence dreams, scare the animals, just little things that make a difference. And if they prove stubborn then I push the limit. I make myself appear.

Not the way I look now. Heh, one thing about being dead is the fact you can choose your appearance and for the most part I do like to keep that same sophisticated look I tried so hard to perfect in life.

When I'm chasing them away from my property it's a different matter.

I pull out all the stops then.

Dripping blood, skin falling off in shreds, my eyes little more than yellow and green orbs that roll about in their sockets, it's enough to drive a strong man to drink. One man left without even saying goodbye. Not that she will ever see that image. I've made sure of that, even when I materialized to them when she's been in the room she's never seen me. I won't have her that frightened of me.

How can I be so possessive about a woman that I'd trade at a card table? It doesn't make sense unless you understand how these things work. Oh I'd let her fuck a dozen men a night but it's like this. Get Melissa to pay a debt on her back and she'd still belong to me. It's me she comes back to at the end of the session. All wet, willing, smelling of sex, ready to curl into my arms and beg to be mine all over again.

She marries someone else and I loose her for ever.

Not going to happen.

I'm dead so how could I share her?

Well did you think I'm the only soul that found a way to stay behind? Of course not, and we have our own amusements. Our games are a little more interesting than they were when we still held onto the mortal coil. So are the payments.

She's tired, almost ready for her to retire for the evening and perhaps this is the night I will be able to convince her soul to cross over. I've waited a couple of years, and I'll wait a little longer if I have to but even a ghost can become impatient.

There are ways, spooking her horse at the right moment.

A push when she's at the top of the stairs, though that might leave me too weak to pull her soul to me. A risk. If I lack the strength she'll go into the light. To the one place I won't be able to touch her. Not something I want to happen.

Gods, the light caresses her form in all the right places. Her nightgown, I can almost see through it. No one else gets to witness this nightly ritual, the soft touches beneath the sheets that ease her into her sleep.

There, the first touch, her thighs parting under the sheets, the way her lips form that soft o. The sheet moves with the first rock of her hips, her nightgown tangled about her waist, pulled down to bare one firm breast.

Pinch it for me.

Her fingers close about the crinkled rip bud, a squeeze, enough to shock her system with that delicious mix of pain and pleasure combined. She wants to cum, she will in time, but she'll draw the moment out just the way I taught her to. In the end she'll bite into her arm in order to stifle the scream but I'll hear it. I'll see the look of exquisite pleasure in her eyes.

Melissa.

My cock throbs, thickens beneath the clothing created by my will alone. I could shed them, stroke it, permit myself that fake release but it won't be anything like the real thing.

No. I'll control it, just as I control her.

I want more than anything else to be able to touch her, to share this with her and I will again.

Soon.

She's mine and we've been separated by the flesh for too long. We'll have eternity, I know that but I'm short on patience for that time together to begin.

About the Author

Originally from England Terri Pray has lived in the USA since 1999 and currently resides in Iowa with her second husband and their two children. Her writing ranges from fantasy to science fiction, romance through to horror and it would be realistic to say that she has as yet not met a genre she doesn't like.

She also, along with her husband Sam Pray and with the help of John Welch, runs www.darkfantasychat.com a site dedicated to online text role-playing.

For further information about Terri and her writing please feel free to stop by her site at www.terripray.com

About the Artists

Diana Harlan Stein/Illustrator/Naiad Studios
http://www.naiadstudios.com/

What the heck is a naiad?

It's a Greek water spirit. It's also an anagram of my name. Water, mythology and my name - perfect! Add the 'studio' part for the artwork and it's perfect.

While I declared business with the government on the millennium, I have been painting full time from 1995. Of course, I've been drawing for years before that. My family is choked full of artisans and patrons. I became a bit of the black sheep when I fell for fantasy themes instead of more mainstream topics. Still, I've had a lot of encouragement, enthusiasm and energy.

Past clients include Analog, Nasdaq Securities, the Dragonstorm Card Game by Black Dragon, several titles at Radio City Comics and many more. My art has been included in magazines, rule books, supplements, card games, art collections, comic books, jewelry, T-shirts and literary anthologies.

My work is seen all over North America. I love traveling to many conventions, selling and showcasing my art. I've worked with the Ronald McDonald House Charity Fund to raise money for families in need. There's always something going on with me!

Richard Savage
http://www.swage.plus.com/art/index.html

Richard Savage was born in the north England in 1962. He has been a figurative artist for twenty years and strives to make his art work challenging and thought provoking, trying to capture something of the celebration of life in all its wonderful shades.

His background is in illustration fine art and technical drawing. He works mainly in acrylics, but is also happy working in oils, pastels, line and wash, watercolour and mixed media. He draws inspiration from classical art, and the styles of the contemporary artists Boris Vallejo and Jack Vettriano.

Current projects figurative art, for illustrations and book covers, for four American publishing houses, private commissions, commercial art projects.

As AvatarArt's Lead Artist, Mates Laurentiu has created

Forbidden Love: Bad Boys

numerous fantasy-based pieces for clients ranging from individuals to companies. He is skilled in various media, enjoying both pencils and digital painting, yet is completely self-taught, drawing since he was three. Mates designed a house in his hometown of Ramnicu Sarat, Romania but his work can be seen anywhere, via the online portfolio at **www. avatarart.com** which also features commission information. He is thankful for his patron's support.

Steve Gerke is the Project Manager for AvatarArt meaning he does all the things that let the artists focus on their craft. He lives in Rochester, NY with a trouble-making cat duo, Pippin and Jolene. For fun he remodels his townhouse, thanks to weekly help from his father, Jack and reminders from his mother, Mary-Ellen. Steve's other hobby is playing in the Seven Stones and Shielding Alliance D&D game campaigns, as Alaina and Turtle respectively.

Thom Scott

Hoosier born and midwestern raised, Thom Scott worked for several years as an Inker in Indie Comics, before returning to school. Majoring in English Literature but Minoring in Fine Arts due to loving art but not wanting to deal with an obsession with canon works at IU. Check out his web site: **www.thomscottart.com**

Veronica Jones

Veronica V. Jones is a freelance illustrator working from the Northern Virginia area, just down the road from Washington DC. Confused in her youth, she didn't pursue art as a living until she had already graduated from college and was working in the real world as a research assistant. It's much more fun to draw swordfights and spaceships than set up spreadsheets.

Since then, she has made her mark as an artist for over six years. Her work has appeared in collectible card games and in roleplaying games, notably Warlord, Legend of the Five Rings, the Game of Thrones, "Spycraft" and "Tales of the Caliphate Nights". Her clients include Paradigm Concepts, Alderac Entertainment Group, and Fantasy Flight Games among others. For additional information, or to contact the artist, please visit her website at **www.moonshines.com**

Genre Web Shop

The Genre Web Shop is the online store for Honor Harrington merchandise, Saganami Island Tactical Game, the games and merchandise of Ad Astra Games, and novels and merchandise of Final Sword Productions, Under the Moon and Terri Pray.

The Web shop also carries a variety of vintage products and merchandise from stars such as Claudia Christian, Commander Susan Ivanova of Babylon 5.

http://www.genreconnections.com/shop

**Under the Moon Publishing
136 Fletcher Ave
Waterloo, IA 50701**